Sergeant Verity and the Imperial Diamond

"Good research, skillful writing and ingenious plotting."
— *The New York Times*

"The action is as thick as traffic in the winding streets of Calcutta, with as much local color."
— *The Booklist*

"Engaging and ingenious."   — *Anniston (Ala.) Star*

"There is nothing like a dogged Englishman to foil criminal minds, especially if his deductive reasoning rivals that of a fellow national by the name of Holmes."
— *Publishers Weekly*

Sergeant Verity and the Imperial Diamond

by Francis Selwyn

𝔰𝔡

STEIN AND DAY/*Publishers*/New York

STEIN AND DAY PAPERBACK EDITION 1984
Sergeant Verity and the Imperial Diamond was first published
in the United States of America by Stein and Day/*Publishers* in 1976.
Copyright © 1975 by Francis Selwyn
All rights reserved, Stein and Day, Incorporated
Printed in the United States of America
Stein and Day/*Publishers*
Scarborough House
Briarcliff Manor, N.Y. 10510
ISBN 0-8128-8038-2

Contents

1

BEAT UPON THE
BIG DRUM

I

Azimullah Khan, Dewan of the Nana Sahib, first servant of the King of Kings, watched the approaching column, the steady, unblinking appraisal of his keen eyes judging the speed and distance of the marching infantry. Raising his spy-glass, he turned one brass cylinder in another and brought the two leading figures sharply into focus. As in the silence of a dream, the Khan saw a fresh faced ensign, hardly more than a schoolboy, bearing the colours of Her Majesty's 105th regiment of foot upon a polished staff. The next man, old enough to be the youth's father, was a thick-set colour-sergeant with ginger mutton-chop whiskers and a rolling, open-order gait.

Azimullah steadied the glass, his lips, edged by a finely trimmed beard, moving in a grimace of irony. The very spy-glass in his hands had been presented to him by Lord Hardinge, the Commander-in-Chief, while Azimullah was in London as envoy of the Nana Sahib. Lord Hardinge had been so eager to impress the Khan and his master with the power of British arms that he had arranged the envoy's visit, as an honoured guest, to Lord Raglan's camp before the besieged city of Sebastopol. And there Azimullah had watched through this same glass as the Russian gunners brought down line after line of British infantry in the slaughter and humiliation of the Redan. The Khan lowered the slender brass barrel, his mouth tightening at the recollection of his enemy's defeat.

That arid summer on the bare Crimean hills had been temperate enough compared with the present heat. In the Deccan afternoon the April sky dulled to a furnace of gun-metal grey. Dust drifted like smoke from the broken earth at every footstep of man or horse, coating the faces of Azimullah's riders and the perspiring soldiers of the little column with the same brickish tan.

Close to the spot where the Khan and his horsemen waited, concealed by the tall spear-grass upon the little knoll, a family of mynah birds ended their raucous disagreement in a peepul tree. Silence, oppressive as the heat, settled far and wide. On the downward slope, the tall fronds stood motionless. Across the entire width of the great river plain the heat of India's spring stunned the landscape of mango and tamarind trees into an eerie stillness.

Azimullah sighed and raised the spy-glass again, the curl of his mouth betraying a professional's distaste at his enemy's incompetence. He knew they must believe themselves safe now, having come so far south, but by God they looked more like a troupe of nautch-girls than an army on the march! Behind the colour-party came the senior survivor of the Sitapur massacre, Colonel Carew-Tremlett. With his fine white moustaches and his face burnt brick-red in years of Indian service, the Colonel held the bridle of his grey in his left hand, his right arm being bound in a grimy canvas sling. Behind him the other survivors of the 105th regiment followed on foot, numbering three ensigns, two sergeants, a pair of corporals and eighteen privates. At the rear, a single bullock-cart carried such supplies as they had salvaged from successive skirmishes between Cawnpore and the river towns of the Ganges or the Jumna. The riflemen shambled rather than marched, their long-barrelled weapons hitched untidily on their shoulders by the canvas slings. Azimullah looked at the guns with satisfaction. They were muzzle-loading Baker rifles, preferred by the British commanders to the old Brown Bess muskets for set battles. But the commanders had yet to learn, the Khan thought, that the greater accuracy of the rifle was cancelled out in an ambush or a close fight by the fact that it took half a minute to ram each bullet down the barrel and fire, compared with ten seconds for the Brown Bess musket. In a well-laid ambush, a formation of riflemen might be overrun before they could get off a single volley.

From where he sat upon his horse, Azimullah could hear the words that the men marching in the column were singing.

Oh, when we got the rout and for In-jer we set out,
Oh, the girls was cryin' round us to the docks, boys, oh!
So we gives three 'earty cheers for the pretty little dears,
And we 'opes they've each one got another so-jer!

"You see?" said the Khan softly to the subadar-major
beside him, "They do not believe that there is a single company of our men within a hundred miles of them! They
dream of the railhead at Raniganj tomorrow, and then the
garrison train to Calcutta!"

Bang upon the big drum, bash upon the cymbals,
Sing as we go marching along, boys, along!
And although on this campaign there's no whisky
*   or champagne,*
Still we'll keep our spirits flowing with a song boys!

The ensigns and sergeants, throwing aside the dignity of
rank, were singing with the men, as though to encourage
them forward. By now the column was close enough for the
watchers on the knoll to see dark stains of perspiration on
the red serge of the tunics and discolouring the chalky belts
and cross-belts. The grime of reddish dust etched the white
neck-curtains of the tall, peaked caps and the cotton drill
trousers.

Azimullah wiped a knuckle across his well-cared-for
cheeks, just below the eyes where the sweat was gathering,
and then at last allowed himself the luxury of turning the
spy-glass upon the most important figure of the entire
column, who rode just to the rear of Carew-Tremlett. Here
was the prize for which the horsemen of the Nana Sahib
had ridden almost under the English guns at Raniganj. It
brought a vindictive satisfaction to the Khan to think that
a demure sixteen-year-old English girl – or rather the value
put upon her body – should be the means of bringing victory to the Nana, from Peshawar in the north to Madras in
the south. The girl was the key which would infallibly
restore the great Sahib to the throne of the ancient Mogul
kingdom and would root every English weed from India's
soil as surely as if the first white-skinned traders had never
touched upon the coasts of Bombay or Coromandel.

He knew, as matters of fact, that the girl's name was Judith Perry and that the image of her which his spy-glass offered was in no way similar to her appearance at a regimental ball in Calcutta or Meerut. On those occasions she might move gracefully in a white muslin gown, the veil of light-brown hair sweeping from her high crown to her shoulders, framing a pale oval face with clear hazel eyes and regular features. She was a tall girl, by Azimullah's reckoning, combining long slender legs with a womanly softness of breasts and hips. No doubt, thought the Khan, the matrons of the regiment took this beautiful orphan into their charge. Since she had no dowry, they would see to it that her ball-dress sufficiently emphasised her trim thighs, her soft young bottom, and her firm high breasts to catch some hot-blooded subaltern. Her body's riches would be her passport in the marriage market of the racecourse or the Maidan in Calcutta. And this, he thought, was the people which affected to despise the ways of Indian women!

Seen through the spy-glass, Judith was hardly the same girl. Her hair had disappeared under a cap, either worn up or cropped. She wore a loose tunic and tight knee-breeches in blue denim. Was it all that could be found to cover her nakedness after Sitapur? Or had some pious garrison missioner dressed her like a boy in the hope that, though she might be butchered, her sex would be sufficiently disguised to save her from the repeated raping which customarily preceded death in the bitter war between Indian and Englishman? Azimullah chuckled at the downfall of all these careful schemes.

The ensign with the colours was level with the knoll. At so short a distance the voices of Her Majesty's 105th sounded ragged but resolute.

A-thirsting to avenge, me boys, the bloodshed that is done
On poor defenceless women, ere Delhi has been won,
We'll make the Pandies for to know, and make 'em
for to feel
That British wrongs shall be avenged with sterling
British steel!

Azimullah twisted his mouth in an expression of contempt and, with a half turn of his head, spat upon the earth beside him.

A-hunting we will go, me boys!
A-hunting we will go!
To chase the Pandies night and day,
And level Delhi low!

The Khan pulled himself erect in the saddle, turned, and waved forward the first line of horsemen, many of them still wearing the royal blue with red facings of their native cavalry regiments which had mutinied at Lucknow or Barrackpore. As a mounted squadron of the Nana Sahib, they jogged carefully forward, guiding their roan chargers to the crest of the rise, the steel scabbards making a light jingle as they fell against the stirrup irons. Then the Khan's sword, consigned to him by the heir of all the Mogul emperors, flashed like a heliograph on the top of the little knoll. In a slithering drumbeat of hooves, the first riders of Dundoo Punt, Nana Sahib, swept down upon the dishevelled survivors of Her Majesty's 105th.

The first movement of the horses brought Carew-Tremlett's head upright and caused him to curb his mount. He acted with caution but without alarm. The 105th had come through too much in the past months to be thrown into panic by the approach of every mounted patrol which the orderly officer at Raniganj might have sent out on duty. Moreover, it was unheard of to find mutinous cavalry in squadron strength, and even in their usual groups of four or five men they never dared come as far south as this, within range of the British strongholds protecting Calcutta. The successes of the sepoy rebels had been in seizing and holding isolated garrison towns in Bengal, not in attempting to maraud hostile territory. The dark faces and the royal blue tunics identified the riders in his mind as loyal native cavalry from Raniganj.

Carew-Tremlett was only too glad to call a halt. His right arm in its sling burnt and throbbed under a swathe of bandages which he had worn for several days. The unchanged dressing was dried and abrasive as an old scab. He watched the approaching horsemen. Where the devil was the British troop commander among all those damned natives? By God, he, Carew-Tremlett, would roast the young jackass for not teaching his blacks to halt and be recognised properly! A great weariness weighed on all his thoughts. Each day he had faced the heat with greater sickness and dizziness, hardly knowing how to bear the brilliance of the morning light. The poison from the sword wound across his arm set up a renewed itching along the artery, acid and virulent.

He heard a shout from one of his ensigns and, looking again, saw the swords of the approaching *sowars* drawn in a ripple of steely light. Almighty God! He still could not believe that there was not some misidentification between the two groups, but the junior officers and sergeants had taken the power of command and were already shouting orders to the bewildered remnant of the 105th. The Indian driver of the bullock-cart had fled at the first sign of an attack and was already two or three hundred yards away.

On all sides the orders rang out.

"Company halt! . . . In close order, dress! . . . Fix bayonets!"

Carew-Tremlett turned in his saddle, angry with himself and his subordinates at the haphazard commands, but there was no time to form a regular defence. The two files of men divided to either side of the bullock-cart and there divided again into two ranks of about half a dozen men each. The first men knelt, their bayonets levelled at any approaching horseman, while the second rank stood upright, ready to fire over the heads of their comrades. The junior officers with revolvers and drawn swords endeavoured to keep the flanks, the youngest ensign wrapping the regimental colour round his own body in order that it should be safe until the last. Carew-Tremlett saw that one of the ensigns had formally shaken hands with a sergeant and several privates who had been under his direct command since the regiment was sent to India.

"With ball and cartridge, one round, load! . . . Commence fire!"

There was a clicking of old-fashioned priming pans and then the crackle of uneven firing. As the smoke from the first volley began to clear, the iron ramrods clanged into the barrels and the men began to load again with desperate haste. The three sergeants had taken spare rifles and were adding their own fire to the fusilade against the oncoming horsemen. They and the ensigns endeavoured to keep the lines steady.

"Company! Will you, for God's sake, look to your dressing, lads, or we're done for!"

The attack was all on one side of the cart to begin with, and the other half of the riflemen had not yet been drawn in. Carew-Tremlett dismounted and found himself a little cooler in the shade of the cart, where his depleted party held all the ground they could. He knew in the moment of their common peril he had failed them as a commander, yet he was so weary that he hardly cared.

"Company! Prepare to receive cavalry!"

Here at last was an order to be instinctively obeyed, as their fathers had obeyed it at Seringapatam or Waterloo, Aliwal or Chillianwallah. The bayonets of the kneeling men sloped upward a little more steeply, just where they would tear open the bellies of the approaching horses. In their combined length, the long-barrelled guns and the fixed bayonets sloped four feet in front of the riflemen. The rear rank stood like sentries, the butts of the long unwieldy rifles firmly into their right shoulders, taking deliberate aim. The colour-sergeant with the ginger whiskers spoke close to Carew-Tremlett, though without addressing his words directly to the commander.

"Must be forty of the 'eathen bastards. But all on one side. They ain't touching us round the back."

"No more they are," said Carew-Tremlett softly to himself, "no more they are."

As he spoke the Colonel was thinking of the girl. He turned and saw her standing behind him, tall and straight, stroking her horse's neck to calm it among the sputtering

15

explosions of the rifle fire. There was one chance for her, the Colonel thought, not a great chance but the only one that remained. He took her by the arm and led her more securely behind the shelter of the bullock-cart.

"Now, missy," said the old man gently, "it's best you should stay clear until we've seen off these fellows. You must mount and ride away in the lee of the wagon. Ride to the mango groves and our men will cover you. You have nothing to fear, the natives are not armed with guns and if one of them tries to come after you himself, our men will shoot him down before he gets past this wagon. Take the path through the grove and follow it back up the hill to the place where we broke the march this morning. You shall be safe there. Ride hard and don't delay. Mr Saunders shall come back to you when this is over."

He watched her slim young leg, bare below the knee, as she braced herself on one stirrup. Then the pale blue denim of the breeches tightened across Judith's full rear cheeks as she swung herself over the horse's back. Carew-Tremlett watched wistfully, thinking that in more private circumstances he would have exercised an old man's privilege of giving the girl an affectionate pat on the backside. Even in the face of death it seemed oddly impossible to banish such thoughts entirely. He laid his hand on the agile young thigh that gripped the horse's flank.

"Away with you now!" he said softly.

She looked uncertainly at him, until he removed the hand. Then she spurred the horse and galloped away across the hard earth.

"Stand to your arms, 105th," said Carew-Tremlett wearily. "Shoot straight as you can at any nigger that tries to go after her." The crouching riflemen watched her draw clear of the skirmish in a trail of dust.

For all the advantage of the ambush, the Nana's *sowars* had by now lost seven or eight riders to the marksmanship of the 105th. The rate of fire was faster than Azimullah had allowed for, as Carew-Tremlett's men, the muzzles of their rifles still smoking from the last round, bit open cartridges to re-load until their lips were black with the powder. Four of the horsemen had received the blast full in the face or chest, their horses now running loose alongside the others. Several more horses were wallowing in their death-agonies on the ground, while their helpless riders were slow and easy targets for the rifles, once they were on foot.

Another Indian cavalryman screamed and seemed to throw himself from the saddle as he was shot through the face. At this rate, Carew-Tremlett thought, there was just a chance the attackers would turn and run. Then he saw a fresh puff of dust from the little knoll and, mingled with the screams and discharges of rifle fire, there was the rumble of a fresh cavalry formation, like a distant avalanche. For God's sake, he thought, why? Two formations of the enemy's precious cavalry advanced almost under the guns of Raniganj to destroy a score of emaciated survivors, few of whom would ever be fit for service in India again! Why? Even if the attack succeeded, the Indian casualties would almost equal the number of Englishmen. It made no kind of sense. But the sound of a second troop extinguished all Carew-Tremlett's hopes.

"Mr Saunders!" he called, drawing his pistol and turning to the nearest ensign, "Set charges to the ammunition boxes, if you please!"

Azimullah, riding down with the second wave of royal blue cavalry was in time to see the line of kneeling riflemen on the near side of the wagon overwhelmed by the numbers of the subadar-major's horsemen. The rear rank, unable to reload in time, found the blows of the sabres falling upon them. Some struggled to parry the blades with their ill-balanced rifles and bayonets, and, when that failed, with their bare hands. The Khan watched in fascination as the desperation to live drove one rifleman to protect his head with his arms until both hands were severed at the wrists. In a moment more, the defenders on the other side of the cart found themselves outflanked and surrounded. Some died where they stood, as uncomplaining as animals in a slaughterhouse. Two men, a private and a sergeant, began to run wildly across the plain, throwing off their webbing and packs as an encumbrance. The native cavalry rode after them with whoops of

exhilaration, closing upon them easily and running swords
repeatedly through their backs, as though it had been a pig-
sticking match. It was soon over. The havildar-major carefully extinguished the fuses and made the ammunition boxes
safe. The young ensign with the colours wrapped round his
body, who had been one of the last to die, lay with his eyes
open, staring at his own outstretched arm.

Only Carew-Tremlett was still alive. He stood surrounded
by dismounted *sowars*, every one of whom held a drawn
sword. But the habit of obedience and authority instilled by
half a century of military training made it difficult for any
one of them to be the first to cut at the Colonel in his topee,
his thin-bridged nose, white whiskers, and piercing grey eyes
the very epitome of a regimental commander. He stood quite
still, never taking his eyes from them, hoping for nothing and
holding the bridle of his horse with his good hand. Carew-
Tremlett was a poor commander but a brave soldier. It was
not in his nature to fear men whom he despised.

Azimullah had dismounted also, and was pushing his way
through the silent *sowars*, cursing them for their cowardice.
Was not the Nana Sahib greater than an English colonel by
as much as the sun is greater than an ant which crawls in its
heat? The *sowars* moved back a little and allowed the two
men to stand face to face. In the smooth profile above his
mouth, the Khan's eyes glittered with hatred of the icy
arrogance displayed by his captive. The Colonel's gaze
remained level and indifferent, as though he contemplated
a point on the horizon which could be seen through
Azimullah's head. The Khan was about to give a positive
command that the infidel should be cut down, when Carew-
Tremlett dropped his good hand from the bridle and, before
any man could move to stop him, drew the loaded pistol
from his holster. It was a gesture which was contrary to all
Azimullah's experience of men in such situations, but the
muzzle of the weapon now pointed unwaveringly at the
Khan's breastbone over a distance of four or five feet. Not
one of the *sowars* could move far enough or fast enough to
cut down Carew-Tremlett before he might blow Azimullah's
heart from his body. Fury, rather than fear, seized the Khan's

brain as he saw the coming destruction of his own life and, worse still, the undoing of his masterpiece of strategy which was to make the Nana Sahib conqueror and ruler of all India.

A long half minute passed in the silence and the glittering heat of the plain. Then, without the least alteration in his expression, Carew-Tremlett turned the barrel of the pistol aside. Incredulously, Azimullah prepared himself to watch the suicide of an English officer, for such a thing was quite unknown before. But the muzzle of the pistol rested gently against the head of the Colonel's grey mare, just by the ear. There was a sharp crack, and the pistol barrel smoked briefly. The mare jolted sideways and then fell like a parody of a puppet-horse whose strings had been cut. Stretched on the earth, she pawed with one fore-hoof in a final spasm, shuddered, and lay still. Carew-Tremlett tossed down the gun. The first *sowars*, as though woken from their trance by the echoes of the pistol-shot across the plain, raised their sabres across their shoulders and bore him down in a rush, hacking him about the head and shoulders with their broad blades, as though they had been using a butcher's cleaver.

Carew-Tremlett made no sound, for the weight of the first heavy swords had almost knocked him senseless. Azimullah saw him fall and watched the body move in reflex convulsions under the blades. The Colonel was dying but not yet dead. The blood which flowed was so dark that the white hair and moustaches seemed flattened against the head by a thick oil, reducing the appearance of it to a featureless ball. But the Khan cared little for such details. He still shook with anger at the calculated contempt of Carew-Tremlett's last action. By that final shot, the colonel proclaimed to all who saw it that such a creature as Azimullah was not fit even to have possession of an Englishman's horse. The single bullet might have served to kill Azimullah himself, but Carew-Tremlett had shown that the horse was of greater account.

The Khan sought quickly for some retribution on the man who bled to death at his feet. When he had chosen the words and hissed them into the dying ears, the insult sounded tawdry enough, betraying the menial origins of the man who spoke it. For all his fluent French and English, the Khan had not always been first servant of the King of Kings.

"Bahin ka chute!"

Any Englishman in the India of 1857 knew too well the meaning of such sardonic promises. Then Azimullah raged, whispering ferociously in Carew-Tremlett's ear not only what would be done to the bodies of the Colonel's own womenfolk (as the insult promised) but pain and indignities which all English women should suffer in India before they joined the heaps of their slaughtered countrymen in the hecatomb of the Nana Sahib's final victory. In his anger, the Khan added to the list the foolish hostesses who had lionised him in London, and the loose-tongued English girl who had promised him marriage at that time and then had betrayed him like a common whore. By the time that the anger had subsided, Carew-Tremlett was motionless except where a pulse flickered at his throat. Azimullah drew his own sword and slashed accurately, near the collarbone. Blood rose in a brief arterial arc, spattered on the hard earth, dwindled away, and then the pulse in the throat was still.

The ambush which had seemed so prolonged and close-fought, was over in less than ten minutes. But as Azimullah controlled his rage he knew that in half that time the girl might hide herself too securely to be found. He left the subadar-major with the main body of horsemen at the scene of the fighting, and rode off with the havildar-major and eight *sowars*. They moved at a full gallop, the uniformed riders rocking low over the necks of their Arab bays, following the direction she had taken across the plain. The Khan knew that she must make for the mango groves and the hills, for there was no other shelter close at hand. But among so much foliage she might conceal herself so completely in half an hour that a whole army, let alone a single squadron, would hardly find her. The Khan cursed himself for indulging the luxury of anger at the cost of losing the girl.

The horsemen brushed past the closing mango and tamarind in a drumming of hooves, and the ground rose a little with the first slope of the hill. There was no puff of dust, no sound of a hoof-beat ahead of them, and no sight of her.

When they reined in, Azimullah heard with growing alarm
the great silence that stretched for miles about him.

"*Sahib-bahudar!*"

The havildar-major was calling him back. The Khan
turned his horse's head and trotted down the path to where
the senior NCO of native cavalry was waiting. But before he
reached the man, Azimullah's heart leapt with relief as he
saw one of the *sowars* leading a riderless horse from a narrow
path that diverged from the trail through the trees. He dismounted and sent a rider back to fetch the subadar-major
with the rest of the squadron. It was something that she had
abandoned the horse, but it might not make her easier to
find. On horseback, the rising dust, the hoof-beats, and the
quick movement would betray her easily in the brightness
and the stillness. On foot she might be moving silently away
from them, or she might be well hidden anywhere within
several square miles of foliage.

"She cannot escape us, Sahib," said the subadar-major
jovially. "If we do not find her, she will die of the heat in this
place."

"If she dies," said the Khan bitterly, "she has escaped us,
and these sons of a white sow shall answer to the Nana Sahib
for it!"

Four parties of men on foot beat out to the points of the
compass. Before them, pairs of riders followed the most likely
paths through bush and scrub to flush her from concealment.
An hour later they had found nothing.

"Water!" said the Khan, baring his teeth at the apprehen-
sive subadar-major. "Where is the nearest water?"

The second-in-command conferred with the havildar-
major.

"Half a mile, Sahib, through the bushes, but it is dry now,
Sahib."

"Find it!"

They came to the place soon enough, a broad bowl which
the rains of August would turn to a miniature lake but where
the tall reeds now grew in a forest from the cracked mud,
their stems bleached like dry parchment. Azimullah drew his
men up in a line and then waved them forward through the

dense growth. As they crunched and rattled the dried stalks, there was a sudden movement, as if an animal had been startled from its hiding place. The Khan smiled and said almost good-humouredly to the subadar-major, "Fools! There was no trick to it! If she would go on foot, she must find water. Besides, there is the story of an English officer who escaped death after Cabul by hiding among reeds. They are all taught it at school, as though it would save them!"

Then they saw her, struggling through the reeds ahead of the *sowars* as though wading through a strong surf, her long hair streaming loose as she stumbled. She gained the bank, twenty or thirty yards ahead of them, and began to run.

"She is to be left to me!" called the Khan to the subadar-major, and the *sowars* reluctantly slackened their pace.

Azimullah rode forward at an easy canter, following the girl's path. She was running determinedly, her long legs giving her more speed than he could imagine any Indian girl showing under such circumstances. She looked back across her shoulder once, and ran more desperately than ever on seeing him, her young hips swaying, as she plunged forward. She stumbled once, but picked herself up at once and ran on, her long thighs quivering under the impact of the strides. Suddenly she burst from the concealment of the mango grove on to the baking earth of the open plain. It was then that the Khan saw her seized with panic, for in that great expanse ahead there was hardly a blade of grass to hide her. She ran this way and that, crossing and recrossing in front of his mount, as though she had given up all hope of escape and was now frantically trying to postpone her ordeal minute by minute. He rode past her and came back again in a tight circle, penning her into a smaller and smaller arena. At last he drove his horse past her, so close that the stirrup brushed her sleeve. She lost her balance and fell, lying face down upon the earth, sobbing for breath and trembling with the exertion of running and the fear of what was about to come.

Azimullah dismounted and stood over her. Then he squatted down and turned her face so that she looked unwillingly into his eyes.

"You have made it very hard for my soldiers to take you

without hurting you," he said gently. "It was very foolish. If you act foolishly again, they will treat you a great deal more roughly."

The Khan spoke English with the intonation of southern Europe, which was not surprising since he had been educated by the soldiers and teachers of France who still served the Indian princes they had once ruled. From these men, who had lately led his own countrymen against the English, the Khan had also learnt to hate British rule and to seek out its weaknesses. Yet he was wise enough to know that to speak the language of the common enemy and to be accepted by them was a powerful weapon in the hands of a warrior.

Two *sowars* rode up and dismounted. Under Azimullah's supervision they raised the girl to her feet, led her back to the edge of the trees, and sat her upon her own horse. Then the entire party rode deeper into the jungle foliage that lay beyond, retracing the route that Carew-Tremlett and his survivors had so painfully followed. Ahead of the Khan and his captive lay the lands of the upper Ganges and the territories which now lay in the undisputed control of the army of the Nana Sahib.

Sergeant Billings of the 105th watched the drama of the ambush through a spy-glass of identical pattern to Azimullah's. At length he saw that they had taken the girl prisoner, though the details of her capture were hidden from him by a screen of trees. In a few months' time, Colonel Carew-Tremlett would be posthumously and discreetly condemned by a court of inquiry as a superannuated old fool, more suited to "a hundred up" at regimental billiards than to commanding a detachment on active service. But he was not such a fool as to have neglected the precaution of positioning a rear scout at the last point where the march had been broken, so that the man might see him safe across the plain. Billings had been grateful for the duty, which had kept him in the shade of the hilltop foliage during the heat of the day.

Like Carew-Tremlett, the Sergeant had not seen Azimullah's *sowars* until the ambush began. After the attack was over, he saw them riding back, close to his hiding-place, with Judith Perry as a prisoner among them. They passed within a hundred yards of him, retracing the route which the survivors of Sitapur had followed. Billings had no idea which mutineers they were, just another bunch of murderous "natives", or "niggers" as they were more disparagingly known to the British regiments. Yet the thought of what they might do to the sixteen-year-old girl before they finished with her made Sergeant Billings glow with righteous anger. Mind you, he thought uneasily, he and Sergeant Tanner had one or two ripe conversations on the march as to the ingenious variety of mounting they would practice on the little chit with a skinful of India Pale in their bellies. But that was soldiers' talk. What would happen to her now, done by a crew of natives at that, was unthinkable. He watched them lead her away, knowing he could do nothing to prevent it. It was one against fifty, and Billings had never fancied himself for "a schoolbook 'ero". Moreover, his orders from Colonel Carew-Tremlett, in the event of such a disaster as this, were strict and unambiguous. His first duty was to ride hard for Raniganj, saving himself at all costs, and to report the news to the senior officer of the garrison there. He was to stop for nothing and for no man, not even to assist a wounded comrade.

Sergeant Billings waited for an hour, until the shadows began to assume their long evening slant. It was dark and growing cool by the time that he adjusted the chin-strap of the white topee, which was to make him distinguishable from a distance to Carew-Tremlett. Self-consciously, he brushed the dust from the three gold stripes upon his sleeve, and straightened his scarlet tunic. He thought that somewhere among the scene of slaughter on the plain below the regimental colours must still be lying. To an NCO who had seen almost fifteen years' service in the 105th it went against the grain of tradition to leave them there. But orders were orders, and in any case Sergeant Billings felt a sudden horror at the thought of walking among his dead comrades who had talked and joked with him as they left him at his look-out only a few hours before. He mounted, spurred his horse lightly, and

24

began the long journey to Raniganj with his mournful news.

Azimullah pushed aside the bead curtain and passed from the cool verandah into the central passageway of the raised bungalow. Its rooms had once housed the Collector of the Sitapur district, before he and the other officials of the East India Company had fled down river to Calcutta as the sepoy mutiny flared and flamed on every side. The trees and scrub came close up to the building and the rasp of cicadas in the darkness was interrupted from time to time by the crackle of the dry undergrowth as a jackal or lynx stepped fastidiously through the thickets. The sounds disturbed the horses, who snorted and shifted uneasily where they were tethered. Occasionally there was a murmured grumbling among the sepoy picket-guard. A man coughed and spat, a musket butt bumped on the hollow boarding of the verandah.

There was a sentry on the first door that the Khan came to. He motioned the man aside and gently turned the handle. Judith lay upon the iron-framed bed, still fully dressed, her back to the door and her knees drawn up a little towards her navel. By the light of the single oil-lamp, Azimullah saw at once that she was still awake. He spoke gently to her, knowing that there was nothing to be gained by frightening her unnecessarily, even if it was expedient to kill her in the end.

"You will do as you are told? You will behave sensibly?" he inquired, his tone implying a statement as much as a question. The wide hazel eyes met his gaze, faltered, and then steadied again. Judith nodded, and the Khan felt a faint pride in her. He had been impressed by her demeanour throughout the ride, during which she had remained demure and self-possessed for all her silence.

"Yes," she said, in a quiet, firm voice.

"Good," said Azimullah, showing his relief, "then no harm need come to you. I wish you no ill; indeed it is very important to me that you should be protected and cared for. You may fetch me the belt from the table over there."

She had stood up instinctively when he entered the room and now she crossed to the table, the lamplight casting a tawny tan upon her pale legs and light-brown hair. She picked up something which, with all its loops and buckles, looked like a diminutive set of harness. The Khan watched her movements, the shimmer of her resilient young breasts under the damp silk tunic; the long light-brown hair sweeping across her shoulder-blades as she walked; the distinctively feminine fullness of Judith's bottom in the tight denim pants as she stooped to pick up the loops of leather. He took the contraption from her.

"You must know what my soldiers would do to you, if the chance were given them," he began, in the distant voice of a man telling an old story. "They would think nothing of cutting your windpipe or opening your body upon their swords. You would not be the first. But before that they would use you as a woman, so roughly that whatever joy was found in it would be driven from you and only bitter sorrow would remain. They would use you so vilely that you would welcome death. Such things are abominable to me, but I tell you only what has happened to others of your kind. Do you understand?"

She nodded briefly, keeping her eyes lowered to hide from him the full impact of his words upon her.

"Very well," said Azimullah, "then this will protect you. Now, you must take off your breeches." He spoke calmly, preparing to meet her defiance, but the threat of what might otherwise happen to her in the hands of the *sowars* had its effect. Judith shook back her hair from her face and looked up with quizzical innocence, or perhaps an amused parody of quizzical innocence. She went to the far corner of the room, where it was darkest, turned her back to him, pulled the denim pants down her thighs and stepped clear of them. Then she waited, still facing the wall, like a little girl sent to stand in the corner, displaying her pale legs and hips, her arms folded patiently. The Khan called her back and she walked carefully towards him, one hand resting on the triangle of light-coloured hair where her legs joined.

"This shall be your protection against them," he said, holding up the leather straps so that they appeared more obviously what they were, the basis of a carefully made chastity-belt.

The Khan was still puzzled that she made no more protest over the whole business but acted with the complete submissiveness which would have been more appropriate to a young Muslim wife who had been consigned to intimacy with her husband for the first time. As she stood before him, he tightened the stout leather belt round her waist, clipping it so that it locked securely. As he adjusted the slender silver chain that ran from the front, down the slight, taut curve of her belly, she flinched from his touch, but controlled herself quickly. She seemed to know exactly what was required of her, shifting her slim thighs astride as the chain followed her pubic cleft and a leather oval was adjusted to bar the entrance to her body. Then she turned her back, leaning forward a little so that he might guide the chain between the pale cheeks of her behind and lock it into the back of the waist-belt. He stroked the velveteen lustre of pale skin, where the little bones at the base of her spine curved out in the swell of her hips.

"You will wear the belt from now on," he said, "until the journey is over. It will be for a few days only. When you require to take it off, come to me and I will give you the key."

He let her go and she walked across the room towards the bed, her head bent, her hands folded before her, taking the small measured paces of a nun. Azimullah watched her as she slept, for her value was too high, he decided, to entrust her to the sentry. In the warm room, which the lowered lamplight illuminated in long deep shadows, she lay in her tunic and the grotesque belt, her breeches still folded upon the chair where she had left them. The Khan's eyes ran the length of her long slim legs, and over the whiteness of her hips, finding a special piquancy in her youth and paleness. It was quite true, as he had told her, that the preservation of her life and her virginity was more important to his scheme than it could be even to Judith herself. Yet he swore that if his scheme should come to nothing, he would take every consolation that her body offered. As she lay half naked in the lamplight she seemed infinitely more desirable to him than the great imperial diamond itself, which sat at the heart of

Azimullah's plot, like some monstrous glistening spider at the heart of a murderous web.

To the gracious presence of the just sovereign and refuge of the world, Dundoo Punt, Nana Sahib, Shah-in-Shah Padishah.

Azimullah Khan, first servant of the King of Kings, offers the poor tribute of his loyal heart with unfeigned respect and reverence.

The taking of the English virgin, whom the Sahib named to his unworthy servant, is accomplished, not many miles from Raniganj. This news shall hardly come to the ears of the great Prince before the woman shall be brought to abase herself before the mighty Shah-in-Shah Padishah.

All shall now follow as the Sahib has commanded and as Azimullah has ensured. Before the heat of the year is half done, the Kaisar-i-Hind, the great jewel of the Mogul Kingdom, that river of light to which the Koh-i-Noor and all diamonds of empire are as glass, shall rest in the glorious sight of the Nana Sahib. It is written that all Princes of India, and all their subjects shall rise in allegiance to the mighty Mogul King who wears this ancient jewel of supreme Empire in his crown.

Azimullah further swears, as he hopes to enjoy the bliss of Paradise, that he has the solemn vow of every Prince and Rajah, from the Ganges Plain to the forests of Burma, that when the great Sahib shall ride to war, with the splendour of the Kaisar-i-Hind upon his brow, every man of their armies shall turn upon the vassals of the foreign Queen and drive them in fire and blood from the ancient lands of the Mogul Kingdom.

Know, O Gracious Sovereign, that all this shall come to pass before the first rains swell the sacred Ganges. The creature of the infidel Queen, Lord Canning, and all his minions are henceforth no more than the walking dead upon India's shore, whose graves wait to receive them!

2

Sergeant William Clarence Verity, "A" Division, Metropolitan Police, private-clothes detail, sat on a hard little
chair and sweated. Since his secondment to the Provost-
Marshal's office in Calcutta, he had sweated often and abund-
antly, but there had never been such an afternoon as this.
When April turned to May, the thermometers in the
barrack-yard of Fort William and the forecourt of the
government prison had stood at a little over 110 degrees.

"Hot?" said Sergeant Martock cheerily, in reply to Verity's
grumbling: "We don't call it hot here, old fellow, not until
you see the mercury bubble in the glass."

"If you only 'ad a decent bit of flesh about you, Mr
Martock," said Verity reprovingly, "you'd know what was
'ot and what wasn't."

The general opinion was that Sergeant Verity had a very
decent bit of flesh about him. His round, thick-set head with
its pink moon of a face, black hair plastered flat and moustaches carefully waxed, was a study in well-fed complacency.
His lumbering figure in a black suit or frock-coat strained
under the armpits, tightened trousers, and tall chimney-pot
hat, was unmistakable. Plodding through the Devil's Acre
of the Westminster slums or surveying the "flash houses" of
the Haymarket, he was rated as the most easily recognisable
plain-clothes peeler in all the force. The young magsmen
and their fancy polls boasted of being able to "see the fat
fool coming a mile off". Great was their indignation when
they fell victim, one after the other, to the same "fat fool".
The professional cracksmen and whore-house keepers knew
better, treating him as "a rummy cove with a hand deep in
the game". For all that, a round dozen of the swell mob now
had leisure to ponder their mistakes as they sat in the damp
fetid cages of a rotting convict hulk moored somewhere off
the Essex marshes or Portland Bill.

Sergeant Verity knew every alley of the Seven Dials, every
snoozing-ken or bolt-hole of the Waterloo Road and the

Ratcliffe Highway, as well as he knew the lines of his own palm. He knew little about India (which he had been brought up to call "Hindoostan") and he cared even less. Yet after the first phase of the Sepoy Mutiny in 1857, the Commander-in-Chief, Sir Colin Campbell, had asked for a draft of volunteers from experienced officers of the Metropolitan Police. They were to assist the Provost-Marshal's office and the Intelligence Department in Calcutta in re-establishing law and order among the civil population and in bringing the guilty to justice. Sergeant Verity had not volunteered. He had protested to Inspector Henry Croaker that he "never was in foreign parts, only for the Rhoosian war". What he had seen of the "Rhoosians" in the battles of Inkerman and the Redan led him to prefer the Seven Dials and the Waterloo Road.

But Croaker, the dry, brittle-voiced administrator with a face the colour of a fallen leaf, had volunteered Verity's services. Having failed to secure the dismissal of the burly, self-righteous sergeant, and having failed to get him convicted as an accessory after the fact in the Train Robbery case of 1857, the Inspector had seized on Sir Colin Campbell's memorandum. The sergeants and constables of "A" Division could not think so poorly of their Inspector as to believe him capable of sending an awkward sergeant to his death in Bengal. But it was generally considered that if Verity should happen to be shot by the Pandies or go off with the cholera, Mr Croaker would "bear up handsomely" under the bereavement.

During his first month in Calcutta, Verity was plagued with an aching head, diarrhoea, and the prickly heat, which tormented his rich blood more searchingly than either of the other two. However thoroughly he soused himself under the tepid water that gushed from the pump in the little yard, the red pimples blossomed afresh in every crevice of his body, itching and prickling like fire. As he sat on the hard little chair by the wooden trestle table of his barrack room, he hardly knew how to contain the suffering. He would almost have wrenched off his clothes and torn the rash from his arms and legs. But the constant *creak-creak-creak* from the passageway beyond the open door reminded him that the eyes of the native punkah-wallah were upon him as the man pulled upon the cord to stir the broad fan sluggishly overhead. From time to time the *bhistee* walked slowly past the building and sluiced down the straw window-blinds with a pail of water. It was said to cool the breeze passing through the blinds by ten degrees, but it did little to alleviate Sergeant Verity's misery.

It was just after three in the afternoon, an hour when the British army and the entire East India Company in Bengal rested from the labours of the day. On the little table before Sergeant Verity stood a small china pot of foul-smelling, rancid, native ink. There were also several sheets of mauvish-blue notepaper. For the third time he took out his pocket-knife, opened it, and sharpened the quill that lay by the ink.

His exile was all the crueller for coming when it did. Three weeks before going aboard an ancient East Indiaman at Gravesend, outward-bound for Madras and Calcutta, Sergeant Verity had become the husband of little Bella Stringfellow, daughter of Julius Stringfellow, cabman of Paddington Green, whose lodger the sergeant had been. Now it was the husband's loving duty to write an affectionate homily from Bengal to his young wife. But whenever he attempted it, Verity found himself sitting and dreaming instead. He dreamt of Bella, the liveliness of her blue eyes, the waywardness of her blonde hair, her plump little arms, and her enthusiasm in making love. She had hugged him tight after the first occasion and said, "Do it again, Mr Verity!" so that he was quite shocked by her boldness.

He put down the quill again. How to address her? She was his beloved Bella. Should he call her that? Darling Bella, perhaps? His own Bella? Or his dearest Popsy-Wop, as he had called her in their softest exchanges together? The choice was impossible. And then, for all the Indian heat, Verity shivered with a sudden chill. What if the letter were to be opened by the authorities? Worse still, what if it should fall into hands other than Bella's in Paddington Green? He sat still, horrified by the thought that their most secret endearments might so easily become the property of strangers. It would be unendurable!

A droplet of sweat rolled from his forehead, down his broad pink cheeks, and splashed on to the table. Sergeant Verity took up the quill, clenched the fragile-looking stem in his large fist, and cleared his throat magisterially. He laid a red handkerchief on the paper so that his moist hand should not stain the cerulean blue and dipped the tip of the quill into the evil-smelling ink. Then he took a deep breath, his tongue pressing through his teeth with the concentration of unfamiliar labour, and wrote firmly across the top of the page.

Dear Mrs Verity,

For half an hour he compiled details of his voyage and safe arrival. Then he wrote a few words about his new colleagues and superiors.

> *Colonel Farr is an elderly gentleman who has passed his life in India. He is no less popular with his men, for all that, seeing he is always first into any danger.*

Who should come next in the hierarchy?

> *The Colonel's assistant in the Intelligence Department is Mr Lopez, a prime thief-taker but a desperate cruel man. He is darkish and, Mr Verity hears, was born Portuguese in India. He has no love for natives and woe betide any mutineers that should fall into his hands! The ways Mr Lopez has, when questioning suspected persons and so forth, would never be permitted in "A" Division and are sometimes enough to turn Mr Verity up.*

So much for his superiors, but how to describe the man who was his immediate colleague and guide?

> *Sergeant Martock is an army man, properly speaking, and his rank cannot count so high as Mr Verity's for constabulary purposes. He is good-hearted, very genteely brought up, but went for a common soldier to spite his father! His language is rather too free for Mr Verity's taste*

*and he is not continent where drink and the fair sex are
concerned. Mr Verity hopes much that he may induce Mr
Martock to attend one or two of Mrs Captain Tolland's
Wesleyan class meetings, that are held in a private house
near Fort William.*

An hour later, Verity struggled towards a conclusion of
the letter.

*That Mrs Verity is in all health and happiness, and that
she may remain an example of purity and uprightness to
all her neighbourhood and family is the sincerest wish of
her loving and respectful husband,*

William Clarence Verity

*P.S. Mr Verity trusts that Mrs Verity will present his
compliments and duty to her father, Mr Stringfellow.*

*P.P.S. Mr Verity hopes that Mrs Verity will believe how
often he remembers their great joy and happiness together, and how earnestly he looks forward to the renewal
of their nuptial ties.*

It was not at all as he had intended. On reading it
through, the letter seemed as though it had been written by
a stranger, with no resemblance to himself, to another
stranger, who bore no resemblance to Bella. He almost tore
it up and abandoned the idea of writing to her altogether.
Very few of his acquaintances ever sent such letters home.
But if he sent it, at least she would know that he was alive
and safe. He felt again the haunting fear of Bella, young and
warm, in the arms of some other man, ten thousand miles
and six months away. How much more likely, if she believed
Mr Verity had indeed succumbed to the Pandies or the
cholera! He sealed the envelope and turned round in his
chair.

"Ramgolam!"

The wizened young Indian, in loin-cloth and very little
else, came into the room half-running, genuflecting at the
door and repeating the obeisance as he approached the sergeant.

"Quart of Abbot and Hodgson's, wet!" said Verity
loudly.

"Yes, Verity, Sahib. Only, Sahib, it is not good for the Sahib to drink when . . . "

"Sharp!" said Verity, and the Indian scuttled away.

Two quart flagons of India Pale hung like Christmas poultry in muslin in the window recess. They were wrapped in wet flannel and positioned to catch the breeze as it came through the straw blinds. It was the traditional British device for cooling ale in India, practised by regimental commanders and private soldiers alike.

Ramgolam polished the glass neck energetically with a piece of dusty cloth and set the flagon on the table. Verity unscrewed the china stopper with a fist the colour of a ham, and raised the bottle to his lips. The level of the dark ale in the upturned flagon quivered and fell by rhythmic steps while the Sergeant's thick throat pulsed in resonant gulps. He put the bottle down again, wiped his lips on the edge of his hand, his cheeks filling out with the sudden disturbance of wind. Ramgolam watched, his fingers twisting together apprehensively. A few minutes later, Verity's tightly-suited bulk began to shift about on the wooden chair with greater impatience than ever. The cooled liquid was notorious for raising the irritation of prickly heat to an unbearable torment, but it was a lesson that every newly arrived "griffin" had to learn for himself.

"Oh, Sahib!" said Ramgolam nervously, as though he might weep on Verity's behalf, "It is not good for the sergeant sahibs to drink ale so cold while the heat is upon them!"

Verity rose with a half-suppressed howl, as though about to turn against the unfortunate barrack-boy. Instead, he threw off his coat and vest, flung himself on the trestle bed, and tore at the tiny blisters that tortured his white, shuddering body. Wallowing in misery, half whimpering with desperation, he thought of his wretched victims who now worked themselves raw on the treadmills of Newgate or Horsemonger Lane Gaol. How eagerly he would have changed his own suffering for theirs, if only to be in London again!

The torment eased a little and Verity's envy of the men

who trod the cock-chafer wilted. The braying of a bugle outside the guardroom of Government House pierced the cocoon of self-pity in which he sought comfort. Pulling himself together, he retrieved his clothes and dressed. Two brushes and an ornamental tin waited by his mirror, arranged there by Ramgolam. When Verity had brushed his hair flatter than ever, with the aid of a little water, he waxed his moustaches into a state of brilliant polish and put on a tight cravat. His black frock-coat was no different in style to that of the London private-clothes detail, but like many Englishmen in 1857 he wore light grey trousers as a concession to the heat. With the added luxury of a white topee he looked the picture of a comfortable John Company clerk. Only the heavy tread of the shiny boots might have betrayed him to a careful and observant criminal.

The ferocity of the sun had dwindled, but the metal doorplate of the barrack entrance still burnt his hand as he touched it fleetingly. Then, with the slow, habitual tread of the experienced thief-taker, he began to walk the short distance past the barrack blocks and parade grounds of Fort William towards the Granary Barracks. These had been turned into a military prison during the emergency and housed native prisoners suspected of some part in either the plotting of the Mutiny or in the massacres which followed. Some confessed their guilt quickly and were sent to perfunctory trial and even more perfunctory execution. Others were detained, either because they had confessed nothing or because the Intelligence Department required futher information from them before they were allowed to die. The work of the gaolers and the interrogators was the subject of numerous nods and smiles in mess-rooms or at the regimental billiard-tables. Well-meaning and liberal-minded letters of protest appeared in the London papers. The men of Fort William ignored them, remembering only the treachery of Cawnpore and a dozen other towns, the butchery of babes in arms, the sight of women's bodies stripped and mutilated by the rampaging sepoys.

Fort William was a city in itself with a bazaar and offices surrounded by the great hexagonal ramparts. Protected by the River Hooghly on one side, and facing Government House and the fashionable drives of the Maidan on the other, its garrison of ten thousand men seemed equipped to defend it against the most powerful attack. But it was no longer a place where most Indians went willingly. Indeed, since the news of Cawnpore it had become necessary to double the guards on every gate at night in order to prevent parties of private soldiers from setting out to "avenge" England's dead among the local Indian population. But hunger was still stronger than fear. Verity had gone hardly a hundred yards when an old man in loin-cloth and *puggaree* shuffled towards him, bowing repeatedly with the rhythmic regularity of a clockwork figure. He was always there when Verity returned to afternoon duty from the barrack-room. The old man snuffled and began a sing-song chant.

"Oh, preserver of the poor, be gracious! Oh, protector of the fatherless, be merciful!"

"You've no right to expect to have a father at your age!" said Verity with some indignation.

"Oh, feeder of the hungry!"

"Hook it!" said Verity. "Sharp!"

He quickened his pace, leaving the beggar to fasten on some other prey, and stepped aside to avoid an officer's *dakgharry* pulled by two rat-like ponies. To his left, on one side of the broad review ground, a drill instructor was putting a small company of defaulters through their penance with goose-stepping exaggeration.

"Balance step, gaining ground! Balance! By the left foot, commence! Step! Step! St-e-e-p!"

Outside the gates of Granary Barracks the two sentries, in scarlet with white helmets, patrolled alternately between their posts. As though at some invisible sign, one of them snapped to attention, shouldering his rifle in three slapping movements on its stock. He turned and marched in a long, loping stride towards his companion, turned about with a heavy-booted stamp! stamp! stamp! and came back with the same rolling gait. Verity presented himself to the orderly sergeant, who greeted him cheerily.

"Your Mr Lopez ain't half in a wax this afternoon. Asking

questions of them natives what was found with the loot from Cawnpore. I'd say that, just this minute, those native twisters must be a-cursing their parents for ever bringing them into the world to suffer like it. 'e's a good worker, your Mr Lopez."

And the orderly sergeant chortled agreeably at the imagined retribution.

The yard of Granary Barracks had been transformed into a prison compound, where Indian suspects exercised daily under the muzzles of several rifles and at the command of Private Sweeney, a burly Irish guardsman who took every British death at the hands of the mutineers as though it had been a personal bereavement and insult. The men to be exercised wore a single cloth twisted about their loins, leg-irons with a length of chain, and manacles. There were several dozen of them drawn up round three sides of a hollow square for "shot-drill", an ordeal which Private Sweeney embellished until it almost rivalled Mr Lopez's inquisition. The shot was a 24lb iron ball, there being one for each man. At the first command, every man lifted the ball at his feet, carried it three yards to his left, placed it where his neighbour had been standing, and returned to his own position. Another ball, positioned by his right-hand neighbour, would then be waiting his attention. Even for hardened convicts in England, shot-drill was restricted to those passed as medically fit, and forbidden for all men over forty-five. It was also limited to seventy-five minutes. In the Granary Barracks all prisoners were drilled and the time-limit was loosely interpreted. Private Sweeney was reputed to have celebrated the relief of Lucknow with a session of over two hours, after which three men died. Colonel Farr, the commandant, was angry but, had Mr Lopez been drafted in at that time, Sergeant Martock swore that he would have "recommended that bloody Irish fellow for the Victoria Cross."

The heat never tired Sweeney. His voice rapped across the paved yard and caught the echo of the high stone walls.

"Lift! Carry! Down! Return! Lift! Carry! Gently down! Gently! Return!"

Before the drill was over, a dozen men would collapse

from causes as simple as "a shamming fit" or as final as a coronary seizure. As each man fell, one of the armed guards would test him with a bayonet point to discourage an outbreak of "shamming". When a man died during shot-drill, Mr Lopez noted it as "death by natural causes".

Though he had seen it so often, the shot-drill shocked Verity as he watched the prisoners moving like bowed and tormented creatures of hell. He never doubted that they were the murderers and defilers of Englishwomen and children, and so had earned their suffering, but in this form the retribution sullied the dignity of British justice. As he entered the inner gate, Sweeney's voice still echoed across the yard.

"Smartly, you damned cut-throats! All prisoners to have wholesome exercise, the Governor-General sez! And wholesome exercise you shall have, you murdering bastards!"

Verity laid his topee and gloves on the tall counting-house desk in the office allotted to the Provost-Marshal's sergeants at the Granary Barracks. A well-thumbed roll of official manuscript awaited him, folded and tied with red tape, as though it had been a barrister's brief. Releasing the cotton ribbon, he surveyed the contents, a list of civilians, women and children not yet accounted for after the slaughter at Cawnpore and other towns which had been in the hands of the mutineers. It was the duty of the Intelligence Department to establish the fate, wherever possible, of those who had not been listed as dead or as survivors. Many were undoubtedly dead already but not yet listed. Others might be dying in a hundred scattered hiding places. A few had found shelter with Indian rajahs like Maun Singh, who would surrender them to the British or to the Nana Sahib, according to which side seemed likely to win the "Sepoy War". From the interrogation of captured mutineers, and by examining such items of loot as they might possess, the sergeants of the Intelligence Department completed the mournful story of the first months of the mutiny.

On the list of names was one with a pencil-mark beside it: Amy Stockwood. Verity turned through the other leaves of the papers until he came to a page headed by her name. The page began with the transcription of her brief "diary" of the catastrophe at Cawnpore, which had been found on a scrap of blue notepaper tucked into the mount of a cameo brooch. The brooch had been found in the possession of a native thief, arrested in Calcutta, and the paper told a simple but horrific tale:

> May 21st News of mutiny at Meerut. Went into barracks for safety.
>
> June 5th Native regiments of infantry and cavalry mutinied.
>
> June 7th First shots exchanged.
>
> June 9th Two cases of cholera in barracks.
>
> June 20th Aunt Mary died. (Mrs C. E. Cotton)
>
> June 26th Uncle Charles died. (Major C. E. Cotton)
>
> June 27th Left the barracks under safe-conduct.
>
> June 28th Boats fired on. Mama and Alice died.
>
> June 29th Taken with others to the Savadu Kothi.

And what then, thought Verity? The girl was identifiable as the niece of Major C. E. Cotton and the daughter of Captain J. S. Stockwood, whose fate was unknown. Amy Stockwood, at twelve years old, had evidently survived the massacre in the boats when the Nana Sahib and his brothers had watched from the temple steps as the sepoy muskets opened a ferocious fire on the helpless occupants of the craft, to whom the Nana had given safe-conduct. And then? She had been taken with the other surviving women and children to the "Ladies House" of the Nana. Had she still been alive on the 15th of July when the Sahib, hearing the approach of General Havelock's relief column, had ordered the butchers of the bazaar to go to the Ladies House and slaughter every woman and child, so that his treachery might be concealed? Had she died before that? Did she die in the slaughter? Or was she, perhaps, still alive, having been taken by the native soldiers as a camp follower? The cameo brooch that she had worn and her sad little scrap of paper could tell no more, but Mr Lopez had promised that the tongue of the native suspect should wag before he was passed on for judgment.

Verity tied the tapes again, crossed the passageway, and knocked at Lopez's door. It was opened by Sergeant Martock, in full regimental uniform, his thinning sandy hair and equine profile suggesting accurately the discreet breeding of a gentleman-ranker. Lopez sat at his desk, his smooth dark face as much Eurasian as Portuguese, his carefully set hair and well trimmed beard giving him the appearance of a prosperous merchant from one of the Goan settlements. He looked up from his papers on Verity's entrance and said in a soft, modulated voice, "Let us return to Mr Dhingra and see if he has found his powers of speech."

There was no humour in the voice, only a great weariness. Lopez's dark eyes were bleak and dispassionate. In his dapper grey coat and trousers he led the way from the room, summoned the two privates who stood guard outside, and turned towards the cells. The crashing of boots on the flagged passageway echoed with a ferocious violence. Then the party came to the iron door of the cell with its single judas-hole, where two more sentries kept guard. Lopez made an impatient gesture, the door was unlocked and the four guards entered. Verity heard the sound of a brief, half-hearted struggle, and then Lopez stood upon the threshold of the barred, foul-smelling little room.

Dhingra was a slightly-built man in his early thirties, naked but for the usual twist of cloth. His legs were "ironed" with anklets and chain, his wrists bound behind him with cord. The four guards or *daragohs* were well used to the interrogation of native suspects. They seized Dhingra with businesslike precision and stretched him on his back upon the floor. Three of them held him so that he could move neither his torso nor his hips, while the fourth crammed a rag into his mouth to stifle his cries for respite. The man's eyes turned desperately from side to side during this sinister pantomime, searching the face of first one and then the other of his captors for some trace of compassion. Verity felt uneasy at what he must witness, though he had no pity for a man who had violated and murdered twelve-year-old Amy Stockwood in the most pathetic circumstances. But what, he thought, if Dhingra had never been at Cawnpore—had never been a sepoy – and was telling the truth when he swore that he had bought the cameo brooch with its hidden diary quite innocently in one of the Calcutta bazaars?

"Now," said Lopez softly, looking down at the frantic eyes, "we shall see how long it takes to dig the truth from your cursed belly."

The prisoner's sinews strained like cord on gun pulleys as he struggled for freedom of movement and shouted something into the gag, evidently knowing what Lopez meant. Lopez himself, with the air of a conjurer showing a long-practised trick, shot back his cuffs and took from Sergeant Martock a small glass bowl and a wooden cigar box. He tipped something frail and light from the box into the bowl, then inverted the bowl so that it covered the bare flesh surrounding Dhingra's navel. It was as the bowl was fixed firmly in place that Verity saw movement inside it. He knew that the black insect was a beetle, though it looked more like a cockroach. Its habits of burrowing hungrily into flesh or fruit were such that he did not care to think of them. Yet with the first touch of cold perspiration upon him he realised that he was about to watch a form of interrogation which he had known before only as a garrison legend.

Dhingra tensed and contorted his muscles helplessly as the black insect began to explore its transparent prison. Slowly its jointed legs touched the warm skin and it made for the recess of the navel. Verity saw with fascination that, for all the heat, the surface of Dhingra's skin had turned to goose-flesh with terror. There was a ghastly prelude while the man felt the tiny feet tickling upon him and howled incoherently into the rag. Verity averted his gaze to the far wall. It was only a question of time before the diminutive pincers began work in the enclosed hollow of the navel, as the beetle ate its way slowly but remorselessly into the entrails. If the man remained silent, he would die after a week of excruciating torment, but it had never happened that any man had withstood it so long. The stifled screams continued for a moment longer. Then Lopez said in a half-lisping voice, "You will put your questions now, Sergeant! He knows what to expect as a reward for lying!"

Lopez and two of the guards withdrew, leaving Verity, Martock, and the two guards of the cell. The guards pulled Dhingra to his feet but his knees and flanks trembled so violently that he could hardly stand.

"Be so good," said Verity calmly to one of the soldiers, "as to sit him on the bunk and to fetch me a chair. Also a glass of water."

"It ain't for 'im, Mr Verity, I 'ope!" said the corporal of the guard.

"Who it may be for is my concern, thank you, Mr Dodgson!"

Dhingra was sat upon his bunk, Verity facing him, and the glass of water fetched. But Dhingra refused it.

"Untie his hands, Mr Dodgson, if you please," said Verity smoothly.

"Can't do that, Mr Verity," said the corporal, "Mr Lopez's orders."

"Much obliged, Mr Dodgson," said the portly sergeant, unruffled, "but this is *my* investigation and *I* am senior officer present. Thank you."

Dhingra recovered himself somewhat and looked uncertainly at his new interrogator.

"Now," said Verity, easing the tight fit of the frock-coat across his plump shoulders, "you was taken in possession of a cameo brooch two days ago, having arrived in Calcutta two days before that from Raniganj."

Dhingra nodded eagerly.

"And you never had the brooch before you came to Calcutta?"

"No, Sahib, never before! I swear it!"

"There ain't no call to swear anything, so long as the truth is spoken."

Then Verity paused, regarded Dhingra with curiosity and said conversationally,

"You must be five-foot-ten. Are you?"

"Five-foot-nine, Sahib," said Dhingra, looking bewildered.

"Are you so much, though?" said Verity, as if impressed. "Why, you might have ridden with the native cavalry. You might, you know."

"Sahib, I swear I am a poor man of Raniganj! I know nothing of wars and armies!"

"Don't swear," said Verity gently, "it makes no odds. Don't

ride a horse then? Not from Raniganj to Calcutta? 'ow
would you have travelled? Rail? River boat?"

"By the rail, Sahib!"

"Not boat?"

"No, Sahib. Never."

Verity spoke aloud the words he wrote.

*"Reached Calcutta terminus four days since, by rail from
Raniganj.* Right. That's that. We ain't getting on too bad,
are we?"

Dhingra looked up with a first light of hope in his eyes.
"Been in Raniganj some time, I daresay?" said Verity casually.

"Ever since the trouble began, Sahib."

"Must 'a been there when the garrison commander closed
the bazaar and drove the native traders out?"

"Oh yes, Sahib."

"And you, being in a small way of business there, must
have been driven out along with them?"

"Oh yes, Sahib."

"And you, buying and selling in an honest way, must have
set up in trade elsewhere in Raniganj."

"Indeed, Sahib."

"Would that be inside or outside the city walls?"

"Outside, Sahib. Just outside."

"Well," said Verity, "I can't say I could quarrel with that.
And you never was a sepoy?"

"No, Sahib, I swear."

"Don't swear, just answer. And you never had a musket
nor fired one?"

"No, Sahib."

"Then," said Verity comfortably, "that just leaves the
matter of the cameo. Bought in Raniganj, was it?"

"No, Sahib, bought here."

"In Calcutta? From a street pedlar, perhaps? From a
tinker's hut in Chandernagore? Wouldn't know the face
again?"

"No, Sahib. From Karim in the bazaar. All true."

"If it is," said Verity placidly, "it's the first truth you've
told in a whole pack of lies."

"No, Sahib! I swear it!"

"Don't swear, if you please, especially now you been found out. You never was in Raniganj in your life, else you'd know the native bazaar never was closed down."

"It was, Sahib!"

"And that there ain't city walls round Raniganj that you could have lived in or out of!"

"Then the Sahib has lied!" cried Dhingra desperately.

"What's more," said Verity calmly, "if you came by rail from Raniganj four days since, you must have had a very remarkable journey. The up-train from Barrackpore was derailed last week and there ain't been a wagon travelling between here and anywhere in all that time!"

"But, Sahib, I have never killed!"

"Stand him up and turn him round," said Verity to the guards. The two men hoisted him and pushed his face to the wall. Verity nodded. "He rides a bit awkward, to let the saddle mark 'im quite like that."

Dhingra sat hopelessly on the bunk again.

"Sahib, I swear I am a man of peace!"

"Well, o' course," said Verity reasonably, "having a horse to ride and not living in Raniganj, and not travelling by the steam engine, don't make a man a criminal. But when a man is taken and kept close prisoner with his hands tied, he finds it hard to wipe off all the evidence of his misdeeds. Now you say you ain't never been a sepoy nor a soldier?"

"No, Sahib!"

"And yet," said Verity casually, "there you sit with your lip black just in the centre, black as my hat, from where you've a-bin biting open cartridges!" He touched his upper lip to show just where he meant. "Now, Mr Lopez is going to want to look at that very close!"

But before he had finished, and before any of the guards could prevent it, Dhingra's hand had flown across his mouth and was rubbing at it in a frenzy of terror. Verity watched calmly.

"You know what you are, my man?" he said. "You're a mutineer!"

Dhingra sprang up, as though he might attack the burly,

44

red-faced tormentor. He spat upon the floor in front of
Verity.

"Leave him be," said Verity to the guards, and then turned
to Dhingra. "You be grateful to me, my friend, for the
favour I've done you. You 'ad your fill of murder and now
you shall die for it. But it'll be a clean death. You lied all
right, but Mr Lopez or me would have found you out. Think
yourself lucky it was me. You'd a-died anyhow. But you might
have had a week of such agony that you'd have blessed the
man who would cut your throat. That's what I've spared you,
Mr Dhingra, and never so much as laid a hand upon you.
Pity of it is, when I think of what poor souls have suffered at
your hands, I half wish I'd given the job up and left you to
Mr Lopez!"

Verity stamped about, jowls quivering slightly in pink
self-righteousness, and followed Sergeant Martock from the
cell. As soon as they were out of earshot, he said sternly to
Martock:

"I 'ope we shall have spared Mr Lopez the need to torture
the wretch further. He's a sepoy, mutinied at Cawnpore,
been running loose ever since, but may now safely be 'ung
for it."

"For Miss Stockwood's murder?" said Martock casually.

"Mutiny's better," said Verity, "mutiny's sure."

Martock stopped and shook his head.

"Well, old fellow," he said thoughtfully, "you do plough
a straight furrow, to be sure! How you happened to know
about the bazaar and the walls at Raniganj, and the train
that came off the line, is a living miracle."

Verity frowned a little at his companion.

"Mr Martock," he said severely, "you been a good soldier,
I daresay, but your acquaintance with constabulary strata-
gems ain't all it might be. O' course, I don't know about
bazaars and trains off the line, but nor did he and that's what
caught him. If you know a man's lying it ain't hard to catch
him. It's a caper that the greenest stickman in London
wouldn't fall for. But your native criminal ain't made the
acquaintance of such questioning until now."

"And the powder-mark on his lips?"

"You don't expect to find one that long after," said Verity knowledgeably, "but, then, the only mirror he's got in that cell is his own conscience. Once he put his hand to his mouth like that, he was hung. But he couldn't think o' that in time. He knew the mark might be there and must come off!"

"Dammit, my old son," said Martock, ignoring the disapproving look with which Verity received his clap on the shoulder, "you're the best-trained faker in the business!"

"And so I may be," said Verity, wiping a hand across his black moustaches, "but I'd a sight sooner deceive a man that way than eat his gut out with some poisonous insec'!"

Martock's face creased in a long smile.

"Why, old fellow, you may rest easy enough as to that. That beetle wouldn't turn a whisker for you. It ain't that kind of beetle, my dear chap. Only the prisoners *think* it is, and when they feel it tickle their belly buttons, why, bless you, there's not one of them that doesn't sing the whole round with chorus and ditto repeto!"

Verity regarded him sceptically.

"Damn it!" said Martock impatiently, "Only think of the kick-up and precious row the Liberal newspapers would start if natives came to have their necks stretched with their bellies eaten open!" And he laughed at the absurdity of it.

The nape of Verity's neck grew crimson above the collar of his black coat.

"Well, Mr Martock, you got your mutineer, and there's the end of it."

"I rather hoped, old chum, we'd got Amy Stockwood's murderer too."

"You 'eard him," said Verity shortly: "I gave him a chance to lie his way out of having the brooch, but he stuck to a story that could be proved."

"He slit her poor little gizzard for her," said Martock, "and worse than that."

Verity's head went forward, in the manner of a fighting cock entering combat.

" 'e's a mootineer, Mr Martock. A *mootineer!* That's all."

Then puffing out his cheeks a little, as though to recover

46

his composure, he wished Sergeant Martock a good evening and plodded off heavily about his own business.

3

With the comforting bulk of a bowl of mulligatawny and a plate of curried mutton in his stomach, Verity set about his evening duty. Perhaps, he thought, it mattered little whether they hanged Dhingra for mutiny or murder, seeing he could only be hung once. "But then," he said, half-aloud, polishing the worn brim of a tall stove-pipe hat on his sleeve, "I ain't been fetched to Bengal to catch mutineers, only to see what poor creatures may still be found alive and saved from the black devils." And as he clapped the hat on his head he thought again of Amy Stockwood.

The evening air of Calcutta was thick with the warm twilight smell of sweet lotus and tallow, overlying the peppery and acrid perfumes of city fires. He strode leisurely between the long rows of white barrack buildings, making for the east gate of Fort William and his escape from the massive, creeper-grown ramparts. The double guard, smartly turned out in scarlet tunics and pipe-clayed belts, watched him pass with impersonal suspicion. Beyond the gate, the broad waters of the Hooghly moved swift, dark, and silent, bearing the corpses and detritus of the city towards the Bay of Bengal. Reflected gleams from the lights that twinkled along the Calcutta Strand or Howrah on the far bank, shimmered here and there on the black water. Above Hastings, the piled clouds caught the last of a crimson sunset. The oil lamps of the city streets turned Government House into a fairy palace of rotunda and colonnades. Verity settled the frock-coat more squarely on his shoulders and turned towards Karim's emporium in the native bazaar.

Before him lay the vast expanse of the Maidan, the emerald green of the open lawns now brown and withered by six weeks of unremitting heat. The Maidan was boasted of as the Hyde Park and Rotten Row of Calcutta: to Verity it seemed the meeting place of polo and adultery, the mingling of the fashions of the west and the vices of the east. In the hour after dinner its gravelled carriageways were busy with London-built landaus, attended by liveried Indian footmen, hackney carriages with native drivers, and the chariots of the wealthy baboo or Bengalee merchant. In the early lamplight, the brilliant whiteness of Indian tunics and turbans contrasted with the scarlet of European officers and the swaying blue or green crinolines of their partners. Among the crowded paths moved the native palanquin-bearers, four to each curtained chair, trotting and grunting with the burden as they bore their passengers to baccarat, brandy pawnee, or a private assignation with an Indian mistress in a secluded villa near the Chowringhee. Verity had a policeman's instinctive aversion to hackney carriages and palanquins. There was no knowing what information a man might miss, once he stopped using his own two feet.

Behind the terraces of fine houses, built in classical proportions with pilasters and frieze, rose the warehouses and cranes of the riverside, for all the world, thought Verity, as though the terraces of Regent's Park had been re-erected in Wapping, or by Hungerford Stairs. Where the gardens fronted the Maidan, bougainvillaeas and almond trees, white blossom touched with pink, shone in the lamplight. By Spence's Hotel and the Great Eastern, hackney carriages with blinds drawn waited discreetly for special clients. There would be plenty that evening, Government House aides and lawyers, young ensigns or portly majors, flushed with champagne and a good dinner. A word to the native driver and they would be driven away by the cabman to whichever house in the wealthier Indian quarter employed him. There, as though they had been sultans in a harem, they might choose their partners from a dozen races and nationalities, Indian, English, French, Russian, Persian, Chinese among them.

Beyond the Maidan, where the buildings grew shabbier, Verity could still hear the notes of a military band drifting from the lawns among the carriage drives. But now the

crowds were denser, in a no-man's-land between the society
of Government House and the native bazaar. Fresh-faced
subalterns and demure English girls jostled with yellow-
faced Anglo-Indians whose livers and constitutions had been
ravaged by thirty years in John Company's service. As the
two nations mingled, the last reflection of sunset gilded the
glittering points of an Hindoo temple. Then Verity smelt
the perfume of burning sandal-wood, and his well-filled
stomach felt sour and nauseated. Yet he could still not bring
himself to avert his eyes from the Burning Ghat.

Under the roof of an open shelter the corpse lay upon an
iron bedstead, only its head and feet visible, the wood packed
round its limbs and torso. The priest and mourners walked
ceremonially round the bier, one man stooped, and Verity
saw the blossoming flame. The brightness danced and
caught, until there was a stirring breeze and the wood roared
with fire. The mourners stood motionless but the corpse,
robed in flame, began to sit upright, the mouth opening and
then closing, and then opening again. When Verity had first
seen this, though from a distance, his heart seemed to stop
with the horror of it. It had taken all Sergeant Martock's
persuasion to prevent him from attempting a rescue, and all
Martock's eloquence had hardly convinced him that it was
only the contraction of sinews in the heat which pulled the
corpse up in this manner and caused the mouth to open and
close. Even this had not reconciled Verity to the well-fed
vultures who sat patiently on their various perches, awaiting
the moment when the remains of the cremation would be
launched upon the river.

He turned into the Bow and Lal bazaars, where the native
quarter of the city came closest to the centre of government.
Glass lanterns were lit before the close-packed houses and
traders' stalls. Coloured fire burnt in the courtyards of little
temples, the burnished metalwork reflecting the glow. He
pushed his way among figures clad in robes of vermilion,
scarlet, blue, and gold, among olive-coloured naked backs,
European topees, and veiled wives with the crimson mark of
belonging on their foreheads. From time to time his path
was blocked by a persistent hawker or bearer.

"Sahib, me very good thing to sell! . . . Palanquin, Sahib, this way! . . . Me very good Khitmudgar, Sahib!"

To each one, he replied, "Hook it! Sharp!" as though he had been dealing with street urchins in St Giles's or Pimlico. When the command failed, he beckoned the native watchman with his tall bamboo pole, who was soon in attendance upon the portly black-clad figure. From time to time there were peals of laughter from above his head, designed to draw his attention, so that when he looked up he saw a window framing the painted faces of several bazaar prostitutes, each of them promising with her eyes every erotic delight of the Orient. Presently the narrow street opened into a square, surrounded by giant trees. There was a sound of drumming and, in a little hut made of matting, Verity saw a grotesque statue of the goddess Kali, naked but for a tinsel crown, a jewelled belt, and cheap bangles. She stood over a prostrate Siva, as though about to impale herself upon him. In front of the statues, under a canvas awning, two very young nautch-girls in transparent saris were dancing a smooth, gliding step to the accompaniment of pipes and drum. A crowd of spectators sat in a circle about the awning, the reflection of oil-light dimly outlining their features, and sang to the Hindoo temple music in a soft, monotonous chant.

Leaving the last traces of English Calcutta behind him, Verity crossed the square and turned into the street of native stores, where Karim's "emporium" was to be found. Karim was a man of many vocations, money-lending and the procuring of native girls for the bungalows of British officers, among them. But Verity knew that Karim's interest lay firmly in the continuation of John Company's rule and in seeing every mutineer from Simla to Trincomalee hanged in a row. The "emporium" sold cloth and trinkets indiscriminately, and was designed like most of the Indian shops in the Bow and Lal bazaars. The counter displaying Karim's goods was well-shaded but the contents were visible to passers-by. Most of the goods were either protected from dishonest hands or else could only be reached by Karim himself from the interior of the dark cavernous store. Between the customer in the street and the goods displayed there was a broad wooden barrier, ornamented by scores of forged coins which had been nailed to it, in order to advertise Karim's acumen in matters of commerce. There were bad rupees and small "silver" coins like four-anna bits. Some were, in fact, merely the metal buttons of jackets filed down until they were barely to be distinguished from the earliest coinage of the East India Company, which was notorious for having hardly any imprint left upon it by the 1850s. But Karim had distinguished the fakes and maintained his boast that no smasher had ever played at "under and over" with him successfully.

In his fez and black tunic, Karim stood in the oil-lit doorway of his emporium as Verity approached. He recognised his new customer as one of the "vigilance officers" who had lately begun to frequent the bazaars.

"What is it that the Sergeant Sahib desires?" he asked softly.

"Mr Karim," said Verity, looking stern, "you always been a straight man, 'ave you?"

"Sahib?"

"You was always a loyal subject of 'er Majesty, and a well wisher to Old England?"

"Oh yes, Sahib."

"And you would assist 'er Majesty and 'er servants, as best you might?"

"All that I have is hers, Sahib," said Karim mournfully, as if to suggest that what he had was too little to be noticed.

"Good," said Verity, "and might you be in the habit of selling any cameo brooches? Proper cameo, I mean, for ladies' wear."

Karim's eyes brightened.

"Ah, the Sergeant Sahib wishes to purchase . . . ?"

Verity sighed heavily.

"Much obliged, Mr Karim, but I ain't particular to buy a brooch. You might tell me, 'owever, whether you sold a cameo of a lady with her 'air in corkscrew ringlets – sold it in the last few days to a scrawny young fellow name of Dhingra. Shabby sort of cove. Must 'a bought it on commission to sell again, I should say."

"A small man with a deceitful eye, Sahib?"

"Couldn't 'a put it better, Mr Karim."

"He was a Hindoo," said Karim disapprovingly. "Yes, Sahib, he bought such a brooch."

"And 'ow might you remember 'im so clear, Mr Karim?"

"Why, Sergeant Sahib! He was the most tiresome fellow! He would have the brooch and he would not take the ring — he had not the money for both. It is no easy thing, Sahib, to sell the ring alone when the brooch is gone."

Verity breathed heavily with satisfaction.

"Now you interest me, Mr Karim. This was a cameo set, then, brooch and ring? And might you still 'ave that ring?"

"Indeed, Sahib, it is upon the metal rod with the others."

"And how might you have come by that ring and brooch, Mr Karim?"

"Sahib, I do not know, the rings and brooches I sell only to please those who will not come to buy my cloth. I have them in hundreds from the hawkers who come to me. If there is something evil about this ring or brooch, Sahib, I swear I know nothing of it!"

"P'raps you don't, Mr Karim," said Verity reasonably, "and even if you did, I might draw it a bit mild for you, provided you was to act sensibly over this ring. P'raps I might just see it?"

Karim bowed, his face somewhat paler with apprehension, and led the way outside. At the front of his display, just behind the wooden ledge with the false coins nailed to it, was a slender brass rod locked into its horizontal position at either end. A hundred rings or more were strung upon it, so that they might be turned and examined by the customers without any fear of theft. Karim's fingers moved deftly upon them, sorting and sliding until he had found the cameo.

"This is the one, Sahib, a fine ring."

"'Just take it off that rod, Mr Karim. And don't start telling me now how fine it is, after saying how cheap you bought it."

Karim busied himself with the iron hinge that locked the rod in place.

"Just tell me," said Verity with impatience, "whether you see the cameo loose or whether anything mayn't have bin slipped in behind the mount."

But Karim had unlocked the rod, retrieved the ring, and handed it to Verity. The cream cameo of a girl's head showed the corkscrew ringlets of an old-fashioned coiffure against a dark caramel background. The inset was the size of an oval half-crown. Karim watched nervously as Verity took out his pocket-knife and opened the small blade. He inserted this under the diminutive hooks which held the cameo in its place, and began to prise them backward so that the little portrait was loosened from its mount. As it came free his heart jumped with excitement. A sliver of paper, identical to that found in the brooch, had been folded into a tiny wad and slid between the cameo and its case. He took it very carefully, then put both the paper and the dismembered ring into his pocket.

"Mr Karim, I have reason to suppose that this ring of yours was formerly the property of a young person who may have met a unnatural end in the disturbances at Cawnpore. Now, I ain't saying that you came by it dishonestly, but it may prove a very suspicious piece of evidence in the case against Dhingra. If you'd be so good as to have a ink-and-dip fetched, I shall write a note for you, on police authority, as a receipt. But one way or the other, this ring goes with me."

Karim seemed only too eager to comply. He shouted for his boy, gave an order, and the little wooden tray with quill and glass ink-pot was produced. Standing at the wooden counter, Verity began the slow and laborious task of making out his personal receipt for the ring to "A. Karim, Esquire." He had almost completed this when he became distantly aware of a disturbance in the street whose volume was far above the normal level of shouting and raucous cries in the bazaar. There was a rush of escaping customers past his back and then, to his astonishment, there came the hollow clopping of hooves as a pair of riders reined in above him.

"Karim, you black ponce! Come out here!"

"Come out, Karim, and we'll settle Captain Groghan's debts with you!"

Before Verity could turn, a hunting-horn blasted a "View halloo!" so close to his head that his heart jumped to his throat with the shock of the din. There were five riders, two of whom now got down from their saddles and seized Karim, who was visibly shaking with fright in the opening of his shop.

"Karim's woman poxed Captain Groghan!" said the first man.

"Karim's arrack poisoned the whole bloody mess!" snorted the second man.

"Karim's going to get the thrashing of his life!" said the first.

"And not a minute too soon!"

Verity failed to identify their corps in the oil-light, seeing only red mess-jackets with white facings, the bare heads and smooth young faces of subalterns, flushed wth drink and food. It was by no means unknown for a lively mess dinner to be rounded off by some of the boisterous junior members hunting out and beating senseless their native money-lender, purveyor of drink, and provider of girls, on whom all their violence was now about to fall. There were three of them still on horseback and two on foot, whose role was to prevent Karim's escape by pushing him back into the cleared space where he was to meet his enemies. Captain Groghan, a blond young man in his early twenties, trotted his sleek powerful mare forward, trailing a long coach-whip. Karim gave a cry.

"No, Sahib!"

Groghan's flushed young face contorted with hate and exertion, the lash streaking across Karim's shoulders with an ear-splitting crack. Karim gave a shriek and stepped backward as the whip rippled again and exploded with a sound like a blow upon the side of his neck.

"Stop this!" roared Verity, neck and jowls purpling with rage. Groghan slashed again at Karim.

"I am a police sergeant and I will arrest the next man that strikes a blow!"

He strode forward until he stood by Karim's crouching body.

54

"He's going to arrest us! All of us!" said a derisive voice from the darkness.

"You shall answer to the Governor-General, if you strike this man again!" bellowed Verity.

"I am the Governor-General," said a voice from the shadows, and there was a hooting of laughter.

"Only one way to teach manners to a bloody peeler!" said Groghan thickly. He flexed his arm again and the lash rang out, wrapping itself round Verity's leg with an agony that took the breath from his lungs. But he had half prepared himself for the blow, though he could not prevent it. Putting the ferocious pain of the cut firmly to the back of his mind, he seized the whip as high up as he could reach and jerked it violently towards him. Groghan had somehow looped it round his wrist, to secure it more firmly, but now found himself pulled from the saddle by the sudden weight of the portly sergeant. Yet he fell lightly enough and was on his feet in a moment, still holding the whip and taking a fresh aim at Verity. Verity watched the arm go back, then sidestepped and came in determinedly with face lowered. It seemed to him that Groghan, swaying a little even though the fall had sobered him, was moving with absurd slowness. It was as though he had all the time in the world to double up his fist like a prizefighter and plant a decisive blow on the loose, grinning jaw. Groghan went down, crawled a yard or two, and then lay still.

"Right!" said Verity, displaying the clenched fist to the others, " 'oo's next?"

They all were. The four red mess-jackets emerged from the shadows, on every side of him. Someone called, "Cut him down, the brute!" As the first subaltern took him from the rear, Verity heard the sound of running footsteps, but it was no longer the scampering of Karim's customers leaving the scene of the violence. These were heavy, rhythmic steps, boots marching at the double, and they were coming closer. When the corporal and the guard arrived they found the fat man in the black frock-coat already overpowered with two red-cheeked young subalterns holding his arms.

The corporal and four privates of the guard were kilted

Highlanders, though their voices were more accurately Glaswegian. Three of the privates snatched him from his captors, one taking either arm, doubled excruciatingly behind his back, a third prodding him on unnecessarily from behind and a fourth clearing the way ahead. To Verity's dismay they began to run him towards the guard room of Government House.

"Stop this!" said Verity breathlessly, "I'm an officer of the law."

"Stash ye'r gab!" said the Corporal from behind him, prodding the fat trouser seat with a sharp but invisible instrument.

"N'listen to me! Those officers 'as committed a common assault on a shopkeeper. Listen . . . "

"Stash ye'r gab!"

The native witnesses stared at the fat man in the frock-coat being trundled unwillingly along by the two Scots in their kilts of green and black tartan, red tunics, and black bonnets with a red cockade. Verity could feel the veins in his neck and forehead gorged and throbbing, his lungs drawing breath in a muted howl. His legs began to fail him and he was half dragged the final quarter of a mile to the guard-house, a white-painted outbuilding of Government House itself. The two men who had dragged him were themselves winded by the effort, but the Corporal and the remaining Highlander took over the duty of gaolers. Before they could do more than box him into a corner, the door of the guard-house opened and a bare-headed young lieutenant with his tunic collar torn open in the recent struggle entered. Verity smelt the drink upon him at two yards' distance and noticed with alarm that the lieutenant was brandishing a horse-pistol with a long shiny barrel.

"That's him!" said the young officer to the Corporal, "That's the man who attacked Mr Groghan! Teach him a lesson with the compliments of Lord Canning's staff!"

" 'alf a minute!" said Verity breathlessly, "I am in pursuance of my duty on the authority of the Provost-Marshal. I have my identification as a Sergeant of Metropolitan Police 'A' Division."

"Po – liss!" said the Highlander with distaste.

"A shiddle-come-shite, kiss my arse wary Sawnie!" said the Corporal contemptuously.

"In my jacket pocket," said Verity confidently, "is a ring and a scrap of paper on which a man may be 'ung. 'ave the goodness to see me conveyed to the provost barrack in Fort William without delay."

The Corporal's green eyes were fixed on Verity's as he approached, thrust a hand deep into either pocket of the frock-coat and drew out the cameo ring and the scrap of paper that had been concealed in its mount. He handed them to the other Highlander.

" 'ere," said Verity sternly, "you just have a care of those, my good man!"

"Ay," said the Corporal, "ye heerd the fat booger, Private Rae, take good care o' 'em!"

Private Rae grinned and popped the little wad of paper into his mouth.

"You ain't half goin' to answer for this!" said Verity furiously "The pair of you!"

Private Rae continued to grin, working the paper to a pulp before crossing to the window, opening it, and spitting it into the darkness. He pocketed the ring.

"I wadnae be too sure who's to answer," said the Corporal bleakly. "A so-jer as strikes a officer goes before a file of muskets. Ye may be sure o' hearin' more o' this fram ye'r oon commander. I suppose ye canna be shot, bein' only a fat bludy peeler, but I hae no doot they'll find summit for ye. But for our satisfaction, just now, ye'll please tae lie on the floor."

"Stand out of my way!" said Verity defiantly.

"Put him on the floor!" said the Corporal to the other two Highlanders who had been recovering their breath, "And you, Rae, take ye'r boots off!"

Verity struggled but his legs were deftly knocked from under him and he found himself staring up at the guard-house ceiling in a manner uncomfortably recalling Dhingra's ordeal that afternoon.

"Now," said the Corporal, "Private Rae is going to

promenade you with his knees. He'll no crack more than a rib or two for ye, and the beauty o' the whole thing is that it never leaves a mark on the skin. He kens the art o' it to perfection, fram havin' guarded poor lunatics in a private asylum. Begin wi' the legs, so-jer, if ye please!"

Private Rae dropped into a kneeling position on Verity's thighs and began to shuffle up and down vigorously as if in some ritual dance. Suddenly the bony knees found Verity's thigh muscles, forcing out a gasp at the intensity of the pain.

"A little harder, if ye please, Private Rae!"

It was like the most excruciating cramp. Verity bit his lower lip till the blood welled from it, to control the howl of suffering that swelled in his breast.

"An' now the belly, a little harder still."

The sweat that ran from him was cold to his flesh as winter rain.

"An' now the ribs, so-jer! Let's hear a pair o' 'em crack for poor young Mr Groghan's jaw!"

Verity could feel the breath upon his own face as Rae panted with exertion and began the "feeling out" of the required spot with his knees. In a moment, Verity knew, he would howl for mercy, beg them to spare him. He was almost weeping when he heard another voice.

"Wot the 'ell's this civilian doing in the guard-'ouse?"

The sudden removal of Private Rae's weight was comfort bordering on physical bliss. Looking up, Verity saw the reassuring sight of an unquestionably English sergeant-major.

"A bit o' a disagreement with Captain Groghan, sir."

"My compliments to Captain Groghan, and I will not 'ave civilians in *my* guard-'ouse. Charge 'im and throw 'im in a cell, or else get 'im out of here. Orderly officer's rounds in five minutes and the Governor-General's carriage coming back in ten! Turn the guard out, and get rid of this civilian!"

"He's no a civilian, sir. Provost-Marshal's office."

"Then, by God, man, let Mr Groghan report him to the Provost-Marshal! Now get him out of my guard-house!"

Verity had risen to one knee by this time. Orders were shouted and the Highlanders of the guard appeared from every side. Under the Sergeant-Major's repeated expostulations, a pair of them helped Verity respectfully to his feet, led him into the open air, and steered him towards the direction of Fort William.

"Leave 'im!" bawled the Sergeant-Major, approaching the dishevelled policeman. He moved menacingly behind Verity, as if to deliver a parting insult, and breathed heavily into the Sergeant's ear.

"If it was you that broke Mr Groghan's jaw, I only wish I 'ad you in *my* regiment, under *my* orders. I'd see to it myself that the likes of you got the bloody Commander of the Bath!"

"Seconded!" said Colonel Farr angrily, the face behind the iron-grey whiskers deepening to a damson purple: "Seconded. In other words, Sergeant, you don't belong to the Provost-Marshal but to the Metropolitan Police."

Verity stood bolt upright, at attention before Farr's office table. He swallowed discreetly.

" 'ave been told so, sir."

"Dammit, man," said Farr abandoning all official procedure, "if you had been transferred and were under army discipline, you'd be court-martialled and shot for striking an officer! And don't think they wouldn't do it, especially when the war's not over and discipline is all the go!"

"Only acted in pursuance of duty, sir, according to instructions."

"Your instructions, Sergeant, were to ask certain questions of a native trader in the bazaar. You were not under instructions to beat senseless one of the Governor-General's aides!"

"No, sir. 'ad to prevent a breach of the peace, though."

"Don't play clever with me, Mr Verity! Not unless you want to travel a very rough road. We don't make barrack lawyers very comfortable here."

"No wish to be clever, sir. Only acted to prevent 'er Majesty's peace being breached."

"And do you think, Sergeant, that the natives of Calcutta

will respect Her Majesty's peace more, after seeing you brawling with a superior officer in the bazaar gutters?"

"Couldn't say as to that, sir. Only acted to protect the man Karim."

"Sergeant," said Colonel Farr, getting up from his chair and coming round the table, "Karim is a native, a nigger! Captain Groghan is a British officer. This isn't London, my lad, and I'm not Mr Croaker. A hundred miles from here there's a native army still on the rampage, and there's ten thousand of them for every one of us. Now, you forget everything you ever learnt at Bible classes and Lady Linacre's meat-teas. There's a war to be fought even in Calcutta. There are spies and turncoats by the hundred among the natives. Don't ever forget that and don't ever forget which side you belong to. If Captain Groghan chooses to go to the bazaar again and horsewhip every native the whole length of it, you know what you'll do?"

"No, sir," said Verity nervously.

"You'll go there," said Farr softly, "on official duty, and make sure that no one interferes with him while he does it."

For an instant Verity thought that he must then and there demand his return to London, but the knowledge that it would be refused checked him. Instead he said, "One other thing to say, sir."

"What's that?" inquired the Colonel suspiciously.

"Request to prefer charges against Private Rae, 42nd Highland regiment, for assault and destruction of evidence, sir."

"Refused."

"Sir," said Verity, "he ate the evidence in Dhingra's case."

"*Ate* it?"

"Chewed it up and spat it out, sir. It was the paper in the cameo ring."

Colonel Farr drew a clean sheet of paper towards him, as though about to begin some other task.

"Your request is still refused, Sergeant."

" 'ave the honour to ask why, sir!"

"Look," said Farr reasonably, "your Highlander may have done all you say but, by our own account, you have no marks and no witnesses except hostile ones."

" 'e destroyed the evidence in Dhingra's case, sir, before it could be seen here."

"Sergeant Verity," said Farr, his eyes levelly upon the indignant policeman, "you did well in your interrogation of Dhingra, you and Mr Lopez between you. But I will hear no more of this."

"Don't see why, sir, with respect."

"Because, Sergeant, yesterday morning, while you were still recovering from your – ah – accident, Dhingra was hanged."

Verity felt as though the breath had been knocked from his body.

"Now," resumed Farr, "the business is over and I will not have questions about 'evidence' being brought up when it can no longer be of the least use."

"And Miss Stockwood's case, sir?"

"That, too, has been settled, Sergeant."

Dismissed from the interview with Colonel Farr, Verity sought out Sergeant Martock.

"Well, old fellow," said Martock, "when you go out on the hi-tiddly-ti of an evening, you certainly kick the traces over!"

"Mr Martock," said Verity helplessly, "they *hanged* Dhingra."

"My dear chap," said Martock laconically, "what else was there to do after your brilliant inquisition? He was a mutineer!"

"I know he was."

"And," said Martock, wagging a finger, "you were wrong about Amy Stockwood, and I was right. He ravished her cruelly on the fifteenth of July when they were all put to death, and then slit her poor little gizzard himself."

" 'ow d'yer know? Was he put to the torment again?"

"Not a finger laid on him," said Martock with surprise. "He kept it all to himself until they were about to kick the platform from under him and leave him dancing in the air. Then he came out with it all and said he was glad of it. Dirty bastard!"

Verity sat down heavily.

"I found 'er ring," he said sadly, "and another bit of that paper in it. But a Highland so-jer eat up the paper and stole the ring."

"Well," said Martock, "it ain't going to make much odds, old chum, they've hung him, he deserved it, and there's an end of everything."

"Oh, he deserved it all right!" said Verity gloomily, "He was a mutineer."

"And he coopered poor little Amy Stockwood," said Martock.

Verity looked suspiciously at his companion.

"Mr Martock, before that sojer eat up the paper, I wasn't so stupid as not to see what might be on it."

"Of course not, my dear fellow."

"And what was on it," said Verity, "was two more dates. One was the fifteenth of July, when the massacre was and Dhingra says he killed her. The other was the twenty-eighth of July when she's bein' took for the pleasure of some cruel native to the 'orrors of 'is zurr-narr-narr!"

"We call it zenanah," said Martock lightly.

"Whatever you call it can't much signfy. What does signify is that Dhingra has confessed to a murder he can't have done, a-cos Miss Stockwood was alive nearly two weeks after, and 'e's added ravishing cruelly, for good measure."

"Well!" said Martock, an expression of ironic wonder lighting the long, well-bred features, "And what does Colonel Farr say to that?"

" 'e don't say nothing!" said Verity, " 'e don't want to know! And I can't prove what I read, there being no witnesses."

"Then I think, old fellow," said Martock kindly, "that you'd best employ yourself with facts that can be proved and cases that Colonel Farr does want to know about. That's my advice."

"Much obliged, Mr Martock," said Verity shortly, "and I ain't greatly in need of advice. When a man goes to be 'ung, confessing a murder he can't possibly have done, there's a smell about it, and that smell ain't got rid of by pretending it's gone away. The orders I take from Colonel Farr is one

thing, but what I may inquire into for my own satisfaction
is another. And you'd oblige me most of all, Mr Martock,
by remembering that I ain't come ten thousand miles for
Colonel Farr's pleasure but to rescue poor innocent souls
from the torments of black-hearted villains. And I ain't
going to be put off easy!"

4

The room where the girl lay, upon a low divan, was carpeted
in white, brilliant as a snowfield by contrast with the dull
emerald of peacocks and birds of paradise upon the rusty
crimson of the woven wall hangings. A smell of musk hung
heavily in the still air of the halls and alcoves, where the
keyhole shapes of archways in marble and sandstone gave
a Moorish tone to the apartments of the zenanah. From the
ornamental lamps a thick ochre light enriched the warmth
of beaten brass upon the small inlaid tables.

Freed of the belt which Azimullah had put upon her
weeks before, Judith lay curled upon the embroidered cotton
of the divan. She had lost count of the days that had passed
since the Khan had watched her enter these private apartments, and had then taken his leave. It might have been a
fortnight. It might have been nearer to a month. The girl
had reluctantly submitted to bathing and "purification"
under the supervision of two Indian women, who treated
her little differently from the matron of the garrison orphanage. Her clothes were taken from her, washed, and then
returned. She was a mere prisoner, a virgin though a slave,
and not yet worthy of the traditional smock and trousers.
Hour after hour, Judith lay alone in the room, not knowing what they planned to do with her and, in the end, hardly
caring.

From time to time, food was brought by a girl who smiled
at her but understood not a word of her language. Occasionally a young and beautiful Indian woman, in the bright

sari and jewels of a favourite wife, looked in at her through the bead curtain. Once a plump, smooth Indian with a bald head and ageless features had stood silently at the foot of the divan and watched. He had neither spoken nor touched her, though he said something in his own language to one of the women as he withdrew. It was from the women who had bathed her and who spoke a little English that Judith learnt to know the man as the Nana Sahib.

During the afternoon of the day following this visit, the Nana Sahib appeared again, accompanied by several of his women. Without a word being spoken, two of the women stood on either side of Judith, each holding an arm gently but securely. Under the white silk of the tunic they could see her blue-veined breasts rising and falling more rapidly with apprehension at what must follow. Then the youngest of the women, who was named Arga and who had the scent of spice strongly on her breath, stooped over the fair-skinned girl and unbuttoned her. For all her twisting and wriggling, Judith was soon naked except for the cotton tunic, which had been pushed up under her armpits. Arga smiled into the wide hazel eyes with evident satisfaction, drawing a hand over the moon-whiteness of the smooth young body. The Nana Sahib stood by, almost unhappily, as though it concerned him little and as if his thoughts were elsewhere.

Presently Arga put a hand to her mouth and took something that she had been chewing. She smiled almost reassuringly at Judith, her hand easing the tense thighs with slow, insistent movements. Still watching the girl's facial contortions, she put her hand to her mouth again, while the other women turned Judith over on to her side. Then Arga repeated the process from the rear. She watched, at the same time, the head of light-brown hair switching from side to side as the prisoner fought to conceal her growing physical agitation. When the moistened spice was finished, Arga poured scented oil from a little flask into the palm of her hand, dipping her other fingers into it. With practised firmness, she massaged the soft breasts until their shape began to harden, then she worked the oil soothingly over the belly and thighs. At a nod from her, the other woman turned Judith on to her stomach, the girl hardly attempting any resistance by this stage. Arga oiled the bare back, the sharp ridges of the shoulder-blades, the inward curve of the spine, and the swelling of the body at the top of the hips. Her fingers followed the cleft of Judith's bottom, touching the enclosed body heat and then brushing the back of the legs towards the final goal. Arga smiled, seeing that this time the girl relaxed herself a little in anticipation. Then Arga practised the most secret art of her massage until she felt the tensing and slackening of the body in a rhythm that was beyond Judith's immediate control. It was time for the women to turn Judith on to her back again, so that Arga could open the legs widely enough for them to hang on either side of the narrow divan.

The bead curtain parted and a naked Bengalee entered, her body small and slender with tight little breasts, her oiled black hair hanging loose to her buttocks. She knelt at the foot of the divan, eyes bright with curiosity, then leant forward over the stretched body and bent deftly to her task. There was an intent silence, broken after a while by the sound of Judith's uneven breath, while the Nana Sahib and the women looked down upon her as they might have watched a fever victim. Several minutes afterwards they saw the brief involuntary arching of the spine and the growing tension in the pale limbs. The Bengalee girl's movements became more darting and more aggressive. Judith's eyes were closed, her lips parted a little, and her face turned aside as though she sought vainly to clench the hard thin pillows of the divan between her teeth. When she opened her eyes briefly, Arga smiled at her, partly as if to reassure her that there was nothing in all this which the witnesses had not seen a hundred times, and partly as though mocking Judith's primness. There was a rhythmic crying, a violent trembling, and then as her arms were released the girl hid her face in the pillow with a long sob. The Sahib withdrew, followed by the Bengalee girl and two of the women. Only Arga remained, sitting on the edge of the divan, stroking Judith's hair, as though to console her, and wiping over the oiled, perspiring body with a cotton square. At length the girl grew calmer, lying face-down against the pillows, stunned by the double shock of the assault and of her own self-discovery.

Judith had recovered her composure considerably when the sad, portly figure of the Nana Sahib reappeared before her several hours later.

"You have been gently treated," he said, as though it hardly mattered to him. "Where you have felt the softness of a girl's touch, others of your countrywomen and mine have endured a burning torch. But if you or your people are stubborn, I cannot be gentle for the future. Now you must show your obedience. Arga will come to you presently and she will sit with you while you write down truly everything that was done in here this afternoon. If it offends your modesty, think how much more immodest it would be to lie exposed to my soldiers, the skin flayed from you as one peels the skin of a peach. Do you understand me?"

She nodded at him, unable to find words to express her eagerness to do anything which would save her from such terror and pain.

"Good," said the Nana, and turned to leave her. At the door, however, he paused, one arm parting the bead curtain. "And you will end your account," he said softly, "with the sad greeting of a dutiful daughter to her father!"

5

Beyond the station yard of Raniganj, where the bare earth road stretched flat as far as the eye could see, the contour of the horizon rippled in the early morning heat. Verity and Martock, in white cotton drill, stood to one side of the auxiliary company of the 60th Rifles, now detrained from the cramped wooden carriages which had rolled and rattled all night from the East Indian Railway terminus at Howrah, across the river from Fort William. The journey had begun in daylight, the platform crowded with half naked Hindoos and serge-clad Irish soldiers of the 60th, searching for missing knapsacks and swearing to have a whole new kit off the first mutinous "Saypoys" whom they chanced to kill. Then the snorting black engine had run at a regulation twenty miles an hour across the flat, lush vegetation of the delta, depositing the 60th Rifles and the accompanying staff of the Intelligence Department at Raniganj in the rapidly brightening dawn.

Verity stood with one foot on the regulation portmanteau, into which he had crammed shirts, socks, brushes, and an extra pair of boots. There was hardly room for more possessions if the bag was to be consistent with the official ruling that no man's luggage must weigh above a hundred pounds. Martock stood beside him, observing the restless files of the 60th, while Lopez waited at a little distance off, as though to distinguish his status from theirs. Colonel Farr, saying something about "tiffin", had disappeared as soon as the black, brass-funnelled engine pulled gasping into Raniganj.

"What I don't see," said Verity moodily, "is why we gotta go to 'im. It'd be a sight easier for 'im to come to us, in Calcutta."

He had not seen it all night, and had said so frequently.

"Rajahs don't dance attendance in Calcutta, my old son," said Martock philosophically, "not even shifty bastards like old Maun Singh. And they can be deucedly tiresome about it when you want something they've got."

"'oo wants it?" Verity turned a face creased with indignation, "'oo wants 'is bloomin' jool?"

"Lord Canning wants it," said Martock simply, "and Maun Singh's more slippery than a bucketful of eels. If he's offering it now, it had better be took, sharp."

"Can't see the usefulness of it," said Verity stubbornly.

"You know," said Martock softly, "these damned native trains are beyond a joke. They leave a fellow feeling as though he must have stood chummage round the whole mess, and finished at three in the morning with devilled bones and anchovy tart!"

"I ain't particular as to that," said Verity sullenly.

There was a sudden movement among the waiting rifle-men, the first red-tunic'd file of the company marching away from the railhead to the waiting wagons of the bullock-train. With two bare-backed *khitmudgars* carrying their port-manteaus, Martock and Verity followed. The score of two-wheeled wagons drawn up in a line at the far end of the station yard seemed an unpromising form of transport. Several of the bullocks were by now lying down between the shafts and defying all the blows of the native drivers and the prodding muzzles of the soldiers who endeavoured to get them on their feet again. The wagons themselves had thin wooden staves mounted upon them, over which painted canvas was stretched to provide shelter from the heat.

"Well, old chums," said Martock, hoisting himself on to the tail-board, "be it ever so humble, this is home for us until we get to Benares."

Verity followed him and sat down heavily. His exaspera-tion at the misuse of his talents had grown every mile from Calcutta. He had been taken from duties which it was his second nature to perform, and assigned to those of which he was ignorant and for which he cared nothing. No one, it seemed to him, showed any further concern for the poor Amy Stockwoods of the Sepoy War. There had been a sum-mons from a devious old reprobate, Maun Singh, and, with that, the Intelligence Department lost all interest as to whether Amy and her sisters in suffering might be alive or dead. The problem was General Havelock's relief column. After the General had driven the mutineers from Lucknow and Cawnpore, his gunners began to engage Tantia Topi, commander of the Nana Sahib's army, close to the territories of Rajah Maun Singh. This elderly Prince, seeing the tide of battle flowing for the English, had judged it time to announce himself as the protector of English fugitives and a well-wisher to the men of the Queen's army.

In Calcutta, Government House was unimpressed, but judged it expedient to appear flattered. Lord Canning's confidential messenger hinted to Maun that he might care to demonstrate his loyalty by putting his great treasure into the safekeeping of the British Raj until the end of hostilities.

Such a gesture, it was further hinted, would officially
absolve him of any subsequent suspicion of having supported the Nana Sahib during the earlier stages of the
mutiny. Maun was terrified of deserting the Nana's cause
and so being liable to fearful vengeance at the hands of the
Sahib's army. But the salvoes of General Havelock's guns,
growing louder and closer every day, proved the more powerful argument. Maun Singh privately agreed to put his
treasure, or at least a part of it, under the General's guard.
Soon after, in a positive passion of loyalty, he agreed to a
further suggestion. His most treasured jewel, a stone worth
more than all the wealth of his kingdom beside, was to be
taken secretly and under heavy guard to Calcutta by three
regiments of soldiers and the officers of Lord Canning's
Intelligence Department. So far as ceremonial meetings
could ever be secret, the ancient gem was to be transferred at
a private rendezvous between British officers and Maun
Singh's Dewan, beyond the holy city of Benares.

At Raniganj, the company of Rifles divided, six men to
a wagon, two men at a time marching beside it while the
others rode. The officers, more fortunate, rode in pairs.
Verity swiftly discovered the drawbacks of travel by bullock-
train. The carts were without springs of any kind, and every
rut or mound in the baked earth of the road communicated
itself to him with spine-jarring vigour. Worse still, he soon
discovered that the only protection against the glare and
direct heat of the sun was to close the flap of the awning
at the back of the cart. But once that was done, the tempera-
ture in the unventilated space rose with alarming speed until
both men were gasping for breath.

Later that day, Verity said, "A hundred jools ain't worth
so much as saving one poor lady or her child from a 'orrible
death."

"Likewise," said Martock with a wave of his hand, "this
don't seem to be an ordinary jewel. That damned old screw
Lopez says they reckon it to be the biggest bit of devil's glass
that was ever dug up, the size of half a hen's egg."

"'oo cares?"

"Well, they do, old fellow, though we mayn't. And it's

69

terribly old, the oldest of them all, you've no idea how many centuries it's been kicking about."

"It still don't entitle them to be a-crying off from being held accountable for poor souls in the hands of black murderers!"

"Well," said Martock reasonably, "there is one other thing about this sparkler. The natives believe that whoever owns it, shall be the ruler of all India."

"But Maun Singh ain't!"

"No," said Martock, "because Maun Singh knows as much what to do with an army as a poor gelding knows what to do with a frisky young filly. But Lord Canning knows what to do with it all right, you just see if he don't."

"I still don't see the usefulness of it."

"Only think," said Martock, "only think, Mr Verity, how many of your poor souls may be saved if that jewel in Lord Canning's hands should make the natives see the error of their ways and return to their allegiance. Likewise, think how many more might be lost, if the jewel were to fall into the wrong hands!"

Verity retired from the argument.

"Think of pie!" he said presently, "Think o' a veal and hammer! It makes me 'ungry as a rat-catcher's tyke just to imagine it!"

Martock reached into his pocket, pulled out a flask, unscrewed the little top, and offered it to the plump sergeant.

"There's no burn in it, old son. It goes down like oil."

"Much obliged, Mr Martock," said Verity distantly, "but I ain't particular to sample it. I was just thinking of a veal and hammer."

During the day that followed, Verity seemed to reconcile himself to the duty that had been allotted him. He said thoughtfully,

"Supposing, Mr Martock, that this Maun Singh were to be what you say he is, slippery as a bucketful of eels, 'ow do you suppose we shall, any of us, get a grip of 'im?"

"I shouldn't get into a wax over that, if I were you," said Martock with a comfortable yawn, "Colonel Farr and Lopez will hold him."

"They'll more likely come up with a handful of shine-rag and nothing else!" said Verity sceptically.

"You don't know the half of it." Martock turned his head away slightly, as though in disapproval. "Lopez was in Delhi when the natives began to run amok, long before there was any British troops there. He got out, saved a couple of others, and almost bloody walked to Calcutta. Killed a dozen mutineers along the way with his silk choker. He had a bit of a reputation in Delhi before this trouble blew up, so I hear. You don't want to underestimate Lopez, Mr Verity. And Colonel Farr ain't exactly green as a leek and soft as new cheese. He was at Cabul, in thirty-nine, a prisoner of Akbar Khan, only he escaped. Went through the Sikh business, Aliwal and Chillianwallah. He knows what's what."

"I daresay," said Verity, "as I could've got out of Delhi, if I'd had a skin the colour of Mr Lopez's."

"Don't you believe it, old son," said Martock, "There were scores of men and women, all of them a damn sight more tawny than Lopez, who had their bellies ripped open by the natives for being English."

After a succession of stifling days under the canvas awning, and restless nights when mosquitoes and blister-flies fastened upon Verity's soft plump body with the appetite of gourmets, the entire bullock-train came to an abrupt halt late in the afternoon. There was a sudden confusion of men leaping from the carts among shouts of, "Stand to your arms! ... Fall in! ... At the double!"

Verity raised the flap of canvas and peered out. "'ere!" he said cautiously, "It's a band o' mutineers!"

Martock joined him and looked. Down the road towards the bullock-train marched a column of uniformed men in long *bokus* or tunics with what appeared to be balaclava helmets made of metal. There were some three hundred of them, a few carrying old matchlock firearms, others with *tulwars* or swords, or even rudimentary lances fashioned by attaching a bayonet to a long bamboo pole. The company of the 6oth Rifles was facing forward across the road, the Lee Enfields held ready across their chests.

"They're coming on still!" said Verity eagerly. "If our

71

rifles can only hold their fire long enough, they can blow the lot o' 'em to Kingdom Come. That's how we held on at Inkerman!"

"Just pray to God they don't," said Martock dryly, "that's Maun Singh's menagerie coming down the road."

There was a brief parley and the weapons on both sides were put temporarily out of view. Then Martock said, "What's really worth seeing is on the other side."

Verity walked round the bullock-cart and stared. Across a broad and level stretch of plain he saw a vision of yellow palaces, mirrored as gold in the waters of the Ganges. Against the intense skies, cupolas and temples quivered with a dazzling lustre. The ochre-coloured stone of the buildings was toned in places by a coating of reddish purple which the rain and sun had faded to pale flesh-colour. In the evening light, the balconies beneath their awnings glowed with the reflection of ruby and sunset fire from the river's surface. Verity stood open-mouthed at the centrepiece of this vision, a pointed dome covered with leaves of chased gold, surrounded by smaller cones, by statues of the eight-armed Kali and peacocks in solid gold.

"And there, old fellow," said Martock softly, "is Benares. Best seen from a distance, because once you get close, it stinks like last week's bloater."

"That dome!" said Verity breathlessly. "That's solid bloody gold!"

"So they say," remarked Martock smoothly, "yet the dashed rummy thing is that even that ain't worth the price of Maun Singh's jolly old sparkler."

Close by the small town of Fyzabad the bell tents of three British regiments stretched in neat rows upon grass as well cared for as the parkland of an estate in England. Since neither the British Governor-General, nor Maun Singh himself would be present at the ceremony or celebration, it was not strictly speaking a durbar, but the distinction was observed only in theory. The officers of the 60th Rifles and the Intelligence Department were entertained for a whole afternoon by the sports of Maun Singh's arena, a brick circle some five or six feet high with seating upon its top. Verity and Martock watched the successive fights between reluctant elephants, a pair of pacific rhinoceros, two unwilling buffalo, and a score of other animals, none of whom seemed disposed to do battle. When goaded by *sowars* on horseback, they turned upon these tormentors and unseated a number of them. In desperation, the master of ceremonies summoned his wrestlers, filling the arena with half a dozen pairs of naked mahrattas, their heads shaved and their bodies trembling with excess flesh which gave some of them the appearance of having female breasts. The grunting, the bulging eyes, the inexpert neck-locks lasted interminably and without any decisive result.

"I don't call this much of a do!" said Verity disapprovingly, "I seen better than this at Mr Astley's circus!"

"You wait till this evening, old fellow," said Martock encouragingly, "I daresay you may see a thing or two that Mr Astley never showed you!"

The durbar tent, a large marquee, had been erected between the lines of the British regiments and Fyzabad itself, surrounded by open grassland. On one side, the warriors of Maun Singh kept the ground, on the other, two companies of British infantry formed a broad lane in double ranks, facing inwards. They wore number-one dress, as a matter of ceremony, but the Governor-General's estimate of Maun Singh was made clear by the muskets which the men carried. It was rare for the British army to carry muskets while wearing number-one dress because of the oily patches which the guns left upon the tunic.

Maun Singh's durbar tent, or *shamianah,* was carpeted with red and hung on every side with yellow and red tapestries of Persian design. In company with Colonel Farr, Mr Lopez, and Martock, Verity surveyed the arrangements for the meeting. Two rows of gaudily upholstered chairs had been drawn up, facing one another across the richly-carpeted grass in the area of the tent. Verity noticed that several baskets of oranges and a few squares of coloured silks had been placed on the near side, being intended in some mysterious way to contribute to the entertainment of the

Rajah's British guests. More to the point, there were cases of bottles of Exshaw's No. 1 awaiting the attention of the visitors.

"Seems in order," said Colonel Farr, resplendent in regimentals and sword: "All it lacks is the ceremony. Sergeant Martock!"

"Sir?"

"You will keep the ground on our side, where our people come and go. No one will enter or leave the tent while I am here."

"Sir!"

"Mr Lopez?"

"Colonel Farr?"

"Mr Lopez, I should be obliged to you if you would keep your feet during the ceremony. The rest of us must remain pretty well where we are, and we shall rely on you to move about quickly if you see a sign of trouble."

Lopez half-bowed his acknowledgment.

"Sergeant Verity?"

"Sir?"

"Sergeant, you will stand at the extreme left of the chairs in which the Governor-General's deputy and secretary will be sitting. I shall be sitting beside them with the commanders, majors, and senior captains of the three regiments. No other representative of our side is to be present."

"Sir!"

"One other thing, Sergeant. The casket containing the jewel will be brought in by their people from their side. The diamond will be displayed and then placed with the casket on that pedestal in the centre where the representatives on both sides can see it. There will then be an entertainment of some kind. At the end of that, you will step forward, bow to the Dewan, take the casket and bring it directly to me. I shall open it and present the imperial diamond to the Governor-General's deputy. Is that clear?"

"Perfectly clear, sir."

"Good," said Farr sourly, "then we can all go and get ourselves an inner lining to see us through this heathen rubbish!"

The scene when Verity returned to the durbar tent, an hour after sunset, in the wake of the Governor-General's officials, the officers in their regimentals and Lopez in his black court dress was not in the least as he had imagined it. The canvas arena was sweltering with the heat of coloured lamps that blazed on every side, throwing blue, red, and green among the deep yellow of the oil-light. The air was all the more oppressive for the crowd of Maun Singh's subjects which had pressed into the marquee on the far side. Behind the chairs were a guard of regular troops drawn up in uniforms that seemed a passable imitation of the Honourable East India Company's own regiments'. Behind these stood the irregular native levies in parti-coloured tunics and turbans, a surging, ill-contained mob that seemed likely to burst forward, overturn the chairs and take over the entire tent.

"'ere!" said Verity to Martock, "This wasn't what we was to expect! There's a hundred of 'em or more."

"Nothing in India ever is what you expect, old fellow," said Martock, calmly taking up his position by the entrance. "That's what every new griffin has to learn!"

The emissaries of Maun Singh had already taken their places, most of them hardly to be distinguished from the crowding soldiery, except for the Dewan. He was a corpulent elderly Indian, clothed in a long kimono-shaped garment of green and rose-pink silk, with a mailed belt of gold, supporting a two-edged sword with a silver hilt and scabbard, both set with turquoise and precious stones. He seemed more like a Chinaman than an Indian in his dress, but Verity reminded himself that they now stood hardly a hundred miles from the Himalayas and amid a culture as foreign to Calcutta as it was to London.

Colonel Farr and the British officers, wine-coloured sashes and gold epaulettes ornamenting their more usual uniforms, stood before their chairs, facing their host as though respectfully awaiting an invitation to sit down. The Dewan rose laboriously to his feet, unbuckled the sword, and threw it down before him in a gesture of friendship. There was a pause of indecision among the British officers, whose suspicion of a trap in such circumstances had become obsessive.

But there were two companies of British infantry behind them, and two of Her Majesty's regiments completely surrounding the area at a discreet distance. Colonel Farr unbuckled his belt and laid down his sword, the other officers following his example. The Dewan and his guests bowed to each other, and sat down, while the warriors of Maun Singh raised a howl of acclamation, either in welcome to the British representatives or as an approval of the Dewan's skill in disarming the commanders of an opposing army.

The uproar continued for several minutes, while the British officers watched placidly and Verity felt a growing unease. Then there was a silence. The Dewan rose and spoke in a tone which seemed to alternate between hysterical proclamation and smiling benignity. The Governor-General's representative replied, acknowledging Maun Singh as the most valued ally of Her Majesty and Her Majesty's Governor-General, Lord Canning.

There was a braying of trumpets outside the tent and a stirring among the crowd behind the Dewan. An officer of the Rajah's court in a dark blue, European-styled uniform, paced slowly forward with his hand upon the pommel of his sword. Behind him came two uniformed sepoys of Maun Singh's guard, bearing two poles upon their shoulders, as though carrying a litter. Upon this, high over all, was a magnificent casket, encrusted with turquoise and sapphire, its lid rising in shape like the roof of a miniature pagoda and crowned at the very top with the flashing green fire of an emerald bauble.

Verity's heart beat faster at the sight of the mere casket in which the fabled diamond was kept. In the frogged black coat which had been provided as his ceremonial wear, he felt alternately hot and cold as thoughts of splendour and responsibility jarred in his mind. The bearers brought the casket to the centre of the richly carpeted space, where Maun Singh's guard commander turned, took the jewelled box, set it upon the pedestal, and unlocked it. Raising the lid with both hands, he lifted out a cedarwood box, which fitted closely into the casket. Opening this too, he took out a small object wrapped in black velvet. Turning to the two rows of representatives, he unfolded the velvet, held it forward in his hands, and cried, "Kaisar-i-Hind!"

The sudden brilliance of it in the mellow oil-light seemed to increase its size to that of a man's fist. A hundred facets caught the light, magnified it to the sun at noon, and threw it back to blind momentarily those who looked directly upon the flashing crystal of its tiny surfaces. Verity watched it in astonishment. He had seen diamonds enough before, at a distance, but this was a species of its own. The fire and ferocity of its light answered all arguments as to how men could have been so stunted by superstition as to bow before the authority which it embodied in its legend.

"Kaisar-i-Hind!"

The crowd behind the Dewan's chair recovered from its awe and roared with approval. It crossed Verity's mind that if there should be a stampede, or any general movement, it would be out of the question to protect or save the jewel. But the shouting subsided. The officer of Maun Singh laid the diamond on the pedestal before its casket, where all could see it, reposing on its black velvet cloth upon a cushion of black velvet. He stood a little to one side, taking up a position by Maun Singh's representatives to match Verity's own. For several minutes there was a rising murmur of conversation, which fell away again with the first faint, insistent beats of the drummers. A hush of expectation settled on Indians and British alike. Presently, Verity heard a whisper from the Dewan's companions.

"Massoumeh!"

He did not understand at first that it was the name of the girl, the prize among Maun Singh's nautch girls, one of the Persian beauties most coveted by India's princes. Then he saw her, the colours of the lamps tinting the hues of her hair and flesh, shining on the gloss of her body, the sleek voluptuousness of her pale gold figure gleaming with fragrant saffron oil. Massoumeh's beauty was classically Persian, the heart-shaped face with the brownish-green lynx eyes echoing the reddish henna rinse of her hair. The diminutive gold discs covering her breasts looked like tiny round shields, while a golden cincture circled her waist, matching the sandals with the glittering leg strapping that spiralled round her calves. Her only other covering was an incongruous pair of close-fitting black briefs, worn by the dancing-girls of the zenanah out of deference to the more prudish sensibilities of English guests. But the effect of the saffron oil was to make the black silk cling suggestively like a second skin, so that it seemed to draw attention to the narrow triangle pointing the way between her thighs. When she turned her back, the satiny tightness of the black seat was cut so high that the round tawny cheeks of Massoumeh's bottom were hardly covered by it.

The two drummers, cross-legged on the far side of the rich carpeting, began a soft rhythm, so delicate that the differing pitch of the stretched skins made its own subtle harmony. The dancer's hands touched together before her face as she went down in a deep curtsey of homage before the harsh brilliance of the Kaisar-i-Hind upon its pedestal. Then she slipped knowingly into the practiced motions of her erotic mime. The demure, gliding steps of the prelude quickened with the tempo of the drums. More and more restlessly, the reddish hair brushed the warm tan of her bare shoulders, every gesture and movement of her head growing more vigorous and abandoned. She shrugged the tiny gold discs from her breasts and let the unfastened cincture fall. The beat of the drums dwindled to a mere pattering of fingers, as though her accompanists were marking time. The sleek body passed momentarily into shadow. When the drumming quickened and she emerged into full light again, Massoumeh had taken off the black silk pants and was naked except for the sandals. Yet it was not her shimmering nudity alone which held her audience in a breathless trance. From its wickerwork basket, she had drawn a snake, a Russelian quite three feet long, a serpent of rich ivory colouring with ovals of chocolate brown. Verity shivered. In the perfunctory briefing he had been given before embarking for Calcutta, the Russelian had been commended to him as the most lethal of all India's poisonous snakes. It was traditionally the greatest challenge to the power of the charmer. There

were those performers who secretly extracted the poisonous
fangs as a precaution – and there were those who did not.

Massoumeh's arm, bent at the elbow, was held out at
shoulder height, the Russelian coiled tightly round it like
some monstrous bracelet. Going slowly down on to one knee,
the girl allowed it to glide forward, the looped pattern of
ivory and brown spiralling slowly against her warm gold
flesh, until the flat, evil head was poised a few inches from
her throat. Then she arched her body back, supporting herself with one palm behind her as she knelt, exposing the full
stretch of her throat to the deadly fangs. Verity saw the
reptilian mouth flicker, though whether it had touched her
he could not tell. The head arched into air, as though seeking a new prey with blind urgency, and then the rippling
coils slithered down across the girl's shoulder towards the soft
mounds of her breasts. Massoumeh, still arched backward,
reached for the snake's neck with one hand and held it so
that the mouth pointed directly at the rounded flesh. She
trained the flickering mouth first on one side and then the
other, until the cold thrill of the caress or the fear caused
a visible excitement in her hardening flesh.

Straightening up, she sat on her heels, using both hands
to direct the writhing head towards her mouth, repeatedly
meeting it with her own lips and drawing away again, as
though stealing kisses from it. Then she opened her mouth
and gently introduced the head, though without ever allow-
ing her lips to close around it. Presently, she pulled it free
and lay backward so that her knees, widely-spread, still
touched the carpeting and both hands behind her supported
the backward arch of her body, the supple bow of her breasts
and belly displayed to the onlookers. She gave the snake
complete freedom as the long sinuous body slithered in its
long undulations across her breastbone, over the taut
smoothness of her firm stomach, until the head found the
opening of her thighs. There was a gasp as the snake nuzzled
further and further between the gold tan of her legs, and
Verity saw a tremor run through the girl's body at the first
contact of the cold leathery hide against warm sensitive flesh.
Then he saw her raise her head and bow forward, until she

was kneeling with her forehead touching the carpet. This was certainly not how he had imagined a meeting between a Prince of India and Lord Canning's representatives, and he heard Martock's words again in his mind, "Nothing in India ever is what you expect, old fellow!"

The snake was wriggling through the rear opening of the girl's thighs, flowing upward where the smooth gold of Massoumeh's buttocks rounded tightly before the spectators as she knelt lower. The head touched the tiny bone-knobs of her spine and coiled its long body about her waist. The girl turned on to her back, her knees apart and slightly raised, holding the snake again by its neck and directing the throbbing mouth towards the arch of her body. The movements of her hips, riding against this caress, became more violent, though even in her pleasure she was still required to obey the tempo of the drums. The finger-tips beat rapidly and vigorously at first, then slow and languorously, then paused, leaving Massoumeh lying slack and limp, her breasts rising and falling sharply from the exertion. Then the drumming broke into a rapid beat, moving towards its crescendo, which the girl reached with abandoned writhing and a wild cry, that was the first sound to break from her.

Sergeant Verity swallowed hard and mopped his forehead with a red silk handkerchief. The majors and senior captains, faces empurpled and eyes round as marbles, puffed out their cheeks and relaxed. The girl had faked both the peril and the pleasure, no doubt, but it was generally agreed that it had been a damn' smart piece of faking.

Verity became aware that Colonel Farr was looking at him, nodding him forward towards the pedestal where the Kaisar-i-Hind flashed like a thousand heliograph mirrors. The pedestal itself was little more than waist height, so that Verity faced Maun Singh's officer, the commander of the Rajah's body-guard, across it, while the naked dancer crouched in a posture of homage to the great diamond, just to one side of them. The guard commander bowed his head to Verity, who returned what he hoped was a fair imitation of the compliment. Then Maun Singh's officer wrapped the back velvet round the glittering facets of the jewel, placed the precious package in the cedarwood box, lowered this into the casket, and closed the lid of the inner box. Then the man took the jewel-encrusted lid of the casket, and, holding it gingerly with both hands, lowered it into place. He extended his hands, palms upward, in a gesture of donation for Verity's benefit. Verity took one step forward, lifted the casket, which was surprisingly light for all its splendour, and bowed to the Dewan as he had been instructed. Then, accompanied by Maun Singh's officer, he paced smartly across to where Colonel Farr was sitting, and placed the casket on a small inlaid table which had been positioned there for the purpose. Colonel Farr raised the jewelled lid of the casket, and the lid of the box which it contained. As an apparent afterthought, he then turned and called across his shoulder, "Mr Lopez!"

Lopez, in his black court dress, came quickly across.

"Mr Lopez," said the Colonel, "you are the senior investigating officer present. You have not touched or spoken to any person in this tent who has had charge of the diamond tonight, nor have you been near the casket. You have absolute authority and positive orders to pursue an immediate and unrestricted investigation. The Kaisar-i-Hind has gone!"

It was a tribute to Lopez, Verity thought, that he saw the most imminent peril. Without replying to Colonel Farr, he walked to the Governor-General's deputy and spoke a few words. Then he spoke to the three commanders of the British infantry regiments outside. These three rose, bowed to their host, and quietly left the tent. The Governor-General's deputy, with his aide and interpreter, crossed the carpeted space to where the Dewan of Maun Singh sat, bowed and began an earnest conversation. It was not the disappearance of the diamond which had perturbed Lopez most but the effect of its disappearance on the mutual suspicions of the two sides in the *shamianah*. For the time being there was complete stillness in the durbar tent, and Verity heard distinctly the tramping of the infantry companies as they surrounded the marquee.

"Sir," said Lopez, his dark eyes glittering with the vigour

of his intention, "I should like the tent cleared of all those who cannot have had possession of the diamond at any time, who were never within reach of it, and to whom it cannot have been passed."

"Who will that leave you with, Mr Lopez?"

"It will leave, sir, the officer of Rajah Maun Singh, who stands with us now; the dancing-girl who kneels by the pedestal; Sergeant Verity, and yourself."

"Myself, Mr Lopez?"

"Certainly, Colonel Farr. The casket was in your possession for almost a minute before I saw with my own eyes that the jewel had gone."

Farr nodded.

"As for myself and Sergeant Verity, there can be no objection. As for the girl and Maun Singh's officer, my authority does not extend to them."

At this point, Maun Singh's officer intervened.

"Sahib, the girl is a slave and yours to command as you choose. I am a man of honour, and therefore must insist that you investigate my conduct, so that no man may say it was I who was a thief."

"Very well," said Lopez, "but we do not yet know that there is a thief."

He paused, as though establishing the necessary routine of the investigation in his mind. Then he turned to Farr again.

"Colonel Farr, will you be so good as to arrange that enough soldiers are brought in to ensure that when the tent is cleared no person sets foot upon any ground where the diamond may have been since it was last displayed, and that no person comes near or communicates with those who are to be the subject of my investigation?"

"Major Golding hears you as well as I do," said Farr, turning to the officer who sat at his right: "I now ask him that your instructions shall be carried out."

Major Golding stood up, bowed, and withdrew. A moment later, Verity, who had not moved from the spot where he stood when the casket was opened, heard a murmuring among the Dewan's companions on the far side of the

marquee. By both entrances to the durbar tent the red-coated
infantry of Golding's regiment doubled to their places,
forming a cordon in the centre, enclosing the ground and
the suspects whom Lopez had specified. The Governor-
General's deputy parted from the Dewan, who led Maun
Singh's followers from the tent among a hubbub of dissatis-
faction. It was a simple matter for the officers of the three
British regiments to withdraw on their side.

"Now," said Lopez, "the soldiers are to file out and form
their cordon about the tent. And perhaps, sir," turning to
Golding, "you would be good enough to send for the
Surgeon-Major of your regiment."

Verity imagined that when a treasure of such value as the
Kaisar-i-Hind was discovered to be missing, those responsible for its safety were instantly seized with a desire for
action and raising a hue-and-cry. In practice, there seemed
to be a great calm about the whole business, as though the
guardians of the treasure knew that this was their only hope
of retrieving it. Lopez began his careful examination of
the casket and its cedarwood box. When the box was lifted
out, the casket appeared a mere shell. There was no base to
it, merely a ledge running round the sides, upon which the
cedarwood box rested securely. Lopez tapped the brass sides
of the casket, which were far too thin to conceal anything.
Then he turned his attention to the box, turning it over
and over in his hands, raising the lid and probing the
hinges. Finally he set it on its ledge within the casket, and
drew a cross in pencil lightly on the floor of the little box.
While the others watched, he closed the box lid and then
opened it again. Nothing had altered.

"I don't see," said Colonel Farr suspiciously, "what you
want with pencil marks."

Lopez lifted the box out again and closed it. He turned
it upside down, and Verity saw to his astonishment that the
pencil mark was now on the outside of the base of the box.
Lopez smiled with professional satisfaction, held the box
high, opening and closing the lid. When the lid was open the
box appeared normal. But as the lid closed, the floor of the
box, which had been hidden by the casket, turned over on a

central pivot, so that its contents fell through the open bottom of the casket. When the lid was opened, the floor of the box completed another half circle to return to its normal position.

"Performing boxes!" said Verity with slow recognition.

"Easily done," said Lopez coolly, "the Kaisar-i-Hind left the casket somewhen after Maun Singh's officer closed the lid, but before it reached Colonel Farr. The jewel might have been retained beneath the casket by some means but Colonel Farr could only have removed it by raising the box or casket, which he did not do. The Kaisar-i-Hind was removed while in the reach of only three persons: the officer of Maun Singh's; the dancing girl, Massoumeh, and Sergeant Verity."

"You have your Surgeon-Major now," said Maun Singh's guard commander, nodding at the entrance to the tent. "I have nothing to conceal."

Lopez called the Surgeon-Major and Martock, who accompanied him and the officer behind a convenient hanging at one end of the marquee. Colonel Farr, relieved of suspicion, walked across to one entrance of the *shamianah*, as though taking Martock's place on guard. Verity, standing alone, suddenly awoke to the Colonel's shout, "Look to her!"

Verity turned and saw Massoumeh, who had so far stood dejectedly by the pedestal, racing naked for the other opening of the tent. Farr himself sprang after her, but her oiled body slipped easily away from him as he tried to hold her. Verity was close enough to bar her path to the other entrance but there was no hope of holding her or grappling with her successfully so long as her body was sleek with oil. There was no fear that she would get clean away but, if she had the diamond upon her, she would get far enough to extend the necessary area of search over an impossible distance. The feline eyes glittered with hatred and her lips spat out some incomprehensible insult. She swerved suddenly, and Verity changed his position too late. Then she swerved again. He stayed motionless until she was close to him and tried to spring at her, but the sleek flesh slipped through his hands. For all that, he was still between her and the tent-opening.

"Right, miss," he said grimly, "we know a trick worth two o' that."

She came at him again, about to swerve clear and reach the open night, when Verity with head lowered like a bull and cheeks crimson, charged straight into her, the impact knocking the breath from her body and throwing her sprawling. Farr and Lopez were upon her at once.

"Nothing on this gentleman," said Martock smoothly, emerging with Maun Singh's officer.

"Then," said Lopez, "he is to be accompanied to Major Golding and put under protective escort until the investigation is over. Search the girl next."

The combined efforts of Lopez, Martock, and the Surgeon-Major succeeded in wiping the worst of the oil from her, and then positioning her so that every possible place of concealment might be explored.

"No," said the Surgeon-Major at length, "nothing. But who's to say what she may have done in that little paddy just now?"

Then it was Verity's turn to submit to the Surgeon-Major's attentions, while Lopez searched his clothing and his possessions. He almost expected to be told that he had unwittingly had the diamond in his pocket the whole time, but he was pronounced innocent of having purloined it. As Lopez pointed out, the diamond must have been released when Maun Singh's officer closed the lid of the cedarwood box, after Massoumeh's dance. It was the only time when the lid had been closed and the only time when the floor of the little box would have opened. In that case the jewel was probably deposited on the black cushion of the pedestal, and would hardly have been noticed in its own wrapping of black velvet. The pedestal and the cushion had been searched without trace of the stone being found. It was possible that it had been retained under the casket by some means while it was lifted from its cushion and then carried by Verity, on its way to Colonel Farr. There was no trace of it on any of the ground covered or on either of the men who had held the casket. The third possibility was that it had, indeed, been deposited on the black cushion of the pedestal (which seemed the most likely result of the workings of the "performing box") and had still been there when Massoumeh began what the Surgeon-Major called her "little paddy". Her chances of escape had been slight, but her chances of moving the black-wrapped diamond from a place where it certainly would have been found to one where its discovery was unlikely seemed somewhat better.

"The fact that she ain't got it stuck up her somewhere," said Martock consolingly to Verity, "don't mean she's an injured innocent. She's under guard for Calcutta."

"And there's half a battalion of rifles round that grass where they pitched the tent," said Verity with satisfaction. "I daresay it'll turn up, and I'd wager they'll find that doxy and 'er fancy man put the whole thing up!"

"Still," said Martock, stretching luxuriously on his pallet, "I wouldn't change your shoes for mine, even so."

"Whatcher mean?"

"Well, old fellow, whatever they find or don't find, the big news in your personal record is going to be how the biggest diamond in the world that's never given trouble in four hundred years, went missing in the two and a half minutes when you were supposed to be guarding it!"

2

THE INDIAN
ROPE-TRICK

6

Government House, Calcutta 21st May 1858

Lord Canning with his humble duty to Your Majesty. Since his despatch of last evening, Lord Canning has spoken further with Colonel James John Farr, of the Intelligence Department, in the matter of the late durbar at Fyzabad and the disappearance of the Kaisar-i-Hind. From his inquiries, Lord Canning believes that no blame can attach either to Colonel Farr or to his assistant Mr Lopez, both of whom behaved with commendable propriety in the emergency, using every means to discover the location of the missing jewel and to prevent an armed conflict between the three regiments of foot and the irregular troops of the Rajah Maun Singh.

It is established from Colonel Farr's testimony, as well as from that of independent witnesses, that no more than three persons were within reach of the diamond from the time that it was last displayed to the witnesses until it was found to be missing.

The first of these was the Rajah's own guard commander, who at once requested that he should be searched to prove his innocence. This was promptly done by the officers of the Intelligence Department and by a doctor of one of the regiments. It was equally impossible for him to have had the jewel about his person or to have found any means of conveying it from that place.

The second man is a sergeant of the Metropolitan Police on secondment to the Intelligence Department. Though the diamond disappeared during the short period when in his custody, it was not found when he was rigorously searched nor was there any means by which, even if so inclined, he might have removed it from the durbar tent.

The third person to be within reach of the jewel was a

native woman, who had shortly before performed a folk dance of the region for the entertainment of the guests. Though she was not permitted to touch the casket containing the diamond, she was for the space of twenty minutes close by the pedestal on which it is supposed that the jewel must have been concealed. At the end of this period she attempted a desperate escape, which was frustrated by the presence of mind of Colonel Farr. The woman was at once surrendered by Rajah Maun Singh to the officers of the Intelligence Department and has been brought under close escort to Calcutta.

Lord Canning is obliged to state to Your Majesty that the closest scrutiny of the persons and place has revealed no trace of the Kaisar-i-Hind, which must somehow have been moved by the woman in her attempt to evade capture. It has not escaped Lord Canning's thoughts that the diamond was abstracted upon the orders of Rajah Maun Singh himself, who has not always been as forward in Your Majesty's cause as might be wished. Yet the Rajah volunteered to place the jewel in the Governor-General's custody without it being asked or expected of him, so that his motive for removing it would be contradictory to this.

It is much to be feared that the Kaisar-i-Hind may now reach the hands of the Nana Sahib, whose present location is unknown, enabling him to proclaim himself the lawful heir of the Mogul Emperors, and to raise the whole of central India, as well as the Kingdoms of Oudh and the east, in a still greater rebellion against Your Majesty. It is known to Lord Canning that recent exchanges between the Sultan of Turkey and the Egyptian government have spoken of the necessity of aiding the Nana Sahib, as a Muslim brother, if the rebellion were to assume such proportions.

Such a development must be attended by the gravest consequences. Lord Canning begs to assure Your Majesty that no means will be left untried, and no avenue unexplored, by which the Mogul diamond may be prevented from reaching the Nana Sahib and returned in safety to Calcutta.

*

Osborne, 10 July 1858

The Queen acknowledges the receipt of Lord Canning's despatch and letter upon the subject of the Kaisar-i-Hind jewel.

At the outset, the Queen must confess her astonishment that a matter of such consequence as the transfer of the great Mogul diamond should have been allowed to proceed in such an extraordinary fashion. From Lord Canning's despatch as well as from her conversation with her Prime Minister, Lord Derby, she is informed that the jewel, during much of the durbar at Fyzabad, was not in the hands of any responsible officer. Her Majesty is informed that the person from whose immediate custody the diamond disappeared is a sergeant of the Metropolitan Police with no experience of India and who is not considered by his superiors to be possessed of any remarkable ability or intelligence as an officer of constabulary. The Queen does not suggest that any suspicion or a major part of the blame should rest upon this man, though he has shown little enough capacity for performing this particular duty. She is, however, greatly disturbed to hear that his immediate superiors are to be commended either for their own conduct on this occasion or for the ill-advised reliance upon their subordinate. Her Majesty trusts that Lord Canning will think of this.

The Queen cannot too strongly emphasise the great evil of which the Kaisar-i-Hind must be capable when in the wrong hands. The manner of its disappearance cannot but give great satisfaction to England's enemies, and will tempt the native population to believe that the Intelligence Department and the resources of the military are no match for the Nana Sahib. There can be no doubt that if this rebellious Prince were to unite behind him a great part of India's native rulers, the temptation to other powers, in Afghanistan and Persia as well as those to whom Lord Canning makes reference, to intervene in some manner in the troubles of India, must prove overwhelming.

The Queen does not underestimate the difficulties of

*the situation with which Lord Canning is faced. She
trusts, however, that the Intelligence Department will
prove more diligent in recovering the Mogul diamond
than it has been in protecting it hitherto.*

7

"Funny thing is," said Verity in his most conversational
manner, "I gone clean off the idea of veal and ham, ever since
we went up country. What I think of now, most of all, is a
quart of Buttery's country-bottled Allsopp. I suppose it must
be the stickiness that comes with a bit of rain."

"Like sitting over a boiler with the lid off," said Martock
helpfully.

They marched on, in step, through the Maidan Gate of
Fort William towards the Granary Barracks. Martock jerked
his head at the rooms in the archway above them.

"That's our most valuable hostage up there, my old son,
the ex-King of Oudh, living in a suite of rooms with a dozen
girls and sentries to keep him company."

"In Fort William?"

"Ever since the panic started. He used to live in a great
house down the river, at Garden Reach, with his court and
zenanah. But once the trouble began at Meerut they rounded
up the lot and put the old King and his slave girls above the
Maidan Gate."

"And his courtiers?"

"Oh," said Martock, "bloody set of twisters. They were
hanged, mostly."

"Hanged?"

"Yes," said Martock. "It was what they called 'Panic Sun-
day', and the court-martial wasn't taking any chances."

Several artillery batteries were at "standing gun-drill" on
the massive creeper-grown ramparts, the shouts of command
carrying on the damp, oppressive breeze. To one side, on a
broad parade ground, a regiment of sepoys, their uniforms

indistinguishable from those of the British except by the dark faces of the wearers, stood smartly to attention. The form of drill was new to Verity, for each man's musket was lying on the ground rather than in his hand. And then he saw that the British regiment parading behind had its rifles at the ready. It looked, for all the world, he thought, as though they were about to fire a volley into the backs of the sepoys. Then an order was given and the native infantry marched smartly forward by about a dozen paces, leaving the muskets where they lay. Another order, and stamping out a right turn, they marched away across the ground, arms swinging high, and disappeared from sight.

"Well," said Martock soberly, "there's going to be wigs on the green all right if they've got to start disarming the native regiments in Fort William. You've no idea how the Pandies take on over it, quite as though it was discharge with ignominy. I'd say it's all about that damn' sparkler of yours."

Verity gasped, winded a little by the pace.

"Mr Martock," he said severely, "you might greatly oblige me by not prosing on so about that particular article. I ain't forgot it, and I ain't given up."

Overhead the hot dull pearl of the cloud banks presented a freak interruption to the progress of the season. The wide, sunless sky rolled in slow procession from the Bay of Bengal across the river plain towards the distant Himalayas. There was a remote muttering of thunder, and the warm metallic smell of an impending electrical storm. Rain had fallen in scattered, heavy drops, the moisture gathering in shallow indentations, only to be steamed off by the heat of earth and air in a foul, disease-bearing vapour. Verity sighed and thought of the bliss of sitting over the most ferocious steam-boiler in Paddington Green.

"It is the Governor-General's wish," said Colonel Farr, his blue eyes flashing and his iron-grey whiskers seeming more closely trimmed than ever, "that all field officers of the Intelligence Department should make their men familiar with the full details of the Kaisar-i-Hind. You will all oblige me by noting them."

Far off, the guard-house bugle of Government House sounded, almost flute-like, in the warm air. Verity, who had been standing at ease before the broad desk with its leather top, produced a small notebook and pencil. Martock, next to him, did the same. Mr Lopez, who sat to one side of the desk, had been provided with a copy of the same notes as Colonel Farr.

"Weight," said Farr sharply, "793 carats, a carat being reckoned as 207 milligrams, Madras weight. A shade over five ounces in all. The jewel is classified as being of the first water, and is therefore flawless. It exhibits a soft pink colouring, and is rose-cut in the approximate shape of a half-egg. It has been cut to exhibit three hundred facets or surfaces. Mr Lopez?"

"As to value," said Lopez softly, "the jewel is unique in its physical properties and in its political significance. As such it is beyond price. However, if such a stone were to come on to the market in London or Amsterdam, its sale would not realise less than £500,000."

There was a long, respectful silence, broken at length by Verity.

" 'ave the honour to request, sir, what we shall be required to do in pursuance of the disappearance?"

"Do?" said Farr, scowling at the round pink face, as though the sergeant had made an improper suggestion, "Do as you are ordered. The suspected thief is here, closely guarded. You, Sergeant Verity, are the detective officer. Do as you did with Dhingra and we shall be well satisfied."

" 'ave the honour to suggest, sir, that this ain't the same as Dhingra. There being no diamond found, and 'er having been in view all the time it was taken, it don't leave much rope to trip her by."

"I fancy, Sergeant," said Lopez, his dark face tranquil with satisfaction, "that once Massoumeh has had half an hour of my persuasion, she will beg on her knees to be allowed to tell you the details of her crime."

"Just it, sir," said Verity, lips tightened with determination. "If this young person is tortured half out of her mind, then she'll say anything you want to 'ear to stop it. And even if she 'adn't thieved the jool, she'll swear she did. Don't see the usefulness of it, sir. With respect, sir."

"Have no fear, Mr Verity," said Lopez, the lisp of the Portuguese intonation almost lost in his half-whisper, "she will not be allowed to go half out of her mind. She will know precisely what is happening, and that it will only cease to happen when she tells the truth."

Colonel Farr turned a cold stare on the policeman, while Verity shifted in his clothes with suppressed disapproval.

"The duty," said Farr, "may be disagreeable, but it is to be carried out this afternoon."

"A interrogation of the prisoner, sir?" asked Verity carefully.

Farr nodded.

"Precisely that," he said.

"Stands to reason, old fellow," said Martock persuasively, "and she could have hidden it anywhere. There were four people and a box."

"A box in a casket," said Verity pedantically.

"Right. Now three of the four, Maun Singh's officer, Colonel Farr, and you couldn't have had it. You were guarded, searched, and guarded again, so that even if the jewel was there you couldn't have gone back to it."

"That's a fact," said Verity thoughtfully.

"Then there was the box and the casket."

"There was."

"And here they are now," Martock indicated the dismembered sides of the casket and the wooden "performing box", the pieces now lying upon the table before them in the "strong-room", which had been the barrack armoury in more normal times.

"Now," Martock resumed, "any fool can see how the box would let the jewel out through its floor. But where could you hide a jewel in the box or casket?"

"Dunno."

"All the sides too thin," said Martock, displaying the pieces as though in the presence of an audience, "no concealed compartments. Nothing but flat wood and brass, with a few little stones encrusted, and an emerald to top the lot, because the benighted heathens believe an emerald will drive away evil spirits. Now, is there anywhere in all of that where the Kaisar-i-Hind could have been concealed?"

"Not as I can see."

"And who does that leave?"

"Look," said Verity, colouring, "I know it leaves Mass-oo-mer. I ain't that stupid, Mr Martock!"

"Massoumeh," crooned Martock "who spent all the time just by the pedestal where the performing box must have let the diamond out, and who tried to run for it before she was searched."

"But what could she 'ave done with it?"

"Well, old chum," said Martock suavely, "that's rather what we're all expecting you to find out. You being a detective officer."

Verity waited unhappily, until the two men heard the footsteps of Lopez and a pair of guards approaching along the flagged stones of the corridor. The door opened, Lopez entered without a word and went through the formality of returning the fragments of the casket and box to the safe.

"Have the goodness," he said tensely to Martock, "to make the preparations".

Martock opened a small green canvas bag, which he had carried with him all afternoon. Verity recognised the glass bowl and the little wooden box which had contained Dhingra's tormentor. There was also a glimpse of coiled black leather. Verity took a deep breath.

"Sir!"

It came out as a frog-like bellow, and Lopez spun round. "Sergeant?"

"Mr Lopez, sir, I 'ave the honour to state that I am prepared to undertake the questioning of the female prisoner as ordered by Colonel Farr."

"Good!" said Lopez, mingling surprise and approval. "Excellent!"

"Likewise, sir," Verity continued sternly, "I can't see my way to being accessory in the tormenting of a poor degraded creature."

Lopez gasped with exasperation.

"Please to explain that, Sergeant!"

"Don't take much explaining, sir. I ain't a-going to refuse my duty of questioning the subject an' endeavouring to elicit the truth. But if that poisonous insec' is to be used, as it was on Dhingra, I shall be obliged to inform the young person suspected that it's a 'armless beetle."

"We shall see!" hissed Lopez, his composure gone. "We shall see as to that, Mr Verity! You be thankful for her if she can be made to speak the truth after nothing worse than the beetle. If not, there are other means!"

"Yes, sir, I 'ave observed, sir. Wish to state, sir, that if you was to physically aggrieve her, like using that whip you got in the green bag..."

"Yes, Sergeant?"

"Then, sir, as sure as I stand 'ere, sir, I will lay an information against you, before the chief magistrate of Calcutta, for felonious wounding and grievous bodily 'arm. With respect, sir."

There was an intense stillness. It was clear to the three men in the room that there was nothing whatever to prevent Verity from carrying out the threat. And once the information had been laid, the magistrate would be obliged to take action. It might have happened on any one of a dozen previous occasions when prisoners suspected of mutiny—or worse—had been driven to confession by the interrogators of the Intelligence Department in the privacy of the cells. However, it had not happened, for the interrogators knew that their own success and the very survival of British rule in India might depend on the private methods of persuasion which they employed. To lay informations for grievous bodily harm had been so absurd as to be unthinkable.

"We shall see!" Lopez was pale with anger as he turned and strode from the room.

"Well, old fellow," said Martock coolly, as the door closed behind Lopez, "you do have a soft touch with a cassowary and no mistake."

"It ain't what's soft, Mr Martock, it's what's right. If the law says this Massoumeh's to be 'ung or beaten, I'll see it carried out. But what's to be done in there by Mr Lopez ain't proper, and it's a downright interference with my duty as a constabulary officer."

"Draw it mild, chum!" said Martock. "She's had worse in the zenanah, I daresay."

Verity's face had deepened in colour from hot pink to port wine.

"Mr Martock! When you've 'ad some little detective experience, I shall be pleased to 'ear your advice in the matter. Until then you can oblige me by remembering that it's no assistance to my questioning to have the girl so frightened silly that she'll confess to every crime in the calendar. There's a jool missing and, what's a sight more important, there's little Amy Stockwood not accounted for."

"Had her gizzard slit," said Martock feebly.

"Now!" said Verity magisterially, "Now! that's more the sort of thing I want to hear the truth of. Then, if she's guilty, the law can be as cruel as it likes with this Mass-oo-mer. I shan't interfere."

"Not half as cruel, my friend, as Colonel Farr is likely to be to you when he hears the tale from Lopez!"

"I got a piece of information for your benefit," said Verity, disregarding the interruption, "about cruelty. Ever since I set foot in India, there's been nothing but cruelty of one sort or another."

"There's a bloody war being fought!" said Martock abruptly.

"That may be. But all of you think if you was only cruel enough, it would be done with tomorrow. It don't follow."

"Doesn't it?"

"No, Mr Martock, it don't. Now, you don't know much of me, and there's no need you should. But I'll tell you this. Not a year since, I had dealings with a villain who was cleverer than you, and Mr Lopez, and the Nana Sahib, all rolled into one. Name of Lieutenant Dacre, a man of education and considerable parts. Now 'e devised a scheme to take half a ton of bullion from where it was sworn no man could take it, on the ferry train to Paris. But he did it, and he need never have been caught. Then he began to act cruel.

He got one of his men drowned, and another sent to a living death. And then there was a girl, Miss Jolly, 'alf native, saucy little chit with black hair and eyes on the slant a bit. To teach her a lesson, he got two of his bullies to bend her naked over a wooden 'orse and leather 'er. When they'd finished, Miss Jolly's backside wasn't fit for sitting on for a month. Very clever, wasn't it?"

"It might be," said Martock cautiously.

"So clever," said Verity, "that she risked her neck to bring him down. And she did such things that our clever Lieutenant was only too glad of the chance to end it all by blowing his own brains out of his skull. That's where cruelty got 'im, Mr Martock. And you aren't to know that cruelty mightn't drive this young person now to fight with the cunning of the very devil."

"And you," said Martock, hardly concealing his amusement, "you of course, know a better way of getting at the confounded jewel."

Verity pursed his lips a little and appeared to consider the proposition.

"Yes, Mr Martock," he said at length, "I rather think I do."

"And so," said Martock, "the Sepoy War shall be ended by a lot of Exeter Hall, philanthropic tosh, and never a native skin touched in anger!"

"Chastisement is one thing, Mr Martock. Chastisement is necessary and wholesome. The law provides for it. Cruelty only puts you where Lieutenant Dacre was, and we may all come to as bad an end as 'im, if we try to save ourselves that way now."

Martock shrugged and turned away towards the small barred window. Heavy booted footsteps echoed down the corridor outside. The door opened and the Corporal of the guard glanced round the room.

"Sergeant Verity to parade in Colonel Farr's office!"

Verity tugged his black coat more squarely on to his plump shoulders.

"Now," said Martock sceptically, "you tell Colonel Farr

about your Miss Jolly and the rest of it. I shouldn't wonder if he was to off with apoplexy."

Verity ignored him, lumbered towards the open door and set off down the flagged passageway, the Corporal of the guard breathing moistly and keeping the step just behind him. When they reached Farr's room, the Corporal belched discreetly, tapped at the door and then opened it.

"Sergeant Verity! Sir!"

Verity's determination faltered a little as he saw that Lopez was standing with an expression of smooth satisfaction just to one side of the Colonel's desk. Worse still, a chair to the other side was occupied by an officer who wore the braid and tassels of a staff officer from Government House. It looked, Verity thought, like a roasting. Chin up and arms compressed against his sides, he waited at attention.

"Sergeant," said Colonel Farr, "I understand that you disapprove of Mr Lopez's procedure in the interrogation of the woman."

"Don't approve of cruelty, sir, on account of its impeding the investigation."

"Perhaps," said Lopez, intervening softly, "you don't approve of *me*, Sergeant."

"Not true, sir. With respect, sir. Captain Abbott, sir, as was at Delhi, spoke very high of Mr Lopez."

"Captain Abbot was a brave officer," said Farr wistfully, and Lopez nodded.

"More than that, sir," said Verity, "Corporal Alfred French, with whom I once served in the Rifle Brigade, and who was then with Mr Lopez, told me in a letter long before the sepoy rebellion that he'd trust his life to Mr Lopez. No, sir. I think of Mr Lopez as a fine example to us all."

There was an embarrassed pause.

"And so may Corporal French be," said Lopez. "I do not know if he escaped alive from Delhi. If not, he is a loss we can ill afford."

Colonel Farr glanced at the staff officer, as though to seek approval for what must come next.

"Sergeant Verity, you are the detective officer attached to this unit of the Intelligence Department."

"Sir!"

"In the event of an active and wide-ranging search for the Kaisar-i-Hind, we must be obliged to you for certain advice."

"But I understood this morning, sir, that there wasn't to be . . . "

"Never mind this morning, Sergeant!"

"No, sir." And Verity thought he saw a glimmer of satisfaction in the eyes of the staff officer, as though at Colonel Farr's expense.

"We should be obliged for your opinion, Sergeant, and let it be only your opinion, as to the manner of proceeding in the case, beginning with the measures to be used for extracting the truth from the dancing-woman."

Verity breathed out, fluttering his waxed moustache a little.

"Let 'er go, sir."

"*Let her go?* Good God, man, she's all we've got! Let the bitch go and that's the end of the Kaisar-i-Hind!"

Verity cleared his throat, as though preparing an oration.

" 'ave the honour to suggest, sir, that if you keep 'er locked in a cell, you'll 'ave seen the last of the jool. And 'owever much you mistreat 'er, it won't be found."

"I think," said the staff officer, intervening for the first time, "you must explain that one way or the other, Sergeant."

"Not 'ard to see, sir. This Mass-oo-mer is a dead ringer for 'aving thieved the stone. But it ain't on her and there's no way she could have brought it here. But if she's guilty, and she moved it from that pedestal, then she's the only one that knows where it is. But whoever put her up to it, she can't tell him."

"Right!" said the staff officer approvingly.

"Now," said Verity, standing at ease uninvited and growing expansive, "supposing she was to escape. What's the first thing she'd do? Either she'd go and get the jool from where it was, or else she'd go straight to the person who put her up and tell him where it was."

"First," said Colonel Farr, "suppose the Kaisar-i-Hind is

already in the hands of the Nana Sahib or whoever planned the theft?"

"Then, sir," said Verity doggedly, "she still ain't to know that, being where she is, and will of consequence lead us to the first man in the chain."

"Second," said Farr, "how shall we do if she goes nowhere?"

"Well, sir, it ain't likely, but if she was given the chance to escape and never took it – why – then she mightn't be our party after all. That'd be something to know, at least."

"Do you suggest," inquired the staff officer, "that the woman be released into your custody?"

"No, sir," said Verity firmly, "but me and Mr Martock is to be sent to Cawnpore, as I'm told, and there is the case of Miss Stockwood still outstanding."

"Not in our book, Sergeant," said Farr shortly.

"Well, sir," resumed Verity, "we're detailed to Cawnpore, first off. There'll be a bullock driver and there'll be a servant. Now, if this young person was released to be escorted to Cawnpore as an evidence, and if she was to be indentured a servant for the party travelling, we might see what's the odds about that. She could be made secure, with handcuffs and that. But there might be times when someone accidentally forgot to make 'er secure. Which is when she'd bolt if she was a-going to. And it wouldn't be hard then to watch her close."

"You don't think, Sergeant," said the staff officer casually, "that she might give you the slip?"

"Two of us and one of 'er, sir. It ain't likely. She'd have to go on foot too, and Mr Martock and me 'ave done a fair bit of rough marching in our time."

The Government House officer nodded, as though satisfied, stood up and shook hands with Colonel Farr. Verity stiffened to attention during the formal leavetaking, and then Lopez conducted the visitor from the room.

"Well, Sergeant," said Farr as the door closed, "we shall see what you can do."

"'ope so, sir, I'm sure."

"But it won't be Cawnpore."

"No, sir?"

"No. Government House has details of an ambush in which the survivors of the 105th were cut down, west of Raniganj. The report gives a girl as having been taken by the natives. It will be your disagreeable duty to proceed to the scene of the event and see what information on the ambush and the subsequent fate of the young lady you can deduce."

"And the prisoner, sir, and the jool?"

"As to that, Sergeant Verity, we must wait to see if she bolts."

"Yessir. Exac'ly, sir."

"And don't forget the other girl, taken beyond Raniganj. Who knows, she may be your Amy Stockwood?"

"What I can tell you, Mr Martock," said Verity condescendingly as they stepped smartly away from the sentries at the Granary gate, "is that there's been ructions at Government 'ouse. After being sour as vinegar on the jool this morning, why, bless you, Colonel Farr can't start looking for it quick enough. Someone somewhere has been a-giving orders, and now they want it found."

"What you mean is," said Martock, "that you're no end bucked at having got your own way out of them."

"Yes," said Verity, as though considering the possibility for the first time, "so I am. Why, it was only an hour ago that I was thinking how I should be writing this evening, presenting my compliments to Mr Inspector Croaker in London and having the honour to request that I might be recalled from here at once."

"It ain't on, old fellow," said Martock wearily, "you'd be here another three months while the answer came back. And they'd only tell you to stay put."

The oddly contrasted pair of sergeants marched several hundred yards more before Verity broke the silence.

"Mr Martock," he said with confidential firmness, "I know that, in a manner o' speaking, there ain't a deal of difference in our ranks. But your stripes, although very good for the military, can't count so 'igh for constabulary purposes."

"Not count?" said Martock uncertainly.

Verity became reassuring.

"Now," he said, "when we're together like this – and seeing as we chummed together so soon as ever I came to Calcutta – I don't want you to think about it at all, but just behave natural. However, in the line of duty, 'owever that may come, we'd work a lot smoother together if you was to try and think of me a bit as your superior officer."

Martock swung his head round and stared at the firm-set head, the pink satisfied face, and the flat black moustaches.

"My God!" he said faintly.

8

The sergeants' *paul* which Verity had been obliged to share with Martock resembled nothing so much as a curtain stretched over a rather broad clothes-horse. During the humid nights of early summer, the moisture of the air dropped to the ground so that the earth began to steam. An hour before dawn, Verity sat on the edge of his pallet, drenched as if in a vapour bath. Insects of every kind dashed or fell against the oil lamp that Martock had hung upon the pole as soon as the bugle sounded at two o'clock. From the darkness outside there was a chorus of frogs and earth-crickets, as the men of the column began to stir for the new day.

Neither Martock nor Verity any longer bore the least resemblance to the soldiers of the infantry regiment which had been detailed to accompany them as far as the scene of the 105th's ambush. Verity, at least, wore the same black coat and trousers, carried the same truncheon, as he might have done in Regent Street or Haymarket. Only the white solar topee was allowed him as a concession to the heat.

He pulled on his stockings to the accompaniment of a rising tumult outside, tents were being struck, horses saddled, and elephants loaded. Above the murmur of voices came the clear abrupt tones of a private soldier who had just broken his shin over a forgotten tent-peg in the darkness.

"I rather feel, old boy," said Martock cheerily, "that we shall do a lot better tomorrow night, when we're shot of this menagerie."

Verity grunted, and pulled on the other stocking. Sleep had been difficult enough with the chanting of the native *khitmudgars*, the shifting and squealing of the tethered horses. But on the first night of all there had been a near disaster. One of the pistols of the left-flank mounted picket had gone off in the hands of a nervous trooper. The right-flank picket heard the shot, assumed that an attack had begun, and rode back towards the main camp. The troopers there were also roused by the shot, and hearing the sounds of hooves bearing down on them in the darkness, swore loudly that "the Pandies were coming". Several unauthorised shots were fired by the riflemen, all of them fortunately inaccurate, before they recognised their mounted escort. By then it was after one in the morning and, as Verity remarked miserably, hardly worth turning in again.

Now, in the four-hour march which preceded breakfast. Verity rode with Martock in a bullock-cart. Massoumeh, under guard, was sitting silent and manacled. At the frontiers of night and day, dark masses of troops moved quietly through the gloom. There was a dull rumble of gun-carriages, the quick trampling and clinking of cavalry, the irregular undercurrent of animal sounds. Verity winced as Martock struck a match and applied it to a black, unappetising cheroot. For all Martock's officer-like pretensions, he thought, the tobacco would be no better than the foul mixture that a common soldier would puff at in his short black cutty.

The ferocity of the sun was matched almost by the speed of dawn, the light growing in little more than the space of a theatrical illumination. The faces of the men and the dust which had collected, even in the darkness, upon their cheeks was plainly visible. It was still an hour before breakfast when there was a shout, repeated at intervals the length of the column. Martock sprang down from the tail of the bullock-cart and stood with hands on hips, looking up at the sky ahead of them.

"I'd rather have had my beefsteak and porter first," he said ruefully, "but I'm afraid, old chums, this is rather what we've been looking for and hoping not to find."

Verity joined him, following the direction of his companion's gaze. Ahead of them, the sky was filled with circling black wings, from which one of the great birds would occasionally descend with the speed and precision of a king-fisher as it dived at the earth below.

"Perhaps," said Martock softly, "you mayn't feel quite so kindly disposed towards mutineers, once you've seen their handiwork."

They responded reluctantly to the general orders being carried by orderly sergeants from company commanders. The scene of the 105th's disaster had been transformed by the ravages of the vultures and the furtive visits of the nearest villagers. The wagon still stood behind the skeletons of the bullocks who had pulled it. Neither the uniforms nor the skeletons of the men were any longer identifiable from the scraps of scarlet serge or flesh tissue which remained. The bare staff of the colours lay by the wagon, but of the flag itself there was no sign. As Verity approached the scene he was struck by the bizarre profusion of documents which lay in an almost undisturbed litter about the scene of the tragedy. Books, letters, cheques, photographs, newspapers, journals, and company records lay where they had fallen, hardly stirring in the breeze. Grain had spilt from the damaged commissariat wagon and in the more humid warmth of the past few days had actually begun to sprout around and even through the decaying corpses.

The major of the forward party struck the ground with the heel of his boot. It crumbled like dry cement.

"Sergeant-Major! Volunteers for the burial detail! Those bodies on ground too hard to dig must be left. No body still in a state of putrefaction to be approached. All others to be buried where they lie."

"Sir!"

The Sergeant-Major began the task of assembling his reluctant grave-diggers, each man issued with an extra ration of rum beforehand to help him through the disagreeable task. Verity and Martock approached the cart. There was no sign of a rifle or musket remaining, and most of the wooden ammunition boxes had been broken open.

"Poor bastards," said Martock, pointing at a box which was still intact, "Look at that!"

"Look at what?"

"That bloody box! That's what did for them! Look at the damn' thing!"

Verity peered. The heavy wooden lid of the crate was held down by two copper bands, each fastened by nine large screws, now rusted immovably into place.

"There's the answer," said Martock knowledgeably. "Imagine being quartermaster and having to open those boxes in a hurry, when the ammunition pouches began to run dry. Why, you wouldn't open a single box in less than twenty minutes. Some of those screws are so rusted in that you'd hardly start them."

"What did for them," said Verity severely, "was fifty or sixty mutineers. Never mind the boxes."

And with that he began to busy himself in collecting up the scattered paper, sorting it into piles, according to whether it fell into his personal classification of "official" or "private", or, in the case of the newspaper pages, into neither. All about him, the burial detail went to work, going at their task with still greater energy in order to have it finished before the full heat of the morning should begin. By eight o'clock a dozen shallow graves had been completed and about half of the bodies buried. Elsewhere, the ground was too hard to bury the men without moving them, and they were left where they lay. A few corpses were still in a state of deliquescence, and the burial party was ordered to keep well away from them. All the papers which had been gathered up were placed in the care of the commander of the column, Colonel Gillis, a youngish contemporary of Farr's. When this was done, Gillis summoned Verity to him.

"Sergeant, you have your orders from Colonel Farr?"

"Yessir."

"Very well. We have escorted you as far as we can. Our duty is done here and we must march on to Hyderabad. From now on, you are responsible to the police commissioners and the Intelligence Officers alone."

" 'ave been so instructed, sir."

"You will search the surrounding area, then, for any further evidence of the attackers. As soon as you have completed that search, you will continue with your – ah – prisoner and report to the Provost-Marshal's office in Cawnpore upon your arrival there."

"Sir!"

"Very well," said Gillis turning away. "Good luck to you, Sergeant."

Later that afternoon, Verity watched the column move off, leaving behind the covered bullock-wagon with its native driver, Ram Lal, the two sergeants, and Massoumeh. The girl sat in the tented shade of the wagon, her ankle securely manacled to the iron frame of the carriagework. Ram Lal, whose loyalty to the officers of the Department had never wavered and who had been chosen for that reason, squatted by the remains of a little fire. Verity turned to his companion, confidentially,

"Mr Martock, you was brought up a gentleman's son?"

"In a manner of speaking," said Martock evasively.

"And might you have been sent to a gentleman's school?"

Martock favoured him with a laconic glance.

"As to that, old boy, you may rest easy. I was."

"And might they have learned you languages there?"

"Not a great deal," said Martock. "Why?"

"P'raps you'd just be so good as to cast your eye over this."

Verity drew from his pocket a sheet of paper, soiled, crumpled, and with the unmistakable rust of long-dried blood upon it.

"Where the devil did you get that from?"

"Lying on the ground, Mr Martock, not ten yards from 'ere."

"And didn't give it with the rest to Gillis?"

"Oversight, Mr Martock."

Martock gave him an unimpressed look and smoothed out the paper.

"Them funny marks," said Verity, "they ain't any letters of the alphabet, and yet they look as if they might be."

"It's Greek," said Martock glumly, "not my forte, old son."

"Is it now?" said Verity, and looked again at the letters.

νατιυε καυαλρυ αττακ – φολλουεδ υς φρομ νορθ υεστ – νο χανσε
νου – θε γιρλ ἀς γονε βακ – φορ γοδς σακε φινδ ἑρ – αλσο τυο
φρου κανπορε – νο μορε τ _____

"I 'eard in Calcutta," said Verity conversationally, "how Sir Colin Campbell would send messages back in code. And 'ow the code he used was Greek, seein' that any gentleman of education would understand it, whereas the natives never could."

"Understand it?" said Martock derisively. "Most of our fellows could hardly make out the alphabet in Greek!"

"Why, Mr Martock! That's just it! O' course, Sir Colin don't write Greek words! Only Greek writing for English words! It's the Greek writing that foxes the natives, them never having had an English gentleman's education. Now that third word along, with them funny 'a's, must be pronounced 'attack', even I can see that. But I can't see more. Might you 'appen to remember the Greek alphabet that your masters in the gentlemen's school taught you, Mr Martock?"

"After a fashion."

"Only fancy that! And you never thinking how one day it might come in so handy in the middle of an Indian war! Now, might you be able to con those first three words?"

"Native cavalry attack," said Martock, as though unwilling to confess his expertise.

"Very good! And then?"

"Followed us from – can't read it. Just a minute. Followed us from north-west. No . . . something . . . now. No chance now. That's it."

"*Very* good, Mr Martock."

"The girl as . . . has . . . gone back. For God's sake find her.

Also two from . . . what the hell's this . . . Cawnpore. No more, and then just a 't' and a line."

"The girl has gone back," said Verity softly, "for God's sake find her. Also two from Cawnpore. No more t - - -." He stood in deep thought for a moment. Then he looked up again. "Mr Martock, I ain't a envious man. In all my life I don't believe I've ever wanted to change shoes with another living soul. And yet just for a bit you made me quite sorry as I never did 'ave the advantages of a real proper Latin-and-Greek, genteel education."

Under the starlight, Ram Lal slept curled on the driver's bench of the bullock-wagon. Two *pauls* had been erected, one for Verity and Martock, the other in which Massoumeh slept, her ankles manacled to the central pole.

"Stands to reason," said Verity, "if we let her bolt now, she'll have miles to go and there's every chance of losing her. Wait a day or two and she'll be much nearer. Then we'll give her the chance."

"So she's to be guarded night and day?"

"Day ain't no problem, Mr Martock, but it means we must take turns to sit out here of a night."

Martock slapped at the mosquitoes which fastened on his face.

"Only a few days," he said, "might bring us to Cawnpore."

"No," said Verity, "not by my route. I ain't exactly thinking of going straight to Cawnpore. Those mutineers that made off with the young lady from the 105th, as Sergeant Billings said, came from the north-west. Now, you may bet they've gone back north-west and took 'er with them. It being our duty to investigate such matters, we ain't quite going straight to Cawnpore, not if there's some evidence of her having passed on the road to Delhi."

"Between the two things," said Martock glumly, "you'll miss your tip and come a header. We shall end up without either the diamond or the poor young lady."

"That's as may be, Mr Martock, but if I can only save one, it ain't a-going to be the jool. And it ain't just one young lady either."

"Isn't it?"

"Mr Martock! You read that Greek writing. Also two from Cawnpore! And if you didn't think before that Amy Stockwood might still be alive, you'd better start thinking now. And you'd also better start thinking why Dhingra, who couldn't have coopered 'er, swore with his dying breath that he did. P'raps you'd like to do first sentry-go. It gives a man a chance to reflect."

With this advice, Verity opened the flap of the *paul* and scrambled awkwardly inside. As he stood there, pulling off his coat and trousers, preparing the blanket on his pallet, his bulk seemed to fill the little space. Perhaps, he thought, it was as well that he and Martock were to sleep turn and turn about. They had set up their little camp for the first night a mile away from the scene of the ambush, just on the fringe of the mango and tamarind groves, where the ground began to slope upwards to the hills. In the eerie stillness, Verity gave one thought to the dead who lay in their shallow graves, and then he slept heavily.

He awoke suddenly, without at first knowing why. It seemed many hours later, but since Martock had not called him to his watch it could not have been. He lay motionless and listened. Faint but audible, lowered voices were murmuring somewhere outside. Pulling on his trousers, and reaching for the musket that had been chained to the tent-pole, he eased himself into the sudden coldness of the open air. The bullock-wagon stood in its place, the animals lying, tethered, close by. The *paul* in which the girl slept was silent. Of Martock there was no sign.

Verity felt a sudden fear that there had been a silent descent on the camp, perhaps by the girl's accomplices, and that Martock and Ram Lal had been either killed or taken prisoner. With great care he stepped towards the other *paul*, laid his musket on the ground and gingerly opened the flap. The oil-light was subdued but after the darkness the surprise of it almost dazzled him. The manacles which had fettered the girl's feet to the central pole had gone, but to his astonishment he saw that Massoumeh herself was still there. She lay uncovered on the pallet, wearing the deep red top of a sari which hardly reached down to her navel or the small of her back, and a pair of black stockings. She was stretched on her belly, looking at the far end of the little tent. At the sound of Verity's movements, she swept a hand behind her, as though brushing dust from her seat, and looked at him over her shoulder. She was chewing something, betel-nut perhaps, and she continued chewing and grinning at him knowingly. Anger began to rival apprehension in Verity's mind. He glanced round, saw the manacles, and snatched them up. Massoumeh turned obligingly on to her back and clasped the tent-pole, at the foot of the pallet, between her ankles. Verity clicked the two halves of the anklets so that they locked automatically, giving the double security of hobbling the prisoner and confining her within the radius of the pole.

Having accomplished this, he backed awkwardly out of the canvas shelter and straightened up.

"Mr Martock!"

As though answering the call of a necromancer, the shadowy figure of Martock rose from concealment beyond the far end of the *paul*, one hand wrestling with a last obstinate button.

"After all, old fellow," said Martock, "it's one way of winning her round. And if she ain't won round, then dammit it's as fair a way as any of getting careless with her and giving her the means to bolt. It's three days now, and precious small chance she's had."

The wagon lurched and bumped, the protecting canvas glowing faintly with the fire of the sunlight behind it.

"You might oblige me, Mr Martock, by not alluding to the matter further."

"Might I?" said Martock. "And you might oblige me by telling me how much longer we must follow a road that won't stop short this side of Delhi, rather than go to Cawnpore, as ordered!"

"My orders is clear enough, Mr Martock. I am to proceed to Cawnpore, *after* investigating all matters consequential on the demise of Her Majesty's 105th Foot."

"That's not what was said at Fort William!"

"It's what I 'eard, Mr Martock."

"And the Kaisar-i-Hind?"

"Mr Martock," said Verity, puckering his face a little, as if to show the effort required to make his colleague understand, "the first night of our march, we found the front of a young lady's locket, left on a pallet in one of the disused bungalows we searched. Next day we finds the back of ditto with a little twist of nut-brown 'air, as a keepsake. Last night we finds a thin gold chain, which fits nothing else in the world but that same locket. Now these three places is the first three nights passed by a poor tormented creature in the hands of savages. She leaves us these sad little tokens to beg our assistance. Think, Mr Martock, of what she must 'ave suffered – of what she suffers now, if still alive. I'll find her, Mr Martock, if I have to go to Simla to do it! And then I'll give my thoughts to the jool."

"Oh, God," said Martock miserably, "why can't you let Amy Stockwood be?"

They rocked and bumped onward without speaking. Then Verity smiled.

"I'll make a bargain with you, Mr Martock. We can't go so far as Delhi without a stop for supplies. That'll 'ave to be Gwalior, where the Maharajah Scindia proves a true friend and the town is loyal. If we ain't caught up with our villains by then and set the poor young lady free, I shall ask assistance from the garrison there to continue on towards Delhi. You may return to Cawnpore, or wherever you choose."

Martock grunted.

"There's three poor captives we know of already, two from Cawnpore and one from the 105th," said Verity firmly. "I'll eat my hat if I can't bring one of them back safe."

"And Massoumeh?"

Verity thought for a moment.

"Well, she ain't tried anything yet, but then she's perhaps too far away from her accomplices. What I'll do, Mr Martock, I'll just loosen the catch on them manacles so that they'll pull open with a bit of trying. She'll soon twig it. Then the man who watches her must pretend to doze."

He looked up at the girl, who sat well away from them at the far end of the wagon.

"Don't worry, old fellow," said Martock, "she doesn't understand a word of our lingo."

" 'ow d'yer know?"

"There are situations, my dear chap, in which one discovers these things."

"Oh," said Verity shortly.

"A few more nights," Martock sighed, "and she'd be eating out of our hands. It's much more the style, old boy. She's never been treated right before, can't have enough of it now. She'll tell you the lot when she's been properly sweetened;"

"No, Mr Martock! No!"

"Old man," said Martock, "you've no idea how warm that sort of golden skin is that Persian girls have."

"I daresay."

"And you've never seen such a pair of well-sprung . . such a pair, anyway."

"I ain't concerned about that."

"She starts shivering with excitement the minute you touch her . . ."

"Oh?"

"And though I say it myself," said Martock happily, "Massoumeh's bum is smooth as butter!"

"You might oblige me, Mr Martock, by keeping your observations to yourself! A gentleman's education you may 'ave 'ad, but not much of it 'as took hold! How you can demean yourself, you being a man of good family, with the first native woman who throws herself in your way is beyond me!"

Martock wagged a finger reproachfully.

"Now there, old friend, you wrong me. She ain't the first by any means. I ain't particular about a shade or so of tawny, and nor would you be if they kept you out here a year or two more. And I'll say one thing about Massoumeh. She may be a thieving little bitch and a lying minx, I don't know. But there's things that an English girl would scream the house down rather than do for a man. Massoumeh, on the other hand, actually asks for them, and enjoys them. And she ain't shy about showing you how much she enjoys them either."

Verity shifted so that his back was half turned to Martock. He stared out through the rear of the wagon at the receding groves of mango and stretches of scrub. In the hours that remained before sunset and their halt for the night, he ignored Martock's very existence.

Two days later, early in the afternoon, they joined a broad road, running between hills on either side. The manacles had been "loosened" as Verity promised, but Massoumeh was still with them.

"She can't be in a desperate bad way to escape," said Martock grumpily. "I don't like the look of it. I'd a sight sooner we gave up this Amy Stockwood dodge and got back to Cawnpore, where the Kaisar-i-Hind might be looked for."

"That's only a-cos you ain't put it all together in your mind," said Verity consolingly.

"Put what together?"

"Dhingra, and the diamond. Can't you see that if Miss Stockwood ain't found, you ain't ever going to see the jool again either?"

"No, dammit!" said Martock, "I don't see anything of the kind. You know something else about it, do you?"

"I only know what you know, Mr Martock," said Verity with tooth-sucking smugness, "but we detective police is accustomed to cast things in a somewhat different light."

The wagon halted abruptly, and Ram Lal gave a shout. Verity scrambled down, followed by Martock. They were in a narrow pass, the hills rising on either side in long flanks of scrub pierced by crops of limestone. Before them lay the city, palace, and fort of Gwalior, the rock on which the bastion was built rising as a tall plateau, sheer on every side. Verity unbuckled the leather case of his spy-glass and drew the brass instrument out to its full length. After a moment's inspection of the rock and the fortress, he said, "What's a yellow flag with a serpent upon it, Mr Martock?"

"Cobra," said Martock. "It's the Maharajah Scindia's standard."

"And 'im a loyal subject of 'er Majesty!"

"And him a shifty bastard like the rest!" Martock took the glass. "The only reason he hates the mutineers is because they wouldn't have him as leader. So now he's our gallant ally, God help us, and there's probably a detachment of our poor bloody infantry sitting it out on that blistering hot rock, just to show how much we love the little sod."

He continued the survey for a moment longer. Then he slid the glass closed and said, "That's Scindia's lot all right, the gentry in the red turbans and the long yellow jackets. Bloody good fighters though. They'd hold that rock against the Nana Sahib or Tantia Topi from now till Kingdom Come."

"And this Scindia ain't likely to be dodgy over 'elping us in the matter o' Miss Stockwood and the jool?"

Martock laughed.

"You'll find him the most helpful native from here to Afghanistan! He hates the Nana and the mutineers, of course. But for good measure, all his nearest and dearest are residing in British garrison towns under the – ah – protection of the Queen's army. So if he should ever think of being unhelpful, he'll just recollect how they may be put, one by one, in front of a file of muskets – with a pause between each firing party, so that he may reflect upon the errors of his ways. There ain't a safer man than Scindia nor a snugger berth than Gwalior, old boy."

"Much obliged, Mr Martock," said Verity smoothly, "then we shall proceed and ask for the senior officer of the British force there."

"One thing," said Martock, as they swung themselves back into the wagon, "you'd better keep our prisoner out of sight, if you want to hang on to her. Scindia's a frisky young goat and won't take no for an answer where his zenanah is concerned. Mind you, he wouldn't touch an English girl like your Amy – unless he acquired her in peacetime by the usual trade. But a randy young Persian piece is different. When he sees a thing o' that sort, he takes it!"

Verity looked unhappily at his smiling companion as the wagon jolted forward. Yet when they approached the great

rock in the lengthening shadows and the sunset tints, he was
almost overawed by the natural glory of the scene. On the
south-western face the rock itself had been hewn into temples
and gigantic statues. Huge and sinister, the tiara'd or
smooth-headed idols squatted under canopies and pagodas,
slender columns of white and gold supporting arches which
stood out radiantly against the ochre colouring of the rock.
In the late sunlight, the gold and purple splendour of
Gwalior assumed the liquid translucence of half fused metal.
Towers and temples with their decorations of tiles blazed
against the pure fading blue of the sky. As the bullock-wagon
drew closer, a little balcony with spindle columns, high
above the precipitous rock-wall, caught the last rays of the
sun with a flashing, gem-like gleam, before the bluish haze
of the night drew in about the mighty walls.

By the time that Verity recovered from his admiration of
the scene, they were entering the cluster of buildings at the
foot of the rock, where the steep ascent to the fortress and
palace began. Benares had dazzled him. He understood why
it was admired, but found it tawdry. Yet Gwalior at sunset
was no mere bauble. For the first time he felt within him
something of that fascination which India held for Englishmen, the beauty and the mystery which had driven such
comrades as Martock to turn their backs upon home and
wealth, in order to seek their destiny and find their graves
among alien beauty. Perhaps, he thought, if they made him
stay a year or two, he also might find his pleasure in the
oiled tawny nudity of Massoumeh and her Indian sisters,
entirely forgetting little Bella and Paddington Green. The
possibility shocked him so much that he ended the reverie.

Under Martock's instructions, Ram Lal was driving forward through the crowd, following the road which wound
upward to the palace and the fort. Scindia's soldiers were
parading in the streets, some bearing javelins, others carrying matchlocks, and a few armed with rifles. White silk
banners and red and yellow flags appeared everywhere.
Verity glimpsed a cow standing unattended by the roadside,
its horns decorated with a garland of flowers. Presently there

was an elephant with its mahout following them, and then a pair of laden camels behind that.

"Lord George Sanger's animal menagerie ain't in it!" he said nervously.

The light of the oil-lamps shone on dark faces and white turbans, more dimly picking out the bas reliefs upon the rock-face, where warriors rode upon elephants and Kalis offered themselves in graceful postures. Here and there were lamplit openings to the green depths of reservoirs, or to small temples whose arcades sheltered massive bronze idols, each set among the blooms and warm scent of flowers.

At the top of the road, they crossed a drawbridge into the fort itself, which was large enough to contain several palaces. Under Martock's instructions they made for the first of these, the Man Mandir palace, whose outer walls with their tall towers and cupolas rose a hundred feet into the air as a continuation of the precipitous rock-face itself. At length the wagon stopped, in a broad courtyard surrounded by the arched storeys of the inner building. As Verity and Martock got down, they were surrounded by a dozen of Scindia's troops in their long yellow tunics and red turbans. It irritated Verity that the men appeared to find great amusement in the black frock-coats and trousers of the pair. Then a solemn-faced Indian of higher rank approached, bowed, and motioned them to follow him. They were led through one of the archways to what must have been the guardroom. The floor was of red-polished marble, but the furnishings amounted to no more than a bare table and several wooden stools. Beyond the table stood an immaculately dressed Indian who bowed his head slightly, as though in acknowledgment of their arrival.

It was not what Verity had expected.

"Wish to report" – he looked at the fineness of the silk tunic – "sir" – no harm in easing the way – "arrival of Sergeant Verity and Sergeant Martock with prisoner. Wish to report arrival to senior British officer, sir!"

The Indian crossed his arms, resting the elbow of one in the palm of the other and stroking his finely trimmed beard. Then he spoke softly, with the correctness of phrase and the awkwardness of intonation which distinguished him from a born English-speaker.

"Hardly a convenient time, Sergeant!"

"Well, sir. No, sir. Bit close on mess dinner, sir. Ain't to be 'elped though."

"Why must it be the senior *British* officer, Sergeant?"

From the hardening of the voice, Verity detected that the Indian was about to take offence. He endeavoured hastily to undo the insult.

"Ain't strictly necessary, sir, only Sergeant Martock and me, 'aving been took a bit out of our way, must draw more rations from the commissary officer to see us to Cawnpore. That's all, sir."

"Ah!" The finger that had stroked the beard rested motionless. "Then you do not know that your mission is accomplished? That your duty ends here?"

"Don't follow, sir. With respect, sir!"

"You have done all that is required of you. But now you are to remain at Gwalior."

"Don't see it, sir!"

"No, Sergeant, perhaps not."

"'aven't 'ad no orders respecting Gwalior, nor the Marajah Scindiur neither."

"No, Sergeant," the voice was softer still, "events have overtaken orders. You, Sergeant, are a victim of history. Some days ago there was very nearly a great battle on the plain below us. But the army of Scindia turned aside. Scindia rode in terror for his life, and all his men, who still occupy the fort, bowed before his successor. For two days, Sergeant, Gwalior and all central India has been in the hands of the army of the Nana Sahib, Shah-in-Shah Padishah, Monarch of Monarchs!"

"It ain't possible!" said Verity doubtfully.

The dark eyes gleamed with satisfaction.

"All things are possible, Sergeant Verity! To me, nothing is unattainable. You know my name, for I am Azimullah Khan, whom all your army sought. Have I not brought you to Gwalior, through no desire of your own and against the orders you were given? You are a little late, but I was told

that though a slow fellow you might be depended upon to
arrive, once your feet were set upon the path. Had you been
here last night, you should have seen the Nana Sahib proclaimed by the trumpets and cannon of his great army as
Peshwar of Gwalior, mighty ruler of Bengal, monarch of
all India, and great emperor of the Mogul Kingdom!"

9

"The door!" Martock swung round as he spoke, half
crouched for a leap towards their only means of escape.
Verity turned his head but saw that two of Scindia's riflemen
were already guarding the archway. Azimullah looked
sharply at the soldiers, one of whom stepped forward, re-
versed his rifle and drove the butt expertly into Martock's
side, just below the rib cage. Verity heard the gasp of pain
as his companion doubled over on his knees choking for
relief. Even as he moved to Martock's aid, the stock of the
rifle was raised menacingly in his path.

"For the short time that remains," said the Khan
smoothly, "you will learn not to turn your backs upon the
Dewan of the Nana Sahib!"

One of the guards held Verity in check, tilting the sword-
bayonet of the rifle so that it was in line with the Sergeant's
throat. The man grinned at his prisoner. The second guard
stood over Martock, who was still kneeling with head bowed,
and drove the wooden stock into the exposed small of the
back, close to the kidneys. Martock's body fell sideways,
squirming in mute agony.

"Stop that!" said Verity loudly, "You ain't no business to
act so in'uman!"

Azimullah chuckled.

"I doubt, Sergeant Verity, whether we could teach the
Intelligence Department any new form of inhumanity!
Never fear, you shall have your share of suffering. I wonder
whether you will bear it as stoically as your friend?"

Verity looked at the dark, cruel face with its Mephisto-phelean whiskers. It was, he thought, the face of a madman. But madmen might be diverted by flattery.

"You been clever all right," he said, urgently trying to distract the Khan from Martock. "You been clever, Mr Azimullur. But you been clever for nothing. We ain't no use to you."

Azimullah sniggered, almost like a girl.

"Now there, Sergeant, you make a great mistake!"

He turned to the guards and said something to them in their own tongue. Martock was lifted to his feet and half-pushed, half-dragged from the room, Verity being prodded after him, and Azimullah bringing up the rear. They crossed another courtyard, passed under more archways guarded by Scindia's troops, and entered an ornate ante-room hung with tapestries of old crimson, on which the gardens of paradise and all their creatures had been woven in blue and green. Somewhere out of sight Verity heard the sound of a fountain splashing against the marble walls of a basin. But when the painted doors ahead of them were opened, they seemed to step from Gwalior into one of the more fanciful drawing-rooms of Portman Square or Carlton Terrace. Sofas in mustard yellow, Coburg chairs, rows of books finely bound, a chaise-longue, and a Broadwood grand piano, were set incongruously among the silks and inlaid brass of India.

As the two prisoners were led in, Verity contrived to position himself so that he was standing next to Martock.

"Chin up," he murmured, "never say die!"

Martock looked at him suspiciously and grunted. Azi-mullah stepped forward with a deep obeisance to the man who had just risen from a settee. Verity caught the words *"Dundoo Punt, Nana Sahib"*, and looked carefully. The smooth, almost hairless head of the Nana was a study in un-ageing evil. It was not hard to see why, Verity thought, he had acquired his reputation for soft, almost effeminate luxury, wanton cruelty, and sexual depravity. In this one man the political wisdom and supreme cunning of East and West had combined. The pleasures of India were seasoned for him by the vices of Europe. He it was who needed now only the promised possession of the Kaisar-i-Hind to lead all central India and Bengal in a mighty war of religion against the white-skinned invaders.

The Nana's companion stood close by him. At first Verity thought it must be a boy, dressed in the breeches and tunic of native cavalry. But the femininity of the body, and the sinister beauty of the cruel lynx-eyed face were unmistakably those of a finely bred Indian woman in her late twenties. Her uniform was embroidered with the insignia of a great commander, far beyond anything to be seen upon the shoulders of any native commander in British service, while her forehead bore incongruously the daub of marriage. She crossed the carpeted room with firm masculine steps and stood before the two prisoners. Then, as her eyes narrowed and glittered, she hissed a single word, which meant nothing to either man until Azimullah translated it.

"Kneel! Abase yourselves before Her Excellency, the Ranee of Jhansi! Prepare to pay the blood-debt of your countrymen for the murder of her people!"

Martock spoke softly from the corner of his mouth.

"Look out for her, old fellow!"

The Ranee spoke again, half to the prisoners and half to Azimullah. The Khan raised his arm, his finger pointing at Verity and a glimmer of triumph in his expression.

"You!" he said, "Kneel! The sepoys at Cawnpore were made to lick the blood of their enemies from the floor before they were hanged by your people. Her Excellency requires that you should lick the ground upon which she walks!"

Verity tried to keep his voice level, but he heard it tremble as much with indignation as in fear.

"I kneels to 'er Majesty the Queen. And I don't lick no ground anywhere!"

Before Azimullah could speak, the Ranee caught the tone of these words. Verity had no chance of avoiding what came next. The woman's hand moved like a flash of light, the gleam of the lustres overhead catching on the dull polish of leather. The sharp whistle of the riding-crop ended in an explosive crack across the full pink flesh at the side of his neck. He fell against the wall behind him, the numbing force of the impact giving way to a blaze of agony. Already the Ranee's arm was raised to strike him again, her dark eyes sparkling with fury. Verity felt the collar of his shirt wet against his skin and knew that he must be bleeding from the weal. It was absurd to suppose that he could escape or that he could even postpone his fate for more than a few moments, but with an instinct born of a policeman's training, he drew his truncheon.

This last, futile gesture produced an astonishing impression of fear among his enemies as the room erupted in activity. He was aware of the Ranee stepping back out of range, screaming abuse at him in her incomprehensible tongue. Azimullah had begun to shout excitedly at the two guards in their yellow tunics, as though urging them on no account to expose themselves to such a formidable antagonist as the sergeant had proved to be. In the distance, like a figure in the background of a dramatic painting, stood the jewelled Nana Sahib, his face drawn into a grimace of stupefied concern.

Verity paused. He had heard that many of the Indians had proved poor fighters when faced with the sturdy professionalism of British regiments, but he and Martock were two against five, in the room, and two against several thousand in the whole of Gwalior. The two guards began to edge warily towards him. Then, beyond the petrified Nana Sahib, a door opened and Verity was fleetingly aware of a girl standing on the threshold between two more red turbaned guards, one of whom came forward at once to join his two comrades.

The three sepoys, with their rifles and fixed bayonets, began to weave cautiously about the two Englishmen. Martock moved resolutely forward towards one of them, which also distracted the second, and gave Verity a chance against the third. He heard, rather than saw, Martock grunting and struggling on the floor with one of the guards, the two men rolling and pummelling in a flurry of clothing. The third sepoy looked briefly aside at this, and Verity danced forward like an overweight prizefighter, aiming the blow of the truncheon at the side of the man's head, just below the protection of the *puggaree*. With a cry of fear, the sepoy swung his gun-barrel upward to take the blow, the truncheon catching the iron tube with a crack that stung Verity's arm from palm to elbow. Verity struck again, but again the sepoy caught it on the iron barrel with a force that almost shattered the wooden truncheon.

To Verity's amazement, the Nana Sahib and the Ranee uttered a wailing duet of protest, as though imploring him not to strike again. Azimullah shouted at the sepoy nearest Verity, who hastily drew back. Verity who hunched forward, searching out an opening in his opponent's defence, now paused and straightened up.

"You bleeding cowards!" he said incredulously.

The other two sepoys had taken Martock. They held him bowed between them, his arms twisted up between his shoulder-blades.

"Drop your weapon!" said Azimullah softly.

Verity hesitated.

"Drop it, or your friend's suffering shall begin!"

Martock gave a cry that was half a scream.

"Run for it, Verity! For Christ's sake get out while you can! Get help! Only hope for us both!"

Verity paused, torn between duty and pity, but there was shouting beyond the doors and a dozen sepoys erupted unceremoniously into the room. They bore down upon him and he knew with complete resignation that this was the end of the matter. Philosophically, he singled out the first man to approach him and felled the sepoy with a bone-ringing crack of the truncheon across his collarbone. Then the others were upon him. They seized his arm so abruptly that the truncheon flew from his hand, arced upwards, hit the floor and skittled across it until it came to rest under a table. With the blood still seeping from his neck, his heart pounding, and his face shining with perspiration, he surrendered to his captors who hung upon him on every side, like so many pygmies bearing down a giant. His arms were wrenched behind him and he felt the coarse texture of rope biting into his wrists. At last the sepoys drew away and the first guards resumed their duty. Martock and Verity stood bound before the Nana Sahib, a bayonet levelled at each of their backs.

Yet even the Ranee had lost interest in them for the time being. There was a great excitement, a babbling of voices, and Verity remembered at last the girl who had stood in the doorway. He glanced again. She wore a close-fitting costume of a metallic looking cloth, woven with gold and silver thread, a bodice and trousers of the idols of the evil goddess Kali. He had so firmly expected to find that she was some accomplice of the Nana's that he was quite shocked to recognise her for Massoumeh, transformed by this costume into her original role of nautch-girl.

The Nana Sahib, his smooth plump face contorted by anxiety, turned to Massoumeh and spoke a command. With eyes lowered, she stepped forward, picked up the fallen truncheon, turned to her new master, and knelt before him. Then Azimullah whispered to her. The girl's hands moved carefully and almost caressingly over the wooden baton in her hands, until it seemed as if she were unscrewing the bulbous end from the handle. Verity breathed heavily with indignation, searching in vain for words to express his sense of outrage. The girl's back was towards him as she rose, stepped towards the Nana and knelt again, while he took something from her hands. The sudden explosion of light from the Nana's palm hit Verity with an almost physical shock. Blazing with the pure white-heat of brilliance dazzling and shooting from each of its facets, the Kaisar-i-Hind lay at last in the hands of the Nana Sahib. The promise of Azimullah Khan had been fulfilled.

"You scheming bastard!"

The voice mingled reproach with professional admiration. Verity heard Martock's words, but only when he turned his head did he realise that they were addressed to him. Prisoners and captors stood in a long moment of silence before the splendour of the jewel. Then Azimullah spoke, first in his own language and then in English.

"Oh, mighty Lord, King of Kings, it is written that he who possesses the Mogul diamond shall possess the lands and the peoples of all the Mogul emperors!"

Now it was the Ranee who knelt before the Nana Sahib, as though softly swearing some new oath of allegiance. Then she rose, crossed to Massoumeh, raised the girl's chin with her hand and looked into her feline eyes. Massoumeh bobbed down on one knee, and then followed her mistress from the room. In the half light beyond the doorway, it seemed to Verity that he glimpsed the Ranee's hand stroking the warm gold of the girl's face, sweeping over the smooth shoulders, stroking the velvet tan of the back, and falling caresssingly across Massoumeh's soft hips. Before he could distinguish reality from hallucination, Azimullah gave an order to the sepoys. A wooden butt hit Verity in the small of the back, so that he stumbled forward and took his first involuntary steps towards the prison that was to hold him.

"All I'm saying," Martock reminded his companion, "is that they'll reckon you up for having thieved the sparkler. Damn it, unless there were a dozen of them at it, which ain't likely, whoever it was must have been at the durbar and must have had access to your portmanteau at Fort William. Who more likely than you?"

The faint yellow light from the sentry's hurricane lamp fell through the bars of the door, illuminating a stained patch of red tiling on the floor and a corner of the lime-washed walls.

"For all that," said Verity gruffly, "it 'adn't anything to do with me. Now, I ain't particular about sleeping on a bare floor, but I'm that pumped at the moment that I shall have a shot."

His hands, like Martock's, were chained before him but he edged his shoulders down the wall until he could curl in a semi-foetal position at the foot of it.

"I tell you what, though," said Martock softly, "you've got something to answer for, old fellow, in not letting Mr Lopez interrogate our prisoner. I daresay we shall have our throats cut for us, but I'd die a lot happier if I'd seen the beetle do its work on her, or else watched Mr Lopez skin her backside with his whip! That bloody little whore's got a finger in this somewhere!"

"Well," said Verity smugly, "so it seems your familiarity with 'er ain't been much to your advantage. However, it can't be her that did all this – not on her own. And it couldn't be you, and I know it wasn't me. That leaves one person who had the diamond in his hand and who had every chance in the world of weighting my truncheon with it."

"Oh?" said Martock. "Who?"

"Colonel Farr."

"Colonel Farr!" Martock sat upright. "What bloody tosh!"

Verity sighed.

"We've all been saying that Colonel Farr couldn't a'took it, because it was took before the casket came to him. But if the jool *was* still in there somehow, when he held it, there must have been a good half minute before Mr Lopez came over to him. If he could have got 'old of it in that time and palmed it, like, he'd get clean away. He never was searched because it was thought he couldn't have the stone. He might have walked out of the tent, ridden to Calcutta with the diamond in his pocket, and hid it in a truncheon or anywhere else."

"Gammon!" said Martock unhappily.

"Is it, Mr Martock? Is it gammon? Who was it who thought the jool best forgotten about? Who was it who decided in the end that this Mass-oo-mer weren't to be tormented? Who was it sent us on a journey that brought us here as prisoners and gave the diamond to that 'eathen Nana Sahib? And 'oo was it that didn't want to 'ear more about Amy Stockwood, even when I could a-told him she was still alive? You think about all that, Mr Martock, before you go to sleep!"

"You accuse Colonel Farr, then?"

"Oh no, Mr Martock! I ain't so forward as to accuse any man. What I am saying is that if Colonel Farr weren't an honest man, then he's had every opportunity of thieving the jool for the Nana Sahib. If he's honest, then it ain't him. Know your man, Mr Martock. Once you know him, then there's no crime that can't be solved."

"Why the hell," said Martock slowly, "would Colonel Farr steal the Kaisar-i-Hind and send it to the Nana Sahib?"

"You'd be surprised, Mr Martock, what men can be driven

to do. Being a colonel or even a lord won't save a man from some things!"

They lay on the damp earthen tiles of the little cell, which smelt to Verity like an unswept stable. It was high in one of the towers of the fort, its small barred window looking across a yard which the British troops had once used as a drill square. Beyond another wall, they could just see the edge of the rocky plateau and a stretch of the dark plain that ran south towards Agra and the great mausoleum of the Taj Mahal.

The stiffness from the bruises he had received in the struggle, and the impossibility of finding a comfortable position on the clay tiles left Verity sleepless and wondering in the semi-darkness. In his mind he contemplated the geography of the prison. Outside the door of the cell one of Scindia's sepoys stood, armed with a rifle. A short passageway on the far side of the cell wall ran the length of the room and then turned away at right angles. In his brain, he saw the cell as a square and the passages leading to the steps as an L stuck on to the side of the square. At the end of the base of the L was a second guard, also armed. Even if they could overpower the sepoy who stood beyond the door, they would be targets for the bullets of the second guard and any other sepoys who might be with him. Given time, he and Martock might break the lock upon the door or find some way out of the cell. But once outside, they would be helpless as birds in a shooting gallery. Their usefulness to the Nana Sahib was already over and the sepoys would shoot without question.

In the darkness, Martock said suddenly, "I don't see it being an easy bullet to chew on this time."

Verity thought at first that his companion might be talking in his sleep, but Martock continued.

"It's one thing to die knowing that your cause may triumph. But this ain't the easy way of doing things at all."

"Meaning?"

"Meaning, old boy, that once the Nana has the whole of central India *and* the Kaisar-i-Hind, there's an end of Lord Canning. Young Scindia will run like a hare to join the new Mogul Emperor, and every bloody rajah will follow him. You could empty the whole of England and they'd still outnumber our fellows a hundred to one. As it is they'll have to pull back our regiments from Peshawar and the frontier. The whole of the north will be open to Akbar Khan and the Afghans. Whatever happens to us, old fellow, is a drop of rain in a thunderstorm!"

Verity rolled over and sat up.

"Might it rain much hereabouts, Mr Martock, should you 'appen to know?"

"What's that got to do with it?"

"P'raps nothing, and p'raps a good deal. Rains 'eavy does it?"

"Any day now," said Martock. "Monsoons. Cats and dogs."

Verity smiled in the darkness.

"I was rather 'oping it might," he said proudly.

Azimullah watched from the shadows as two of the Nana's women escorted the girl past the flaming torches of the marbled corridor, towards their master's bedchamber. The flames in the brackets flapped and wavered as the air stirred at their passing and the shadows cast upon the wall-hangings warped grotesquely. It was not mere jealousy that prompted the Khan's misgivings, there would soon be enough white-skinned girls besides this one and he might take his pick of a dozen. But what was happening now plainly suggested to him that the Kaisar-i-Hind had not come to Gwalior in quite the manner intended. He watched Judith's long, easy steps, as the nut-brown hair floated across her shoulders like a bridal veil. They had put a transparent sari on her, made of single white chiffon, so that her tall elegant figure seemed to shine with a pale translucence through its veil.

The door of the bedchamber closed behind them, and Azimullah drew deeper still into the shadows, sensing that he had been somehow betrayed. He heard, as though it were a matter of routine, the voices beyond the door, Judith's protests growing more urgent as the women removed her sari. The Nana Sahib spoke, and then there was weeping.

followed by the sounds of a girl losing her virginity. The Khan heard the protests, the reprimands, the frantic moaning, and then the shrill cry which echoed faintly among the arabesques and the vaulting of the great palace. He heard the rhythmic sobbing which continued until it was no longer sobbing, and then a cry of a different kind. The voices began again, and the Nana Sahib laughed. After some while the first sounds recommenced and continued to their natural conclusion. The Khan drew back still further, behind a marble latticework, and watched the door. As the first of the torches began to gutter the Nana spoke to his women again. This time Azimullah heard the sound of Judith struggling and the Nana laughing sardonically, as though at some perverse joke. Then the girl squealed for all the world, thought the Khan, as though they were cutting her throat, and even after it was all finished her weeping at the degradation she had endured was still clearly audible.

None of this had prepared him for the opening of the door again. The two women held her by the arms, while the girl bowed and twisted between them, struggling to be free. As she strove harder, she began to scream hysterically, finally breaking away and running back down the corridor. The skirt of the sari came loose and fell away, so that she ran naked from the waist down. At the end of the marble corridor an open window set in a fine keyhole arch opened upon a prospect of stars and a crescent moon. To his horror, the Khan saw that she was running full tilt towards it, as if determined to throw herself through the opening and on to the sharp angle of the rock-face of Gwalior, forty feet below. There was no time to catch her. Azimullah dashed out into the corridor and shouted at the top of his voice. Judith never faltered, but he had never supposed that she would. Instead, his warning alerted the two palace guards at the far end of the corridor, who stood beyond the corner, and brought them running to cut off her approach to the window.

The two men seized her, though she tried to dodge between them, and held her until the Khan came up. Azimullah stared incredulously. For all the stories about "dishonoured" women and the fury which seized them, he had never seen one like this. She twisted and screamed in the grip of her captors, shrieking aloud the shame which now branded her and the defilement of the final act. She begged to die, more earnestly than the Khan had ever heard a woman, under other circumstances, beg for her life. He was shaken by the sight of her and said softly:

"Take her to the place of the women and see to it that she does herself no harm."

When she had been led away, he turned and saw the Nana standing a little distance away, having been roused by the commotion. The plump, ageless face bore no sign of either pleasure or concern.

"Why, my Lord?" said the Khan incredulously, "Why? A hundred women, far more beautiful than this, shall be yours for the taking in a little while more! But this one might still serve our cause!"

"My friend," said the Nana wearily, "we have the Kaisar-i-Hind and all that we require from her. Now she must come to this. Have no fear, some of our ways are repugnant to her, but she will be broken to them in a week or two."

"The letters she was made to write to her father," said the Khan anxiously: "They spoke of a promise that such things as this would not be done to her if our commands were obeyed."

"The man has never seen them," said the Nana contemptuously, "and never shall."

"They were not sent?"

"They were sent elsewhere," said the Nana, "in Calcutta."

"My Lord, I beg to know what has been done!"

"Lord Dewan," said the Nana, "what has been done is this. You would have brought me the Kaisar-i-Hind at the cost of the girl. Instead, I have made myself the master of both. I require no more from our enemies. And now let us speak no more of the matter."

10

The brief doze into which Verity had fallen ended abruptly with an explosion so close that it seemed to shake the very tiles of the floor on which he lay. It was just daylight, and he saw that Martock too was lying awake after the sound.

"Mr Martock!" he whispered hopefully. "That's never our gunners?"

"Listen!" said Martock impatiently. There was a moment of silence, and then they heard the *rub-dub, rub-dub* of drummers beating "Old trousers" as a morning reveille. Martock pulled himself up on tip-toe to the small barred window and peered out.

"Natives," he said. "We've trained 'em so long that they can't do without a morning gun and tattoo even when they can do without us!"

"Oh," said Verity, as though he had lost interest. Then his voice became confidential, "Mr Martock, you being a bit taller than me, might you be able to see if that native with 'is gun is still outside the door?"

"Of course he is," said Martock without looking. Then he stretched and peered through the barred opening. "Sat there asleep, however."

"Ah," said Verity, "and would you object to just stand there and tip the wink if 'e should 'appen to come to himself?"

"Why?"

"A-cos they ain't took my pocket-knife, Mr Martock and I mean to get a bunk-up on the wooden stool they left us and 'ave a look at the ceiling in the far corner."

Martock looked unconvinced, but none the less took up his position by the door. The lime-washed cell was some twelve feet square, solidly built at the top of the fortress tower. Straw had been thrown in one corner of the red-tiled floor and a single wooden stool remained the one article of furniture. The manacles which held Verity's wrists in front of him were light enough and in no way prevented him moving the stool. He tugged the pocket-knife from his black coat, opened the blade, and probed the ceiling in the corner.

"Why!" he whispered, "It ain't no more than daub and wattle."

"It might be solid steel for all the good it is to us!" said Martock sourly. "It leads nowhere. If you were to start cutting it away, there'd be such a mess as the first native would see as soon as look. And if you *could* get up there, you must come down again either in this cell or in the passage outside with a musket at either side of you."

"If it was night," said Verity wistfully, "they wouldn't see what was happening in here."

"If it was night," said Martock severely, "you could hear a pin drop in Gwalior. Imagine the precious kick-up and row we should make, smashing open the ceiling in two places with a bloody native guard not fifteen feet off."

"P'raps you may be right, Mr Martock." Verity climbed down from the stool. "And yet we ain't ever going to get out through the floor or walls. I been feeling them all night. Not a 'ollow anywhere."

"It doesn't follow that you can vanish through the roof!"

Verity sighed. He crossed to the little window and put his hand out between the bars, as though testing the air of freedom outside. When he drew the hand in again, his palm was filled with small stones and detritus of every kind deposited by the storms on the broad ledge. He sat in a corner and sorted through these like a miser counting a pile of small change.

"You won't bust the lock on the door," said Martock. "It's all on the outside. Best wait until they take us from here and try to break away somehow."

"Mr Martock," said Verity quietly, "I rather fancy that when they take us out of here, it ain't going to be 'Brighton and back for three-and-six'. In fact we mayn't be going back anywhere at all."

Martock grunted. Then Verity looked up from his corner.

"Might you be able to see what weapon the native is carrying, suppose we could get outside?"

Martock peered through the bars.

"Well it ain't a Lee Enfield for sure, old fellow, and it ain't a Brown Bess musket either. It's a muzzle-loader, though. He's got his ramrod with him. I'd say it was loaded already."

Verity joined his companion, shouldering him aside.

"If you'd a-bin in the Rifle Brigade with me, Mr Martock, you'd know that for a old muzzle-loading Baker rifle. It'll load without a ramrod, though lots use the rod too. You drop the ball down the barrel and it falls into a narrowing breech inside, where it sticks fast when it's as far down as it can fall. Some men use the rod to ram it fast home. There's no danger of it going through the breech, the rod not being long enough to drive it so far. Yes, Mr Martock, that's a Baker rifle what they probably took from the poor fellows of the 105th."

Martock stepped back, faintly dismayed by this display of knowledge. Verity smiled and brushed his moustache with the edge of his hand.

"Just how," said Martock, "did you come to know all this?"

"There ain't no trick, Mr Martock. If you'd been with the army before Sebastopol, in the Rhoosian war, you'd know it too. Times like that, a man's rifle means more to him than father, mother, wife and children all put together. 'e gets to love the gun as 'is only friend."

There was a stirring outside, and the two men drew away from the door. The nearer of the guards was awake now and began a conversation with his comrade. More footsteps echoed on the distant steps of the tower, then grew louder as a third man entered the landing corridor. Keys rattled and the cell door opened.

The guard whose duty was at the far end of the corridor now stood in the doorway holding his gun. The newcomer with a pitcher of water in one hand and a bowl of rice in the other, handed these to the guard who had kept watch outside the cell door. In order to receive the bowl and pitcher, the man was obliged to put his rifle down. He propped it against the open door, where its long barrel stood more than three feet high, and locked it by its trigger-guard to a bolt low down upon the heavy door. Then, holding the bowl and pitcher, he advanced carefully into the cell, about to set them down upon the threshold.

Unappetising though the rice and water might seem, it was the first food which the prisoners had seen since noon the previous day. Martock stepped hungrily forward, only to be knocked off his feet by the weight of Verity charging at him from behind and throwing him full tilt into the Indian who had just put the food down. The pitcher rolled across the floor and shattered against the wall, while the bowl of rice spun over, scattering the cooked grains in every direction. Martock saw that Verity had reached the door and was scrabbling for the rifle which the sentry had locked to the bolt of the door. The plump sergeant's hands seemed to slip as he twisted frantically against the restraint of the chain holding the weapon. It crossed Martock's mind that perhaps Verity, without freeing the gun, might be able to twist it until the muzzle pointed at the other guard, but it was soon clear that this was impossible.

The Indians too had realised the hopelessness of the attempt and stood by, grinning, until Verity's struggles diminished and he knelt there, head bowed and hand to his eyes, as though weeping in despair. With great deliberation the man who still carried a rifle took a step forward and, two-handed, drove the muzzle of it into the soft belly, as he might have used a sword-bayonet. Martock heard Verity's cry and the sounds of violent, retching anguish which followed. Verity rolled clear of the door, desperately trying to evade the next blow. The sepoys, still grinning, drew back and slammed the door to. Martock watched gingerly through the bars. The sepoy outside had taken great care, for although he had locked the rifle to the bolt of the door it had not even been loaded. Now he loaded the gun with its metal ball, driving it home with the ramrod down the barrel for good measure. The clang of the iron rod in the metal barrel echoed through the little cell.

Verity was stirring, tears of pain in his eyes.

"Not even loaded!" said Martock. "And now no food either! All that for nothing!"

Verity shook his head.

"Worth every penny," he said weakly.

The hot, stale air of the cell trembled again to the sound of a new explosion.

"Noon," said Martock. "I wish to God they'd bring some water."

Verity sat in silence, as though his thoughts were far away, perhaps with Bella, perhaps with his comrades of the camp before Sebastopol. The afternoon dragged on until the ferocity of the sun's direct rays gave way to an airless and stifling gloom. There was a distant rumble.

"Thunder," said Martock indifferently.

Presently there was a sound of native music, mingled with the rhythmic tramp of marching men in the courtyard outside. Martock moved to the window.

"Sepoys," he said, "by the hundred. Chairs being set out round a big square. Natives crowding on the edge to watch. Seems to be a show of some kind."

Verity seemed not to hear.

"I wish it was dark," he said softly, "I wish it was dark and raining. I don't care for the sun and the warm."

Martock looked anxiously at him, as though fearing that hunger and desperation might reduce the fat sergeant to delirium.

"Dark!" said Verity. "And rain!"

"I say, old fellow," said Martock encouragingly, "come and look at this! That bastard of a Nana, all dressed up and wearing the Kaisar-i-Hind."

Verity stood up, as though reluctantly, and joined his friend at the window. The great courtyard below them looked, he thought, for all the world like Mr Astley's Circus. Uniformed sepoys kept the ground on every side, guarding the row of silk, canopied seats where the Nana Sahib sat with his court. It was easy enough to make out the figures of Azimullah Khan and the Ranee of Jhansi close by him. Behind the cordon of sepoys, the population of Gwalior in bright silks and turbans or white tunics and *puggarees* pressed forward to witness the spectacle.

But as yet there was no spectacle, only three holes, or rather shafts, dug into sandy soil in the middle of the courtyard, with a small pile of earth beside each.

"Here's a rum go," said Martock uneasily.

There was a stirring among the crowd and a renewed surge forward in an endeavour to glimpse what was about to happen. From an archway somewhere below their cell, Verity and Martock saw that an Indian in tunic and *puggaree* was being led out into the centre of the courtyard by a pair of sepoys. A second pair of soldiers, one with the insignia of a havildar-major, followed them. The prisoner stood at length by the first of the three narrow holes.

"I know 'im," said Verity softly, "so do you. It's Ram Lal, our driver!"

By now the man was standing in the hole, his arms pinioned behind him, with no more than his head and neck above the level of the surrounding ground. Two of the sepoys began busily shovelling the earth into the hole, stamping it down, until nothing but the man's head was visible. It was then that Azimullah Khan, who sat close by the Nana Sahib, rose and addressed the crowd on each side of him. From the height of the cell window it was impossible to make out his words, but when he concluded there was a shout of approval from the leaders of the crowd. The Khan salaamed before the Nana Sahib and turned to where the Ranee sat. She rose, still in her military costume, knelt before the newly-acknowledged Emperor of the Mogul kingdoms, and turned to where the subadar-major was leading into the arena a finely caparisoned horse, a bay stallion.

The havildar-major ran forward and attached to the harness belt of the stallion a long leather trace, which trailed backwards to where Ram Lal was buried shoulder-deep in the earth. The Ranee mounted her stallion, while the leather loop at the end of the trace was slipped over Ram Lal's head. She brought her switch down upon the rump of the powerful horse, jabbed the razor-edged spurs hard into its flanks and drove it forward at full gallop. Like a bareback rider, she rose a little from her seat, pulling the stallion round in a tight speeding curve. The loop of the leather trace tightened with the speed of a snake round Ram Lal's neck, the coils of the harness winding more and more powerfully about his throat as the Ranee rode circuit after circuit, urging the horse with a vindictive satisfaction. She watched the distended eyes and the face gorged with blood, while Ram Lal fought unavailingly for breath through his closed windpipe.

The horror that lasted in reality for only a few minutes seemed to Martock and Verity never-ending. But the climax was more grotesque than anything which had gone before. Ram Lal was already dead when the Ranee reined her stallion round and rode hard towards the edge of the courtyard. With the hollow crack of a melon being broken apart, the head of the corpse was torn from the trapped body, by the power of the great horse's gallop, and spun violently across the dusty square. Though the blood had long ceased to move in the body, enough was spilt by this to make a large irregular star of brownish-red in the sand where the headless body was buried.

"Murdering bastards!" said Martock heavily. "What had Ram Lal ever done to them?"

"Driver for the Intelligence Department," said Verity, as though he was thinking hard about something else. He saw that three of the sepoys had turned and were hurrying back towards the building. With his heart thumping wildly he heard their footsteps on the stairs. They crashed down the little passageway outside and gave their orders to the guards of the cell. Verity placed himself just inside the door.

"Mr Martock," he said, "if it ain't no odds to you, I'll just go down the first. And if you should be left, don't forget that ceiling when it's dark. And don't fear that their bullets may hit you."

Martock looked at him in dismay, and for an instant Verity thought his companion might let a tear fall at parting. But, as if by instinct, each man held out his right hand to the other in a firm grasp. When the sepoys opened the cell door, they found the two sergeants shaking hands as officers and men of a regiment might do before being overwhelmed in the carnage of defeat.

"For Old England and 'er Majesty!" said Verity softly.

The two hands drew apart, but not before the hard metal shape of Verity's pocket-knife had passed into Martock's palm.

There was a brief struggle as the sepoys unlocked Verity's wrists and roped them behind his back. Then he was pulled and driven between them, the cell door slamming to on Martock, now the solitary prisoner. The first hole, Verity thought, had been for Ram Lal, the second for himself, and the third for Martock. If he should die now, there could be no doubt that Martock would be dead in a little while more.

As a matter of habit he noted the way they took him, down the first mark of the L alongside the cell, then sharp left into the other. There was no more to the upper level of the tower except for another left turn to the opening of the stairs. Down and down they pushed him, the descending spirals of stone receding like a dark vortex at his feet. And then, with a blinding abruptness, they brought him out through an archway into the brilliance of the afternoon light. A hush of expectation settled on the spectators packed round the improvised arena, for now they were to see the first of the Englishmen die.

When they led him towards the centre of the ground, where the rusty star of blood beside the two holes marked the fate of Ram Lal, Verity heard the silence broken by cries of "Feringhee! Feringhee!" but his thoughts were far away. He was remembering Paddington Green and the best bed, with the brass rails, where he lay with Bella on the night of their marriage. He recalled how he had broken the news of his secondment to India, broken it tenderly after their first embraces. He heard with absolute clarity the pride and sadness in her voice as it echoed in his memory.

"Will it be like the camp before Sebastopol?"

" 'ow d'yer mean?"

"Will it be for Old England and the Queen?"

"Oh," he had said, understanding her at last, "Oh yes, it'll be that all right."

And so it was to be. To die for England and Her Majesty, as many another brave fellow had done in India the past few months. To die alone, before a jeering crowd of heathen, with no hope of rescue and no detachment of an English regiment within three days march. But there was no shame in dying as Ram Lal had done, he told himself, so long as a man kept steady to the end. He knew that he ought to pray but when they brought him level with the hole he had still not found the words. It was easy for the preachers of his childhood to seize the mood, but extempore prayer had never come to him in that manner.

There was something to be said, however. Not said to his country, nor to his God, but to his enemies. It would make little difference to himself or Martock, it might make for a harder death. But if he spoke the words clearly enough, he might save India. By now he was standing in the hole, though the tops of his shoulders as well as his head and neck were above the ground. Two of the sepoys were packing earth around his collar to remedy this. They would kill him, he thought, by the sheer weight of earth that was being stamped tight around him, for already he could only draw breath in shallow movements of his lungs which grew more rapid with his own exhaustion. He gathered all his strength until his cheeks, above the level of the earth, were a bluish damson-red.

"I gotta message for His Excellency Azimullur Khan!"

One of the sepoys spat at him. Another slipped the leather noose over his head and adjusted it to the fat neck. The Ranee on her Arab stallion waited while the fastening of the trace was secured. Verity took breath in a long painful sigh.

"From the Intelligence Department!"

Azimullah had not moved from his seat, as though merely waiting for the execution to begin. But at these words he rose, salaamed to the Nana Sahib, and crossed the dusty square.

"A message?" he said disdainfully.

Verity tried to turn his head on one side, squinting up at the towering height of his enemy.

"More like a request," he said feebly. "If I'm to die for

'aving brought you the jool, I'd like to 'ave a proper sight of it before it's too late. I never seen it close up."

Azimullah roared with laughter, throwing his head back at the absurdity of the fat Sergeant's self-abasement before the triumph of the Nana Sahib. He turned away and crossed to where the Ranee sat upon her stallion, spoke to her, and stood back. Verity tensed his body against the searing, throttling agony of the leather trace. But still the Ranee waited. Azimullah was returning, but he was now preceded by the Nana Sahib and an escort of sepoys in yellow and scarlet. The Nana, with an expression of contempt, looked down at the helpless prisoner. He took the diamond from its place upon his breast and passed it to Azimullah. The Khan squatted down, grinning, and placed the flashing stone some twelve inches in front of Verity's face. Verity breathed again, deeply and painfully.

"Thank you, Mr Azimullur Khan. And now, if you please, I can die quite 'appy."

The Khan tittered with amusement.

"For having seen the beauty of the Kaisar-i-Hind?"

"Oh no!" said Verity, as if surprised that any man could suppose such a thing, "I can die 'appy because now I know that you ain't got the Kaisar-i-Hind. An' if you was ever to make so bold as to say you 'ad got it – why, your friends in Bengal or Afghanistan 'ud take one look at that there stone and laugh in your face!"

"Fool!" said the Nana Sahib contemptuously. "He thinks to save himself a moment longer by this nonsense."

But Verity saw that Azimullah's eyes, as they flickered sideways at the Nana, were smouldering with rage, as though his misgivings in the matter of the diamond had been realised.

"Mr Azimullur," said Verity, speaking so feebly that the Khan had to squat again to catch his words, "have the goodness to send for a little scale and weights. And in the meantime p'raps you'd be so good as to keep turning that stone about for my observation!"

Two sepoys doubled away.

"Pray," said the Khan, "pray that you are wrong and that

you may die quickly. For if you have indeed deceived us, you shall be put to such torment as shall make death seem a blessing. We will have the truth from you."

"You can only have from me what I know," said Verity stolidly, "which is that this ain't your jool. Come to that, it ain't any other jool either. You only gotta look on two of the corners there. There's what they call contusions, consequential on you having weighted my truncheon with it and me having struck blows with same. That ain't a diamond! A diamond is the hardest stone there is and won't be bruised by wood or metal!"

Azimullah turned to the subadar-major of the sepoys and swore violently in his own language. The scales were brought.

"Now," said Verity, "you just weigh that. You ain't got to take my word for it. The description of the diamond is out all over Calcutta. Six and three-quarter ounce weight without mountings or fastenings. Now you see if that corresponds."

Azimullah squatted by the scales. He put the diamond into one of the small brass pans, which promptly sank under the weight. Then he put the first ounce weight into the other, and then a second. The scales still remained up ended. He added a third, but neither of the brass pans budged. Then a fourth. The Nana's smooth face began to crease in a smile at Verity's impending downfall. Azimullah took the fifth weight and added it to the pile. He was reaching for the sixth when, as though with a great effort the unoiled scale tipped, coming down stiffly with a clatter on the side of the little pile of weights.

"There!" said Verity triumphantly, "It ain't nearly the weight of the Kaisar-i-Hind! And if you knew about diamonds, which it seems you don't, you'd know that they're brightest in half-light. The way that so-called jool 'as been flashing out here, any fool of a cheapjack could tell you it was glass! You been seen off, Mr Azimullur, ain't yer? Your new Mogul Empire ain't 'alf come a cropper! A man can die 'appy, knowing that."

As Verity spoke, he noticed how the shadows of the men,

cast by the thickening sunlight of late afternoon, had lengthened. The night that was coming promised horrors beyond description, but it was not devoid of hope.

"Let the stone be examined at once!" said the Nana softly. "If he has lied, let his tongue be cut out that he may not blaspheme, and let him die in torment. If he speaks the truth, let him be tormented equally, but let him keep his tongue, that he may tell the rest of the tale! See it done tonight. Let the heads of both Feringhees be mounted on lances at dawn, high on the battlements where the crows may reach them!"

I I

Far away to the south there was a dull, prolonged rumbling.

"Thunder," said Martock, "you may have your rain after all."

Verity shivered; they had left his arms roped behind him, and Martock's patient picking at the knots had now set his hands free. Martock himself still wore manacles, his wrists cuffed before him.

"We can't wait for rain any more," said Verity grimly, "not when they may come back any minute and tie my hands again—or worse!"

There was a louder booming, whose vibrations ran through the tower.

"Sunset gunfire!" said Verity "Now's our time, Mr Martock, if you please! I know it ain't perfect dark but we daren't delay longer. The minute they've reckoned up that stone, they'll put us both to the torment. I 'eard of one poor devil after Cawnpore. They put him to such agony as made him arch his body with the torment. In the end, they drove him so wild with pain, and he arched up so violently, that he snapped his own spine! Sharp's the word, Mr Martock, and quick's the motion!"

He lifted the stool to the corner again and stood upon it,

his pocket-knife open in his hand. Martock peered through the grill of the door, saw the guard walking outside, and half-turned his head to Verity.

"Just how," he inquired softly, "did you happen to know that the stone *wasn't* the Kaisar-i-Hind?"

Verity took off his black frock-coat and laid it in the corner so that the fragments of plaster would fall upon it and their sound would be deadened. His coat and trousers were smeared with a caramel-coloured clay, as if they were the grave-clothes of a hastily exhumed corpse. He stretched upward on the stool, in the gathering darkness, and began to work cautiously at the white plaster in the corner of the ceiling.

"I didn't exactly *know*," he said, frowning hard at his work. "More like something at the back of my mind that I somehow couldn't exactly place. You see, Mr Martock, a man as carries a truncheon gets to know its feel. And a man like me, that's never carried his truncheon loaded, would soon know if it was. It ain't so much the weight, it's the balance. A five or six ounce weight can make a deal o' difference to the balance and handling. And I could a-swore that there was no weight like that in my truncheon when I used it last night. But that stone was in there. And then I thought, p'raps the stone wasn't so much as they thought it weighed. And then I thought, if it didn't weigh so much, then it couldn't be the jool. But I wasn't sure, you see."

He paused, wrestling the blade against an obstinate lath.

"Watch out!" said Martock softly. Verity stepped down and sat on the stool, assuming a posture of dejection. The sepoy glimpsed Martock through the bars and grinned.

"Masuur send for sahibs soon! Masuur make sahibs glad to die!"

"Bugger off," said Martock, turning his back. The sepoy chuckled and walked slowly away, patrolling to the corner of the L, where he was within sight and conversational range of the other guard.

"Carry on," said Martock, and Verity remounted the stool.

"So you didn't *know*?" Martock inquired.

"I knew," said Verity, "that they wouldn't kill us until

they heard all about the Kaisar-i-Hind. So I asked to see it and swore it had blemishes, from being knocked by wood, which no diamond could have."

"Had it?"

"'ow should I know? I wouldn't know a blemish if I saw it. Then I told them to weigh it, if they didn't believe me. And I told them the weight checked in Calcutta was six and three quarter ounces, whereas Colonel Farr gave it as five and a half. So even if it was the real jool, I could make out it weighed wrong and must be a fake. I reckoned that ought to save us for a bit."

"Cunning bastard!" said Martock.

Verity turned his face round, his pink cheeks and black moustache whitened by plaster.

"Ah," he said, "but when they weighed it, it was between four and five ounces. The way their scales were sticking, it probably wasn't so much. Now whatever that is, it ain't the Kaisar-i-Hind!"

"But a diamond of some kind?"

Verity dodged a shower of plaster, and said, "Funny thing. Out there in all that sun it flashed brighter than it ever did at Fyzabad, or last night."

"So?"

Verity stopped work and turned indignantly.

"Mr Martock! I don't call myself a man of great education. But I do take the trouble to familiarise myself by a little reading with subjects I 'ave to investigate. Don't you know about them jools? Don't you know that they sparkle like white fire in candlelight, but look like nothing at all in the sun? That thing ain't a jool at all! It's cheap glass!"

"Then where the devil is the Kaisar-i-Hind?"

"We'd all like to know that, Mr Martock!" said Verity smugly.

Martock stood for a moment as though struck speechless by the revelation. Then he pulled himself together.

"For God's sake!" he said, "Get on with that hole or let me do it!"

"Much obliged, Mr Martock. I'm getting on with it all

right, and I ain't particular to listen to profanities while I do so!"

By the time that Verity had cleared the plaster between two beams, cutting through the flimsy laths and opening a hole in the ceiling some eighteen inches square, it was fully dark except for the tawny oil-light from the passageway outside, falling through the barred opening in the door.

"I rather think, Mr Martock," he breathed, "that we're ready. Please to do just as I say!"

"Ready?" said Martock incredulously. "For what?"

"To climb up here and come down in the passage outside."

"No!" said Martock. "They'll hear us the minute we start moving up there. Just think of the row and the time it'll take to open another hole in the ceiling. You saw that bastard out there load his gun this morning. They could both of them put a hundred bullets into us before we cut our way out!"

"Mr Martock!" said Verity severely, "Listen!"

Martock listened fearfully, expecting to hear footsteps on the stairs of the tower. There was almost complete silence, except for a hardly perceptible hissing. As they listened, it grew louder and steadier.

"Rain!" said Verity with a proprietorial air. "While you been indulging in profanities, I been praying for that this last hour and a half!"

"It still won't get you down into the corridor. Even if it did you'd have a gun at either side of you!"

"Mr Martock, I ain't giving you orders. All I'm saying is that *I'm* not staying 'ere to be 'orribly murdered by beastly 'eathen. I got more self-respect than that!"

Martock's thin face was a study in anxiety by the faint light of the lamp outside. But the hissing of the rain had grown to a rhythmic pattering on the tiles above them. He watched Verity put on the black frock-coat and mount the stool. The burly arms grasped the ledges of the hole. There was a snorting, grunting heave. Then, slowly, the stout body rose from the stool, the plump shoulders squeezing with difficulty through the opening and disappearing into the roof space. For a moment longer, the fat legs and large buttocks in the baggy black trousers hung motionless, as though Verity might reappear with a tremendous crash. Martock hurried forward, cupped his hands as a stirrup, and hoisted the large, booted feet upwards. As soon as Verity was safely up, he stepped on to the stool, gripped the edges of the cavity, dragged himself up as far as he could, and was then lifted almost effortlessly by a powerful heave at the scruff of his neck and the belt of his trousers. He lay in the dark space, recovering from the shock of realising how much physical strength was concealed by Sergeant Verity's portly indolence.

Although the rain was drumming harder on the tiles above them, the confined space of the roof was suffocatingly hot from the intensity of months of summer. There was virtually no light at all, but he just heard Verity slithering on his belly towards a spot above the upright of the L-shaped corridor. In his mind's eye, he saw it as being about half-way down the upright of the L. The corridor, at this point, would be in full view of the sepoy who sat outside the door of the cell, but it would be hidden from the view of the other armed guard whose position was round the corner at the other extreme of the L. The rain was now drumming harder on the tiles above their heads and Verity could just hear the first rivulets beginning to churn and chuckle in the gutters of the roof. He lay flat along one of the beams, where it would support his weight, and unclasped his pocket-knife again. With great care, he began to saw gently through a row of laths, until a whole area of the ceiling over the spot he had chosen was precariously weakened. He slid back a little, cupped his hands over Martock's ear, and whispered moistly.

"Mr Martock, there ain't no reason why that shouldn't give now with a good jump upon it. It's no more than eight feet from ceiling to floor, so if I keep a hold on the beam I shall just about drop to touch the floor. Now, p'raps you'd oblige me by following so soon as I'm through. I shall remonstrate with the native outside the door of the cell and show him the game's up. But the other guard is sure to come running at the noise. So if you'd be good enough to stand just behind the corner and fetch him a clout on the side, we shall get along famously. I know you got your hands ironed, but if you could just hold him up while I deal with the other, I shall be with you in no time at all."

Martock turned his head and hissed into Verity's ear, "Not a chance of it! You saw that sepoy outside the cell door loading his rifle this morning! If you come down through there, you'll be six or eight feet from him and it'll be quite a while before you're free of the debris and can get a hand on him! He'll shoot you ten times over before that!"

Verity turned.

"I 'ad thought of that, Mr Martock!" he said reproachfully.

"And," Martock added, "you might break a leg or an arm in the fall!"

"So I might, Mr Martock. Only it ain't the first time in the course of constabulary duty that I've had cause to break into a 'ouse of infamy through a ceiling. I ain't that green!"

Martock gave a forlorn sigh.

"I suppose," he said grudgingly, "there isn't a good deal of choice."

Verity slithered awkwardly along the beam again to the place where he had cut through several of the laths. He raised himself so that he crouched on the beam, facing the weakened lath and plaster, with another beam running parallel about two feet in front of him. It crossed his mind that he might be dead in a moment more, but he had sworn never to let them take him again, never to be at their mercy in such a manner. And for the first time he shuddered at the memory of what had happened that afternoon in the courtyard.

Gathering all his strength, he drew himself up and hopped. two-legged, like some monstrous black frog, from the beam. crashing all his weight down on the flimsy ceiling. To his astonishment, it shook violently but held him, and he heard a shout of alarm from the passageway below. With a sense of panic that something had gone inexplicably wrong, he gripped the beam in front of him, hopped up and down again, and disappeared through the ceiling in a roaring avalanche of plaster. He still kept his grasp of the beam, so that he appeared below as a portly, whitened figure, dangling by his hands in a cloud of thinning dust. He let go of the beam, dropped the remaining few inches to the floor, and heard Martock scrambling after him.

The sepoy who guarded the cell door had swung round, his eyes widening with anger, and his rifle levelled.

"Now then!" said Verity, as though delivering a caution, "Put that thing down or you'll have something to be sorry for, my man! Savvy?"

A half-smile of contempt flickered across the guard's features. Verity was in his sights, about eight feet away with no means of shelter or escape. It was impossible that a bullet could miss such a target at this range. In a moment of intense stillness the click of the priming pan echoed sharply in the stone passageway.

"Right!" said Verity, shouldering forward. He could hear the other sentry, beyond the corner, moving cautiously to investigate the disturbance. There was no more time to spare. Watching the sharp black hole of the rifle muzzle and the whitening of the guard's finger as he began to pull the trigger back, Verity took a step forward. Behind him he heard a sudden blow and a choking, gurgling cry, suddenly cut short.

"Take cover now, Mr Martock!" he said firmly.

"Run, you bloody fool!"

But Verity took one more step, and then the guard fired.

The flash was brilliant as a magnesium flare in the oil-lit passageway but it was red with the burning powder. There was a scream which chilled Martock's blood and he saw the face of the sepoy disintegrate, like a wax doll in flame, through a sheet of fire. A nauseating stench of burnt powder and flesh began to fill the corridor.

"My God!" he said wonderingly.

For a second he stood beside Verity, staring at the blood-soaked and powder-blackened bundle which was all that remained of the sepoy. The rifle was bent and buckled like a snapped twig.

"It wasn't that I intended it," said Verity sternly, "but when a man won't listen to the voice of authority properly constituted, 'e must bear the consequences of his action."

"Never mind that," said Martock impatiently. "How did it happen?"

Verity brushed his black clothes down with his hands.

"You mean, Mr Martock, that you really thought I was soft enough to try and grab that rifle this morning to use it, when it was locked to the door? And me 'aving been in the Rifle Brigade! That's what I wanted *them* to think, o' course. No, Mr Martock, what I did was to drop the biggest pieces of stone and earth I could down that barrel, 'aving palmed 'em specially for the purpose. Natives never cleans their guns proper and I knew that once they thought we might try to escape they'd load those rifles. But when the ball and ramrod went down that barrel, the stones and earth were driven through the breech into the chamber of the gun where the powder is. And when that powder was ignited, by 'im pulling the trigger, the obstruction would jam the breech and the whole weapon blow up in his face. The breech is narrower on the inside and what gets in very often can't get out!"

"It's a bloody miracle!" said Martock softly.

"No it ain't, Mr Martock. It's observation. There's no knowing what a man mayn't do, if 'e'll only make a habit of observation."

They turned to the second guard, whom Martock had laid senseless. Verity took a ring with several keys upon it, trying them in turn until he found the one which unlocked Martock's handcuffs. He took the rifle and several rounds of ammunition, handed Martock the sword-bayonet, and strode towards the head of the tower steps. An iron-barred gate, where the guard had kept watch, was locked across the opening of the spiral stairway, but one of the keys fitted its lock. Verity closed and fastened the gate after them. As they moved softly down the stone steps, they heard two or three men running across the courtyard below, making for the tower door.

"That rifle going off!" said Martock. "That's done it!"

Verity began pounding down the steps, gasping like a drayhorse.

"Deny 'em cover, Mr Martock. If we let them bottle us up in here, we're done for!"

They reached the archway at the bottom of the stairs, which led out into the darkened courtyard. Four ill-defined figures were moving towards them, dimly illuminated by an oil-lamp and recognisable as sepoys of the Nana's palace guard. Without hesitation, Verity dropped on one knee, raised the Baker muzzle-loader to his shoulder and fired. There was a cry and the sound of a body falling. The three survivors ran for the protection of a buttress.

"Now," whispered Verity, "over to the right is the gate and the road beyond leading down the side of the rock. P'raps you'd be so good, Mr Martock, as to run for the buttress just inside the gateway while I cover you. Once you're there, I'll come after."

"There's still three of those buggers with rifles cocked!" said Martock indignantly.

"Much obliged," said Verity condescendingly, "and I don't fancy they'll bother you."

"Why not?"

"A-cos the way they're standing out there in this down-pour, their powder will be soaked by now. Not one shot in twenty would go off. I ain't a griffin where rifles is concerned, Mr Martock. And now a clean pair o' heels, if you please."

With evident reluctance, Martock edged out from the cover of the archway and ran, crouching, across the court-yard. Once he stumbled on the uneven ground and Verity thought he must fall, but he regained his balance and ran on. With a sense of pride in his own judgment, Verity heard the repeated click of the sepoys' firing pans, as their guns failed to go off in the steady rain. He wrapped the butt of his own gun under his frock-coat for protection, as he took a deep breath, hunched his shoulders, and then lumbered off across the darkened courtyard to join Martock.

The two men crouched in the shadow of the buttress, breathing heavily.

"Gate!" said Verity. "Sentries!"

Martock shook his head.

"Those were the sentries, the ones we shot at!"

"Right!"

Still crouching, they edged round the buttress and ran for the open gateway. There was no sign of a guard, though an oil-lamp flickered in a corner of the wall.

"Take that," said Verity, "but keep it low."

He went down on one knee again, aimed the rifle and fired two ear-splitting shots in the direction of the hidden guards. Then the mechanism clicked and failed to discharge.

"Never mind!" he said, "Keep them back for a bit!"

Still clutching the useless rifle, he trotted with Martock down the slope for twenty yards or so.

"Shine that bull's-eye over here, if you please, Mr Martock! Just 'ere, on the wall!"

They were level now with the foundations of the great fort, where an archway blocked by a rough wooden door was set into the wall.

"Right," said Verity, "this one's for us! Sword-bayonet in the jamb, if you please!"

The hinges moved stiffly under the pressure, but Martock opened the door sufficiently for the two men to pass inside and then pulled it to after them.

"Better not hang about too long," he said nervously, "If we can't put a dozen miles between us and Gwalior before sunrise, they'll be round us like flies on a black pudding!"

"Leave Gwalior?" said Verity with indignation, "Leave Gwalior, Mr Martock? I shouldn't leave Gwalior if you was to offer me a gold sovereign for every step I took! Can't you see that's just what they expect? 'ow far down this road do you suppose two Englishmen in frock-coats 'ud get before there was a mob of 'eathen savages after them? And supposing we could get through, there's the Nana Sahib's army for miles around. I don't know which way we should have to walk, and nor do you. And there's another thing, Mr Martock."

"Yes?"

"Yes. One poor young lady may be even now suffering the 'orrors of that villain's zurr-narr-narr. She may be Amy

Stockwood or she may not. But I ain't leaving here without her."

"The devil take Amy Stockwood and the rest of them!" said Martock loudly. "Dammit, man, don't be such a fool that you can't fear danger!"

Verity looked unhappily at the floor.

"Mr Martock, there's times when I could almost be ashamed of you. The fool ain't always the brave who can't smell danger; it's the man who'd give in and suffer worst of all from his enemies. Now, you may come or not, as you choose. But I'm taking that lantern and this rifle, and I'm following this passageway into the foundations, or cellars, or whatever it may be that lies under the palace and fortress. Above ground, you couldn't walk ten feet through the building without having to face more guards. But this way, we might find a road to the very 'areem of the monster. Now, I ain't anxious to do it alone, so if you could see your way to carrying the lantern I'd be greatly obliged. But do it I will, alone or not!"

Martock pulled himself from the wall, grumbled, and then took up the lantern. The floor of the subterranean passage was littered with stones, fragments of carvings and broken bricks. It seemed as if the place had been used as a catacomb or burial place long ago, since the ledges on either wall bore a number of small stone sarcophagi with Jain motifs carved on their sides. Here and there the walls were adorned with rough inscriptions and sketches of Shiva or Kali, as though they might have been drawn by soldiers or prisoners to pass the time.

About a hundred yards from the entrance, the arched tunnel was blocked by the bars of another iron gate. Verity tried it. The hinges were almost rusted into place, but the gate itself was unlocked. Panting with the exertion, he pushed it wide enough for the two of them to get through.

"Leave it," he said quickly, "we may 'ave to get back through in a hurry."

Ahead of them, the vaulted passage was angled a little to the left. Verity moved with greater caution, while the lantern in Martock's hand threw grotesque, looming shadows on the roof and rough stone walls before them. As they turned the angle of the corner, he hissed at his companion.

"Stop!"

The tunnel seemed to widen gradually. To one side, about twenty yards in front, a row of bars walled off what looked like the cage of some wild animal. There was no sound from it.

"It ain't dogs," said Verity softly, "else they'd have let rip by now."

Soon they were close enough for the pale light of the lantern to shine through the bars into the recess itself.

"My God!" said Martock, "Look at them!"

Verity looked. The two prisoners hung against the wall of their dungeon, suspended by their wrists from iron rings in the stones above them. They had been dead for weeks, perhaps even for months, but the dry air of the catacomb had mummified their features. One had the *puggaree* and loin-cloth of an Indian bearer, the other wore the pale blue uniform with silver facings of a British officer of the Bengal Light Cavalry. Verity looked once more at them, stiff and contorted in their postures of death.

"Come on," he said grimly, "they're past any help of ours."

"Wait!" said Martock, "There's a guard ahead of us!"

In the murk of the passageway a shrill voice screamed, *"Kôn hai?"*

Martock closed the lantern shutter.

"It's a woman," he said softly, "that's a sentry's challenge in their lingo."

"Guarding the zurr-narr-narr?"

"Not likely."

"Tell her, " said Verity softly, "that if she's sensible and will lay down her weapons peacefully, no harm will come to her."

Now there was a light in the tunnel and again the shrill voice.

"Kôn hai!"

"Gora lôg," said Martock, stepping resolutely forward.

Then they saw her, a giantess of a woman in a white tunic and baggy trousers, wielding a double-edged sword of the kind used by native acrobats at great feasts and popular entertainments. She came at them, whirling and twisting the long blade with both hands, in a manner that momentarily bewildered Verity. He snatched the rifle to his shoulder, lined the sights with the centre of the moving body, and pulled the trigger. There was a click and nothing more, as the wet powder still failed to ignite. The woman was almost upon him, towering over him it seemed with her raised sword, when Martock rushed in with the sword-bayonet and sank the sharp blade into her midriff. The woman drew back, making no attempt to remove the blade, gave a fearful shriek and bore down upon them again. Once more Verity raised the rifle and once more there was nothing but a click. He pulled the trigger a second time and there was a deafening roar which seemed to shake the very rock about them. The bullet tore into her body and still she struggled on, forcing both men to back away, until she paused, swayed, and then fell at full length.

Verity turned away, and sat trembling on the stone ledge at the side of the passage.

"Drugs," said Martock contemptuously, "they fill them so full of bhang that they'll charge anything and bear anything until they drop like that! I say, old fellow, you ain't seedy, are you?"

Verity shook his head and pulled himself up.

"No," he said, his throat constricted by shock. "Never thought I'd have to kill a woman, that's all."

"No," said Martock, "you thought of Bible classes for the natives and temperance teas for the rest of us. If you can't stand seeing a native woman bleed, my friend, India ain't for you!"

"Don't prose so!" said Verity feebly. He busied himself in looking about the alcoves which the woman had been guarding. One of them seemed plentifully stocked with coils of rope, picks, and shovels.

"Just help me, Mr Martock," he said softly, "to wind a coil or two of that rope about my waist. It may come in useful to pull us out of here."

When they were ready, Martock said, "I'll just keep the rifle and bayonet. It's a good blade, even without bullets."

Verity turned away, not wishing to witness the grisly retrieval of the sword-bayonet. He selected a pick from the store.

"I'd as soon have this," he said. "A tin-miner's son can't help getting to know about the uses of such things."

In a moment more they came to the end of the passage and found themselves in a small, subterranean amphitheatre with steps, a portico, and a statue of the goddess Kali on the far wall. They examined the portico, but it was merely a sham suggestion of a temple which led nowhere.

"It's where the temple dancers perform," said Martock thoughtfully, "so somewhere the other side of this is your precious zenanah".

Presently they found a deep tunnel-like window set in the thick wall to one side. Bars at either end of the recess, and the narrow calibre of the far opening, blocked their way.

"Mr Martock," said Verity gently, "there's a way round one side. If you'll stay here, I'll take the lantern and pick and see if I can't get in somehow. I do believe that's the start of the zurr-narr-narr in there!"

He disappeared into the narrow alley-way. Presently his voice echoed back.

"All right, Mr Martock! Stay where you are! I gotta kind of ventilation grill here. You watch and see I get in safe before you risk it!"

Martock heard the metallic plucking of the pick-blade at the masonry. Then he turned to the window, clutching the bars, knuckles against the glass inside, and watched Verity's entry into the ante-chamber of the zenanah. It seemed that Verity had left the lantern outside, so that it shone in along the floor of the room, dimly illuminating the bare white-washed space, devoid of all furnishing. Martock saw the shadowy, frock-coated figure slithering laboriously across the floor. Then he saw, with some surprise, that Verity was lying there casually unwinding the rope from his waist. He took the end of the rope and threw it upwards, where it remained, quivering slightly but quite straight.

"But it can't!" said Martock desperately.

He stared incredulously as the rope remained standing upright in the air, except for those coils which Verity still held in his hand. To his still greater astonishment, he saw the dim shape of his portly comrade beginning to climb with great effort up the length of unsupported rope. Puffing and gasping, Verity pulled himself to the top. Then he seemed to swing in a cartwheel of black clothing and disappeared. Martock, at his window, surveyed the room from corner to corner. The rope remained, defying gravity, but the room was empty.

"Good God!" he said softly, "The Indian rope-trick!"

He turned away and sat on the temple steps close by. Then, at the sound of footsteps, he tightened his grip on the rifle and looked towards the sound. It was Verity.

"Right, Mr Martock," he said, "I rather think we've found the way to the 'areem!"

Martock stared at him.

"Is that all?' he asked.

"Whatcher mean, 'all'?"

"What I mean," said Martock slowly, "is that I have just seen you do the Indian rope-trick. No white man has ever seen it done before, let alone performed it!"

"What the 'ell are you on about, Mr Martock?"

"Look through there!" Martock indicated the window, with its view of the rope standing straight upwards, unsupported. Verity looked.

"Gimme your gun and bayonet, if you please!"

He unclipped the sword-bayonet, smashed the pane of glass inside the bars and slid the long slender barrel down the embrasure. About half way along it stopped. Verity grunted.

"'ave the goodness to follow me, Mr Martock." He led the way into the alley, down some steps, and through an open door. They stood in the plain white room, the inner end of the window embrasure set beside the door. The rope swung gently in the draught, dangling from the ceiling.

"Now," said Verity, "you just take a look back through that window."

Martock pressed to the bars and looked. The dimly lit scene of the temple portico and steps hung, as in a dream, upside down.

"Lenses!" said Verity contemptuously, "Like a magic lantern to deceive ignorant savages. What you saw was me come in along the ceiling, having first tossed a rope over that hook there, and then shinned to the floor. Only the floor just there is a trap. When a man touches on it, he falls through a foot or two quite safely. Then I unbolted that lower door you couldn't see from outside."

"So that's it!" said Martock, "That's the precious secret of it!"

Verity smirked.

"Why, Mr Martock! Only fancy you being took in like any 'eathen! I do believe they knocked more sense into us at Hebron Chapel than ever they did at that gentleman's school of yours!"

Martock stood in glum silence.

"And this," said Verity, touching a door on the other side of the embrasure, "leads to steps: at the top of which I distinctly 'eard young persons' voices. If you please, then, we'll move very careful just here."

12

The torches in the brackets of the stone-flagged room burned steadily, deepening the warm colours of the rose pink archways. A drift of incense rose in a thin cloud from the chafing pan, concealing the grosser scents of warm bodies. The Ranee stood back, eyeing Massoumeh's nudity with professional distaste. The girl was suspended by her wrists in the centre of the room, her toes just touching the floor.

"A whore may be dealt with as a whore," said the Ranee softly, "but for treason there is one penalty alone. A woman who betrays her race, her nation, and her Emperor is not permitted the luxury of an easy death!"

Massoumeh twisted her face round, her eyes wide with fear as she shook her head vigorously and the red henna'd hair brushed against the light tan of her shoulders. She mewed urgently through the cloth that gagged her.

"Slut!" said the Ranee scornfully. "Whore of the Feringhees! Who else could have stolen the true Kaisar-i-Hind? Would they be fools enough to send two of their own men here with a worthless stone?"

Massoumeh's head dropped forward again and she waited in apparent resignation.

"I greatly regret," said the Ranee in her most matter-of-fact manner, "that I must leave you after so short an experience of my vengeance. Tomorrow, the army which I lead shall be victorious in a great battle, and your body shall lie crumpled at the foot of the deep well of oblivion under this rock of Gwalior. Before then you shall be passed to the care of Masuur and Hanment. All that you have heard of fire and rack shall be practised upon you, until the bowstring releases you from this life. Both of these butchers are tongueless, that they may not tell the secrets of their trade. And they are deaf, so that no prayers or cries affect them."

The Ranee saw with satisfaction that the Persian nautch-girl was shaking visibly with fright. Then the Princess clapped her hands, the curtains of an archway parted and the two robed and hooded executioners emerged from concealment. The Ranee gave an order, Masuur and Hanment bowed, and then she withdrew, leaving them to their grisly trade.

Massoumeh watched them over her shoulder, the hysteria of uncontrolled terror rising like a choking flood in her lungs. The first man stepped purposefully forward, ignoring the crescendo of gagged screams, steadied her by the shoulders, and looked deep into her eyes.

"Right, miss!" he said softly, "Now if you'll just undertake to be very quiet when we get that cloth out o' your face, we shall all get along real 'andsome together!"

She stared in disbelief, until the second man held the curtain of the archway well back and she saw the bulging eyes and struggling, muscular limbs of Masuur and Hanment, the bald-headed executioners, trussed like fowls, their *puggarees* thrust in their mouths.

While Verity cut her free, Martock went quickly round the room securing the outer and inner doors, so that they would be safe from any sudden intrusion. Once the girl was released from the rope suspending her, she collapsed into Verity's arms, weak from shock rather than anything that the Ranee had done. He struggled to hold her up and, at the same time, endeavoured to keep his hands free of the more suggestive areas of her body. It was not easy. As he lowered her, he caught sight of their reflection in a glass, the image of two figures in a wildly obscene dance. One of his hands appeared to be clawing frenziedly at Massoumeh's backside, while his other supported her shoulders, its fingers somehow splayed across her breast. He straightened up at last, his face the colour of port wine and glistening with perspiration.

"Quick!" said Verity, turning to Martock, "Ask her as much as you can in 'er own lingo! We ain't got much time and the young lady 'as to be found!"

He turned his back as Martock comforted the naked Massoumeh, soothing and reassuring her. Then he heard Martock put the questions to her. Even Verity recognised from such phrases as "miss-sahiba" and Massoumeh's quick nodding that the Persian must have seen or heard of an English girl in the zenanah. Martock stood up.

"She's here," he said, "in a room beyond the part where the other girls are kept. And this doxy swears there's only one white girl, all the others are black as midnight, so there's no mistake."

"Then we'll leave Mass-oo-mer 'ere, find the young lady and bring her back, and then leave the way we came."

"No, old fellow," said Martock, "she won't be left here. She says if we can't take her now, will we please cut her throat rather than let the Ranee and her bullies have her again. She'd better come."

Verity began laboriously stripping off the white robe which he had taken from Masuur.

"Then she'd better cover herself with this. I ain't particular to go about dressed like a flash 'ambone. And I never did like incognito."

Cautiously, Martock unfastened the door and they slipped out into the warm, vaulted corridor, where a dim oil-light showed the keyhole Jain arches, the marble lattice-work, and the softer luxury of the zenanah. Martock held Massoumeh firmly by the arm, both as a reassurance and as a precaution in case she should bolt in sheer terror. Verity heard the sound of girls' voices and saw a pattern of light falling on the floor ahead of them.

"This corridor," said Martock softly, "is where the owner of the girls walks. He can see without being seen. All along here is a lattice-work of marble, and he can walk past, seeing every room and every girl in it before he takes his pick. A bit like a French Introducing House I once knew of."

Verity ignored this.

"Mr Martock," he breathed, "I'm going to have to look room by room to see where she may be."

"Undoubtedly, old boy."

"Then I wonder if you would mind obliging me?"

"If I can."

"It's just this," Verity paused and stood still. "If we should be spared, and come safe out of this business, I wonder if you'd just mind not saying anything of this part to anyone? It ain't Mrs Verity. She'd understand it was duty, though I'd rather not concern 'er with it. But, Mr Martock, if some of the sergeants in 'A' Division was to hear the tale, my life 'ud be misery from then on."

"Never fear," said Martock, "a thousand pounds wouldn't get it from me!"

"Why," said Verity, as though moved, "that's spoken like a real gentleman."

They moved forward circumspectly, examining the softly-lit rooms and their occupants through the diminutive squares of the marble lattice. There were two rooms in which several girls squatted on a richly carpeted floor, or lounged on brightly coloured cushions, some smoking a hookah, others talking, laughing, and one playing what looked like a mandolin. Some displayed bare midriffs and legs, others were more fully clothed. Further on, there were glimpses of girls indulging a mild mutual affection in the form of furtive horseplay. Some were of the same Persian build and colouring as Massoumeh, others had a smooth glossy darkness to their skins. A few were slender and many were fat. Most were young. But among them all there was not a single girl who could be taken for European.

Martock touched Verity's sleeve.

"Just beyond here, old fellow, and she says there's a guard on the door."

Then, without consulting his companions any further, Martock released Massoumeh's arm and strode forward, the loose white folds of his executioner's robes still covering the bottoms of his black trousers. As he approached the end of the passageway, where it turned sharply to the right, one of the Nana Sahib's palace sepoys stepped out and barred his way. Martock went up to the man, as though about to speak. Then Verity saw the sepoy double up with a violent groan, as though he had been hit in the stomach. Only when Martock stepped clear did he see the hilt of the sword-bayonet protruding from the Indian's belly, and realised that Martock had continued to carry the blade under his robe.

By the time that Verity was level with his comrade, Martock had forced the door of the room and was shining a lamp into the interior. There was no sound, no stirring of limbs, no whisper of breath. At first it seemed that the small chamber must be empty. Then, as his eyes adjusted themselves to the gloom and the shadowy distortions of the lamplight, Verity saw the shape of the girl hunched on the divan. In the moment of first seeing her, he felt a sudden shock at the certainty that she must be dead. But as they drew closer, he saw that the wide hazel eyes set in the pale oval of her face moved once and were then still again.

"It's all right, miss," he said very gently, "you ain't got cause to be frightened now. We've come to take you home."

She hugged her arms more tightly round herself, the fingers of one hand stretching far enough to stroke her veil of light-brown hair with sharp, repeated movements. She stared dumbly at him.

"Miss," said Verity coaxingly, "I'm a police officer. Whitehall Police Office, Scotland Yard, seconded to the Provost-Marshal, Calcutta. I come here to get you out and see you safe back to those you belong to."

Her eyes widened, her breasts rising and falling more rapidly under the translucence of the white chiffon blouse, and she began a wail of terror which rose quickly towards a shriek. There was no help for it, Verity seized her, clapped a hand over her mouth and hissed into her ear.

"You stop that nonsense here and now, my lady! What we've come through to find you don't bear talking about! And there's three other lives as well as your own to think about now!"

He felt her body go limp and he cautiously released her. She made no sound.

"Stupid little bitch!" said Martock vindictively.

They got her to her feet and she allowed herself to be pulled along, half reluctantly, between the two men. As they passed the body of the fallen guard, Martock stooped and picked up a pouch of cartridges. The passageway beside the marble lattice was deserted and the chatter of girls' voices still rose from the rooms of the zenanah. At last the four fugitives reached the door of the room where Massoumeh had been at the Ranee's mercy, and from which the narrow stone stairway led down to the scene of Verity's "Indian rope-trick" and to the warren of tunnels below the fortress of Gwalior. They passed through the room, and Verity held back the hanging that covered the archway, behind which lay the bound figures of Masuur and Hanment, and the door to the stairs. But Masuur and Hanment had gone.

"Fools!" Verity turned slowly at the voice and saw Azimullah Khan, flanked by two sepoy riflemen, emerging from the archway on the far side of the room.

"Did you think," said the Khan casually, "that it was so easy to enter a royal zenanah?" Then his voice hardened. "Stand where you are and throw down your weapons."

Martock put the sword-bayonet by his feet, opened the cartridge pouch and threw the contents into the centre of the carpet, one of the cases, half broken, scattering a pattern of black grains.

"Turn your backs!" said Azimullah loudly.

There was no alternative but obedience. Yet, as he turned, Verity was willing himself to do what his whole body seemed to rebel against. Half way through turning, he reached out for the pan of burning incense, swung back, and cast the sparkling, red-hot grains like seed upon the soil, so that they fell across the carpet, on the loose and packed cartridge powder. As he did it, he fixed his mind on an image of Bella coming out of her father's house in a summer dress, and only when it was done did he acknowledge the searing pain of the hot metal in his hands and drop the pan with a gasp of agony. But now there was a roaring heat behind them, and the room seemed to fill with a cloud of flame. Martock was through the door and, followed by the girls and Verity, led the way down the narrow steps. Verity had time to glimpse one of the sepoys, who had begun to cross the room, thrown back by the blast, and Azimullah's face maddened by rage.

At the foot of the steps, Verity said, "N'listen, we ain't got long. They'll be down 'ere in a minute more. We gotta 'ave weapons. Anything. Picks from that storeroom 'ud be better'n nothing!"

"Still got a rifle," said Martock breathlessly, "and two rounds in hand."

They crossed the steps by the portico of the temple and headed for the tunnel through which Verity and Martock had first entered the subterranean level of Gwalior. No one had been to the storeroom since, and the body of the female guard still lay where it had fallen a little way beyond.

"There ain't much choice here, old chums!" said Martock disapprovingly.

"Rope," gasped Verity, "an' you can fell a man easy with one of those picks!"

Snatching up what they could, the two sergeants prepared to escort the pair of girls towards the opening on to the road. Then Verity paused.

"It ain't on!" he whispered. "The Pandies are coming in through there! We must go back a bit!"

Slowly they retraced their steps.

"No chance!" said Martock suddenly, "There's a dozen of them with rifles coming that way too."

The fugitives turned into a narrow side opening just as a shout from one of the sepoys confirmed that they had been sighted. They heard the guards coming after them, the voices raised high but the footsteps cautious. The passageway grew narrower until it was little more than a tunnel again. A structure of supporting logs laid vertically, two by two in alternating cross-positions, rose from floor to roof, almost blocking the way. Martock paused, waved the others on, raised his rifle and fired back in the direction of their pursuers. There was a silence; a few voices in the distance seemed to grow fainter and then louder again. Someone was giving orders and something heavy was being moved. Then there was a roar which abruptly raised the pressure of the air until the pain of it against their ear-drums was intolerable. The roaring ceased and a cloud of dust rolled towards them along the tunnel, bringing with it a stench of cordite. After that came a deep total stillness, the dust clearing to reveal the mountain of fallen earth which had turned the subterranean cul-de-sac into a convenient tomb.

"Listen!" said Verity with growing impatience. "Just keep still a minute and listen!"

They listened. The sound of distant hammering grew slower and then stopped altogether.

"I'd say they were walling us in," Martock observed. "Deuced if I can see why, when they still ain't got the story they want from us. They could have come in after us, if it mattered so much to them."

"Something else matters more, Mr Martock," said Verity, looking satisfied, "and what they 'aven't got now is time! Go on asking that Mass-oo-mer about what the Ranee said!"

As Martock turned to the girl, shivering in her shroud-like robe of white cotton, Verity tested the movements of his hands. His left hand, though sore along the head of the palm, was still of some use to him. But his right hand, which had borne the weight of the hot pan of incense, throbbed in untouchable pain. The skin was pink and smooth, the fingers so bloated from palm to tip by their burns that they seemed to press tightly together however much he splayed them.

"All she knows," said Martock at length, "is that the Ranee swore they were riding off last night to win a great victory today."

"What victory?"

"No idea," said Martock. "There's no British force closer than Sir Hugh Rose's column at Kalpi."

"And might they be close to here by now?"

Martock thought about this.

"By forced marches they might," he said. "They'd beat Tantia Topi and the Nana in a fair fight. But don't forget the natives have got the fortress and everything behind them. Our men have nothing but two hundred miles of hostile villages."

Verity looked at the other girl. She squatted in a corner of the dank cavern, her arms still clutched about herself. In the light of the lamp, which Martock had turned lower to conserve its oil, the slim pale legs, the softer fullness of her thighs, and even the pink aureoles of her breasts shone smoothly through the fragile white veil of her tunic and trousers.

"What about her?" said Martock softly. "She must know something."

Verity put the pain of his right hand resolutely from his mind and went over to her.

"Miss," he said gently, "you ain't even told us your name."

She shook her head, refusing to lift her eyes to his. Verity was suddenly possessed by the thought that she might have been a slave for years rather than weeks.

"Do you know your name, miss?"

Again she shook her head. He got up and returned to Martock.

"Either she don't know or she ain't saying," he remarked unnecessarily. "I 'ave seen it 'appen like this before, when a young person is so hurt or shocked that they can't say nor think of anything. Happens after railway tragedies and so forth. She might go for months like this – p'raps for ever."

Martock looked about him.

"One lamp," he said, "that might last for an hour or two if not turned up too far. One rifle and bayonet, with one round to fire. One pick and a coil of rope. No food, no water, and not enough air. That's about the size of it."

Verity crouched down and tried painfully to manipulate his right-hand fingers.

"And three hands between the pair of us," said Martock sympathetically, concluding his inventory of the situation.

Somewhere, as though in a world beyond their comprehension, there was a sudden reverberation.

"Sunrise gun," said Martock.

"Listen!" said Verity. There was a long pause and then the remote booming echo was repeated. Martock frowned.

"That ain't a morning gun," said Verity triumphantly. "Whatever that is, it's shooting on a target. Come on, Mr Martock! We gotta get ourselves out of here. No one else can do it for us!"

"It's all very well to talk like that," said Martock indignantly. "How the hell do you suppose we shall get out of this, with solid earth or rock all round us? You heard just now the sum total of our stock-in-trade!"

Verity nodded, as though agreeing with every word.

"But then," he said, "you left out two things. My father, Mr Martock, lived and died a miner. What he didn't know about the old Wheal Mary Ann and every other shaft in the county of Cornwall wasn't worth knowing! And I ain't just a miner's son, Mr Martock. When I was so high, and wasn't at the Chapel School at all, I turned a penny or two pulling barrows in the shaft with a gang of youngsters."

"And how," asked Martock, "does that get you out of here?"

"It don't, Mr Martock. But I do know when a man says what ain't true. Which you did."

"I don't recall, old fellow."

"Why!" said Verity proudly, "You said there was no water! Now just look at all the wet on that wall there. No water, indeed!"

"Much use that may be," said Martock sourly.

"Not to drink, I daresay," Verity conceded, "but that water talks. At least it does to me. It says that it's going somewhere, because it's running down that wall, and yet it ain't collecting anywhere in here. Now, if water can pass through, so can air. We shan't suffocate, Mr Martock. And if we do die, it won't be thirst that does it. Now, p'raps you'd just buck to and bring that lantern. If the natives should win their victory, they'll have time to come back for us, and I ain't anxious to be found here when they do."

Verity beckoned Martock round the walls of their improvised prison, saying from time to time, "Now you might oblige me by taking the guard off the lamp, holding the light just here, and see how steady the flame can be."

When the blue-rimmed flame stood straight as a sentinel, he said, "Very good, Mr Martock," as though it had been just what he wanted.

They came to the far corner, where the earth and rock of the tunnel glistened with moisture. Verity squatted down and peered into the lowest recess of the corner.

"The flame just here, Mr Martock, if you please."

As Martock lowered the naked light, the tall slender flame wavered just perceptibly.

"It ain't much," said Verity doubtfully, "but it might do. There's water running away down there somehow, which says to me that it's more clay than rock. It must feed an underground pool or run away somewhere. You've no idea, Mr Martock, how a steady flow of water used to loosen up the soil and stones in a Cornish clay mine."

"We'll never get out by digging down," said Martock sceptically.

"P'raps not, Mr Martock, but the minute you try going up through this roof, you'll bring a ton of earth and rock down on us all. Now, if your Mass-oo-mer ain't no objection to hold the lantern, and you could do a little with the pick, I still got one hand good enough to hold a sword-bayonet in."

Martock took the short, axe-like pick and began to strike hard at the earth floor, just in the corner, Verity loosening the small pebbles of rock and scraping clear the damp heavy loam.

"Stop a bit!" said Martock presently, "I'm pumped, old fellow! Must take a breath!"

"You have a rest, Mr Martock, I'll just see what else I can loosen here."

Verity hacked and stabbed with his left hand at the earth, watching intently as he saw the moisture gathering into diminutive puddles in the hole whenever he stopped work. From time to time he seemed to break into a small hollow space which the passage of the water had worn away in the heavy soil. Martock, having revived a little, joined him again, and the two men toiled breathlessly at the shaft which was now about fifteen inches across at its mouth. From time to time they heard the rumble of field artillery from somewhere beyond the thick walls of earth and rock which formed their tomb.

"We've backed the wrong nag, old fellow," said Martock softly, "I can't see there's anything below us but earth and solid rock."

Verity paused.

"Does that sound like water running to you?" he said with a frown. "It don't to me!"

The tiny movements in the earth continued, until Martock peered further into the hole and with an expression of contempt said, "My God! It's a bloody rat!"

He raised his pick to deal with it, but Verity interposed his good arm.

"'Don't you touch him, Mr Martock! He might save us all!"

"Little bastard!" said Martock, unpersuaded, but Verity was watching thoughtfully as the plump creature's bright eyes caught the lamplight, the whiskers and nose twitching suspiciously. Then it turned and scurried away along its burrow.

"There!" said Verity, "It must be able to get somewhere from here!"

He seized the bayonet and clipped it on to the rifle again. "Hold the butt, Mr Martock! Now, help me to turn it round and round. See if we can't bore a hole down three feet with it. Quicker than digging."

Probing and twisting, they drove the bayonet into the wet clay, until its point was embedded some two feet deep. Then the resistance of the earth gave way, the blade ran easily forward, and just as suddenly came up against a hard, impenetrable surface.

"And that's all about that!" said Martock derisively. "Solid rock!"

"But didn't you feel the space before the rock, Mr Martock? Just help me clear a way down to it!"

While Verity continued to loosen the soil with short, twisting stabs of the blade, Martock dug out the loam until they came to the smooth, inclining rock surface about three and a half feet below the level of the tunnel.

"Nothing!" said Martock.

"The lantern if you please, Mr Martock. Let it down gently and watch the flame."

Unmistakably, the flame wavered and flickered.

"There's a draught, Mr Martock!"

"More like a lack of air," said Martock miserably.

"We'll just see about that, Mr Martock."

No longer inviting the aid of his companion, Verity began to clear the earth from a wider area. It was now clear that the hard surface was a broad, man-made gulley, long ago filled in by the alluvial deposits of clay and debris brought down by the constant passage of water.

"It's like a drain, Mr Martock!" he said excitedly, "and that ain't all!"

Martock looked at what Verity was holding in his hand. Yellowed and discoloured, it was none the less recognisable as a human femur.

"The well of oblivion!" said Martock softly. "It must be a channel running from the bottom of the shaft!"

With his enthusiasm renewed, he lowered himself into the widened hole and began to hack away at the earth and stones which had fallen in an almost compact mass upon the gulley. Presently he said, "There's just a way through this refuse, a few inches. And there's light beyond it. But it's not daylight!"

He went at his task again, breaking through the remaining barrier of clay and pebbles.

"It's a sort of cave, with a pool," he said presently. "This channel empties into it somehow."

"There!" said Verity with pride.

"Only thing is," Martock reported, "once you're there, that's an end of it. Solid rock the whole way round!"

"Must be luminous rocks in that water," said Verity, as they stood in the echoing cavern, "though I never knew limestone to be luminous before. Would you object, Mr Martock, to just tie a rock to our length of rope so that we might sound the depth?"

Martock obeyed, and began paying out the cord into the green translucent water. Once it had come to rest, he hauled it back again and said, "Fifteen feet, or thereabouts."

"Indeed?" said Verity. "And might you be a strong swimmer, Mr Martock?"

Martock shook his head.

"No swimmer at all."

"Thing is," said Verity, as though it greatly disturbed him, "'that luminous glow keeps coming and going, which it shouldn't do. And now it's going altogether. Luminous rocks don't act in that fashion, Mr Martock. But I tell you what does."

"What?"

"The sky," said Verity smugly. "That's daylight we can see, coming from a very long way off. I don't see how, but I intend to find out!"

Having insisted that the two women should turn their backs, Verity stripped off his black coat and trousers, appearing in vest and long pants, for all the world like a pugilist running to fat. Apart from the ledge on which they stood, the walls of the cavern rose sheer from the water, but with Martock's grip on his left arm, he contrived to lower himself gingerly into the cold green pool. Martock watched the wavering white bulk, as Verity allowed himself to sink into the depths below the ledge. Then he disappeared from view, as if trapped beneath the stone ledge itself in some way. A succession of large air pockets bubbled to the surface, and then the pool was still. Martock waited, his heart beating faster, as he listened anxiously for some movement. The time was almost past when Verity could still be alive under the water. Tormented by the anxiety, he began to unbutton his coat, preparing to search for his comrade. Then, with a lunge like the black glistening pelt of a seal breaking the surface, Verity's large head appeared, the black hair flat and streaming with water. Martock hauled him gasping to the ledge and helped him out. For a moment the plump sergeant lay spluttering and choking. Then he recovered his powers of speech.

"Mr Martock! That rock ain't luminous over there! About ten feet under this ledge, where we can't see for standing on it, there's a kind of shaft slopes up through the rock into another pool. It ain't difficult. With you and I to help, both these young persons could be got through. We shan't get through dry, of course, but what's the odds about that?"

"What's so special about this other pool?" Martock asked uneasily.

"Oh, it's special all right," said Verity with evident satisfaction. "It's a pool to do with some 'eathen idol of the natives. And it's on the outside of the rock, where a man might walk to Calcutta, if he had a mind to. And being as it's nearly dark, Mr Martock, we couldn't have picked a better time for it!"

13

The temple consisted of little more than a dilapidated porch of yellow sandstone, decorated with carvings of animals and flowers, and an idol of the goddess Kali with her many arms, sheltered under a pillared canopy of white stone. The pool itself was behind this, set back in the rock with green vegetation all about it. Under cover of this, Verity slept in the warm darkness, nourished by the mango and pomegranate fruit which Martock had contrived to pick.

The next day, gunfire was renewed soon after dawn. Cautiously, Martock crept forward, and then returned with his news.

"British regiments," he said softly, "about five miles away. There's a right royal row going on with about twenty thousand natives between here and there. Not that it's going to help us."

"No?" said Verity uneasily.

"No," said Martock. "If the Nana Sahib wins, there's the finish of it. If our fellows win, then the Nana's lot will retire on Gwalior. That'll be the end of our chances, and General Rose and the entire British army can't take this place by storm."

Verity thought about this.

"Did it look as if our men would win?" he asked.

"Tomorrow, if not today," said Martock.

They passed the remainder of daylight in hiding. As the light began to fail, Verity said, "We might try to reach the lines by night."

"One of us might," said Martock, "never four."

Verity slept until the early morning. It was still dark when he woke Martock.

"Mr Martock, you know more about the ways of the army here than I do. Where might the Provost-Marshal's office have been in Gwalior?"

"Behind the room where we were shown when we first arrived, most likely," said Martock. "Why?"

"Never mind why. Would the natives take any great care to guard it, should you think?"

"Nothing worth guarding, old fellow. Papers, a few bits of ceremonial for special occasions. Not a gun or a cartridge. Nothing worth guarding.

Verity appeared to consider this.

"Mr Martock," he said presently, "with my hand like this, I couldn't even fire a musket. But there is something I might do, and I been thinking about it all night. And now I'm going to do it."

Martock helped him get slowly to his feet, wrapped in the crumpled black coat, the trousers almost unrecognisable in their shapelessness. As he watched, Verity moved forward step by step, slowly and soundlessly, until his black clothing made him indistinguishable from the surrounding darkness.

Major-General Sir Hugh Rose, commanding the Central India Field Force, pushed away the plate which had held his breakfast steak. With a glass of cool rich porter inside him, he lit a cheroot and contemplated the Mirzapore carpeting and the four stoves which brought an appropriate degree of luxury to his dining tent. After the battle of the previous day there had been a dinner for his senior officers which had had the agreeable atmosphere of a Cambridge feast, and from which all suggestion of the campaign hardships had been excluded. Rather grey and a little overweight, Sir Hugh enjoyed a sense of having earned the luxuries of rank. Having had two horses shot under him at Inkerman, and been three times recommended for the Victoria Cross, he had now beaten Tantia Topi, the Nana's commander, into the bargain.

His aide entered the marquee to find the Major-General wreathed with cigar smoke.

"Well?" said Sir Hugh, "What news of Tantia and his army? Running, I suppose!"

"Withdrawing across the plain, sir," said the aide nervously.

Sir Hugh blew out a long cloud of smoke and made a click of resignation with tongue against palate.

"Well," he said, "they'll sit tight on their rock at Gwalior until Domesday. No point in wasting time and men trying to assault it. I shall address all regimental commanders at seven-thirty. In the meantime, preparations will be made for an advance past the rock and on to form a junction with Sir Robert Napier's force at Jaora-Alipur."

The aide hesitated.

"Sir . . . "

"Well?"

"Sir, the enemy are not retiring upon Gwalior. They are

withdrawing beyond it. Only a handful of their men hold the fortress."

"Withdrawing beyond it?" said Sir Hugh suspiciously. "Why?"

The aide looked extremely wretched.

"It seems, sir – that is to say, our forward battalion reports that there is a Union Jack, sir, flying from a flagstaff on the fort. Upside down, sir."

Sir Hugh's shaven gill grew several shades redder.

"*Upside down?*"

"Sir, Lieutenant Rose and Lieutenant Waller of the 25th Bombay Infantry request permission to assault the fortress by way of the main gate at the foot of the access road."

"Do they?" said Sir Hugh thoughtfully. "Do they? Upside down, did you say?"

The main gate blew suddenly inwards under the force of an explosion and the two companies of the 25th Bombay Infantry, with bayonets levelled, charged through the smoke, slashing and stabbing at the few stupefied defenders who remained in their path. One by one, the five intervening gates on the steep road to the hill-top fortress were blown in, and the guards of the Nana Sahib's palace overwhelmed. At the final gateway, Lieutenant Rose seized the regimental colours and bore them onward, leading his men in frontal attack. They met a scattered fusillade from the last of the defending sepoys. Lieutenant Waller saw his brother officer fall and the colours fluttering in the dust. Then the flag was lifted by a private soldier and borne forward. When the few remaining sepoys had been despatched, there was a shout of jubilation from the men of the 25th and the sound of doors being smashed open. In a moment the plunder of battle, fine embroidery, gold and silver brocade, banners, drums, shawls. and mirrors was being pitched into the courtyard.

Ignoring this pandemonium, Waller ran determinedly on. With one hand on the holster of his pistol, he climbed the spiral staircase of the tower until he came out under the open cupola at the top, his red tunic dusty and his face streaked with grimy perspiration. And then he stared in astonishment at the fat dishevelled man in the crumpled black clothes who sat slumped against the wall in the shadiest corner.

"You!" said Waller sharply, as the man turned his head, "Yes, you sir! Is this your handiwork?"

He indicated the tall pole with the flag drooping from its top.

Verity nodded.

"The Major-General," said Waller, "does not take kindly to men who show so little respect for the flag as to hoist it upside down!"

"Oh," said Verity, as though it had never crossed his mind.

"Dammit," said Waller gently, "a Union Jack upside down is never used except to signal distress. Not hard to remember, is it?"

Verity sighed.

"My compliments to the Major-General," he said feebly, "and 'ave the goodness to inform him that for the last few days I been more distressed than he could ever imagine."

The long room was light and high-ceilinged.

"You had a spot of luck, old fellow, in not losing that hand of yours," said Martock cheerily.

Verity sat in the bentwood chair, his bandaged right hand in his lap. Distantly, from the foot of the rock, he heard the trumpeter sounding evening-stables for the three troops of the 14th Light Dragoons which remained at Gwalior.

"Providence," he said thoughtfully. "I got a lot to be thankful for."

Martock laughed.

"You'd have a sight more to be thankful for, if you'd only buck up and get out of here. Why, if I'd been the hero of Delhi ridge and the man who saved Lucknow, all in one, I couldn't have been more handsomely treated in the sergeants' mess of the 71st regiment. I can't score down anything. As soon as I *look* thirsty, there's a glass waiting, and nothing to pay."

"Me all the kicks and you all the halfpence!" said Verity philosophically.

Martock thought about this.

"Some have been kicked worse," he said. "The Nana Sahib and Azimullah Khan have bolted for their lives. No one knows where. The Ranee of Jhansi is dead."

"How come?"

"'In the big battle near Morar. Seems the rest of her riders turned and ran as soon as the 8th Hussars advanced. She tried to turn and face our troopers at the river bank, but her horse slipped and down she went. She was dressed like a regimental commander and our fellows cut her up, never thinking she might be a woman."

"I never knew so much killing," said Verity glumly.

"Well, old boy," said Martock, "there's good news too. That English doxy we saved from the zenanah still won't say who she is, but we found out all the same. She's the one who was taken when the 105th was cut down. From that we found her name is Miss Perry. Judith Perry."

"Why was she took?"

"Well, that's the dashed rum thing, old fellow. Seems they did all sorts of things to her in that zenanah. Each time, when it was over, they made her write it all down, in a letter to her father, saying that it would be worse next time."

"I knew it!" said Verity savagely. "I knew that there was some dodge there to suborn a man of ours, so that he'd push the jool their way! I suppose you don't 'appen to know who her father is?"

Martock shook his head.

"That's the rummest part of all. She's got no parents and no family. Brought up in a garrison orphanage. Mother and father dead years ago. There's not even a man who acts like her father, and they made her put her own name to the letters. Work that out, if you can."

"It's got a smell about it, Mr Martock. Those villains knew what they were doing, though I can't see what it was. I s'pose that Massoumeh told you all this?"

Martock nodded.

"That little bastard Scindia had the neck to say that Massoumeh belonged to him, when he came back with our fellows to Gwalior. But he condescended to let us have her so that inquiries into the whereabouts of the Kaisar-i-Hind could continue. Very touchy over his zenanah is young Scindia."

"But where did your Mass-oo-mer 'ear this tale?"

"From a girl in the zenanah," said Martock evasively.

"Of course it was a girl, Mr Martock. But what girl? Was she likely to know the truth. How did she converse with this Miss Judith?"

"Just one of Scindia's doxies in his harem," said Martock wretchedly.

"Mr Martock, I won't 'ave the truth hid from me. I swear I'll have it one way or the other!"

"Very well," said Martock, "the girl who spoke to Massoumeh knew English as well as a bit of the native lingo. That's how she found out so much."

"Yes, Mr Martock? You just keep telling me the tale."

"She said – oh, God – well, this girl *said* – only said, mind you, that her name was Amy Stockwood."

Verity's face lit up, as he rose slowly from his chair.

"Mr Martock! We done it! We saved 'er! I told you I'd find her! Didn't I tell you so?"

"Sit down," said Martock coldly, "and listen to me. She's in Scindia's zenanah, and there she stays."

"Oh no she don't, Mr Martock. I ain't leaving Gwalior without her. I ain't come this far to rescue a poor lost girl only to be put off by you nor Scindiur, nor no one else. If I 'ave to tear down them walls myself, I'll 'ave 'er out of it!"

Martock shook his head.

"No you won't, old friend. There's something else that you don't know about Amy Stockwood, and I don't suppose any-one would have guessed."

"What's that?"

"Amy Stockwood," said Martock, "is black as your hat."

Verity's mouth opened, closed, and then opened again.

"You mean she's a native?"

Martock nodded.

"Massoumeh has no cause to lie and she swears she's a lot more tawny than her own colour."

"But how can it be, Mr Martock?"

"It can be the same as a lot of things in India, old fellow. Deuced odd, but true all the same."

The two men sat in silence for a while. It was Martock who spoke first.

"I suppose now, old fellow, you'll give the subject of Amy Stockwood a rest?"

"You suppose whatever you like, Mr Martock. The first thing I shall do now is to write out a request for an interview with the Major-General. I'm owed that, at least."

"First," said Sir Hugh, "a native girl might easily enough call herself Amy Stockwood or Jenny Lind or the Princess Royal, for that matter. Second, Amy Stockwood might *be* a native girl, even your Amy Stockwood, who wrote the diary. In fact, if she hadn't been a native girl, they'd have done for her at Cawnpore. Don't you see? That's why she's still alive. As for having an English father, I don't have to tell you, Sergeant Verity, how many tawny little boys and girls are produced by Englishmen with their Indian concubines every year. And, dammit, most of them see to it that the children never want for anything. Can't you see that it must have happened that way, sergeant?"

Verity tilted his chin a little higher and stood more rigidly to attention.

"No, sir. With respect, sir."

There was a silence of exasperation. Then the aide-de-camp at the Major-General's right said, "With your permission, sir, perhaps I might ask Sergeant Verity what it is that he wants."

"Very well, Charles, you ask him."

"Sir," said Verity, not quite certain which of the officers he should address, as a matter of etiquette, "she must have questions put to her, to see what the truth is. Then, if she has been took and held in that evil place, she must be got out. Don't see that her skin makes any odds about that, sir. With respect, sir."

Sir Hugh sighed and looked helplessly at his aide. The strong sunlight gave a yellowish glow to the coarse canvas of the command tent.

"Sergeant," said the Major-General slowly, "I'm sure you think of me as an old fool with not the least interest in anything but the affairs of the battlefield and the campaign."

"No, sir. By no means, sir."

"However that may be," continued Sir Hugh, "I have some thought for other matters, even for the fate of such girls as this. As soon as Gwalior was taken, I inquired of the Maharajah Scindia whether his enemies, while they held the palace, might have brought any English captives there. I asked specifically whether any English ladies might be held in the zenanah. The Maharajah undertook an investigation. He assured me that there had been one young lady, a Miss Perry as it seems, who had already been released by the efforts of yourself and Sergeant Martock. There was a native dancing-girl, who has been in your charge, and who was now also free. The remainder were native girls, all of whom he, as ruler, declared to be his own concubines."

"Don't alter the facts, sir. With respect, sir."

"The facts, sergeant, are these. And I will trouble you to remember them. In the whole of Central India we have one ally, the Maharajah Scindia. He has no great love of the British, but he is our ally for the time being. He is quick to take offence and bitterly jealous of his possessions. He assures me that there is no English lady in his zenanah, that all the girls are his of right. You wish me to call him a liar and to break open his palace. Though even by your own admission this young person is a native Indian."

"I ain't actually seen her, sir."

"But your informant has. Now, Sergeant. Scindia may be a knave, a libertine, and a murderer. But by the grace of Scindia we hold the Central Provinces, and only by grace of holding the Central Provinces can we hold Bengal, and only by holding Bengal can we hold India. Do I make myself plain, Sergeant?"

"Yes, sir. Very plain, sir."

"In short, Sergeant, if you were to tell me that your mother and sisters, your wife and daughters were all prisoners in the zenanah, and if I knew that I could only release them by a breach with Scindia and by spreading rebellion all around us, I should tell you to put them from your mind and send you about your business. Do you understand me, Sergeant Verity?"

"Yes, sir. Very clear, sir."

"Good," said the Major-General with audible relief, "then good morning to you."

"Now listen to me," said Verity to Martock, glancing aside at Massoumeh as he spoke, "you sure she got the idea? When she goes back to collect her things, she's to try and speak with Miss Stockwood. First she's to tell Miss Stockwood that we ain't given up and that we won't forget her, not if I've got to write to every newspaper and missionary society in London. Then she's to ask Miss Stockwood if she's there willingly, or if she was took. And last she might ask about the jool. O' course, if Miss Stockwood could manage to write on a bit of paper, begging to be fetched out of a den of infamy, I'd see that got to Lord Canning if I had to take it myself. And if 'is Lordship wouldn't help, I'd see it went direct to 'er Majesty. There. See if your doxy can remember that."

Massoumeh stood beside them in the courtyard, dressed as if for a long journey, her sari shawl draped over her head and brought across her mouth, decorously concealing her lips from the surrounding soldiers, like a well-taught Muslim girl. Martock explained what Verity had said. Then, with a proprietorial pat he sent her on her way. She looked back once, eyes bright with amusement, and entered the archway.

The bullock-cart that was to form part of the column returning by the Grand Trunk Road to Calcutta, awaited the sergeants of the Intelligence Department and their witness. Verity anticipated a long delay, but the girl soon returned. From Martock's murmurings and head-shaking he understood that Massoumeh could have had only a brief chance to speak to Amy Stockwood, and perhaps none at all. Martock handed her into the shade of the canvas-covered wagon, then followed with Verity. They drove for the last time down the steep road from the fortress of Gwalior, past the burnt and twisted frames of the five great gates. At last they took their position in the convoy of wagons, commissariat supply carts, and ammunition drays. It was still early morning but the cool night was giving way to a hot, overcast day with a threat of rain.

When the column had begun to move south-east and the mighty rock of Gwalior was almost level with the horizon, Martock said, "All right."

He was speaking to Massoumeh. As Verity looked up, she was unwinding the silken scarf of the sari. Where the reddish, henna'd hair had been there were now close-cropped black curls.

"'ere," he said indignantly, "what's this?"

"This," said Martock gently, "is Miss Amy Stockwood."

Before Verity could speak, the girl flung herself upon Martock and burst into a tumult of sobs.

"Then where's Mass-oo-mer?"

Martock jerked a thumb backward.

"In Scindia's zenanah, where she belongs."

"Mr Martock!"

"She went willingly, old fellow. As she said, it's where she belongs. You can't take a high-class courtesan and dancing-girl, give her to the missioners, and then send her out scrubbing floors. She belongs in the zenanah, and she was miserable as sin outside it. She said you wouldn't understand."

"Nor do I, Mr Martock! Fancy any young person lusting after such things. Think how she may be abused!"

"I rather fancy, old boy, that Massoumeh ain't averse to being what you call abused. There's no game she's not ready for."

"And this young person?" said Verity more softly.

Amy turned her face and he was surprised to see that the dusky gold of her skin had begun to show somewhat lighter streaks where the tears had run down.

"I had to!" she sobbed. "They were such beautiful gold curls! Mama says they're the beautifullest a mother ever saw. But Ayah cut them and blacked them, and blacked me all over. And a girl at Gwalior, she helped me to keep doing it. And the others were dead, and I was so frightened."

"Well, miss," said Verity gruffly, "you ain't got nothing to be frightened of any more. I rather fancy it's the villains who did such 'orrors that had better start getting frightened now!"

In the darkness of the room, which he shared for the night with Martock in the dak bungalow near Raniganj, Verity said for the hundredth time, "She was a state prisoner, in a manner of speaking. You had no business to let her go to Scindia's 'areem nor anywhere else."

"Tosh," said Martock irritably, "you wanted Amy Stockwood out, and now you can't bear to give the credit for it."

"I'll give credit where it's due, Mr Martock. One thing you did, and I'll be first to say it: you put the lid on this story of Dhingra murdering her. I can't reckon that up at all. Did you actually hear him confess to it?"

"No," said Martock, "but Colonel Farr did."

"So we only know because Colonel Farr told us! And if Colonel Farr wanted Miss Stockwood forgotten, and no further investigation, he had only to *say* that he heard Dhingra confess it. Strikes me, Mr Martock, that Colonel Farr may have one or two strong questions to answer before this is done. Might you be prepared to return me favour for favour?"

"Meaning?"

"When we get back to Fort William, we shall have to report how Mass-oo-mer got left behind in the zenanah, and how the jool that got there was a fake. But would you be so kind as to say nothing to Colonel Farr about Miss Stockwood and the other young person? Call it modesty if you like, but just let it lie and don't say a word."

"If you like," said Martock uneasily. Then, after a pause, he inquired, "So Massoumeh had no part in the theft, after all?"

Verity propped himself on his elbow.

"Mr Martock, I generally act slow, but it ain't always because I think stupid. I *know* who thieved the jool, and I knew it before ever we left Calcutta."

Martock began to laugh helplessly in the darkness.

"And instead of telling us all and getting the thing done with, you nearly killed the pair of us at Gwalior!"

"I said I knew *who*," Verity remarked irritably, "but I didn't know *how*, and I couldn't prove it. Until I can prove how, they'd laugh in my face if I was to ask for a warrant."

"Does the man know you suspect him?"

Verity made a puffing sound of amusement.

"I should just about think not. Why, I interrogated him without 'im knowing it, and caught him sure as I caught Dhingra."

"And you're not saying?"

"No, Mr Martock, with great respect I ain't saying. I learnt one thing from constabulary work. It ain't the quick, flashy officer that gets his man. You have to weave a snare, and you have to weave it sure. Now, I just about finished weaving my snare, Mr Martock, and unless I'm very unlucky, I shall have my man safe inside it in a few days more."

"And the Kaisar-i-Hind too?" Martock asked sceptically.

"Now that's another thing," said Verity, a little crestfallen. "The jool, the Nanar, and Azimullur, is 'orses of a different colour. But if you could be patient a little longer, Mr Martock, I think I could promise you ain't seen the last of them."

DEVIL'S GLASS

14

"Love Divine all loves excelling," sang Verity loudly, "Joy of Heaven to earth come down!"

Hands clasped behind him, he stood at ease. The other members of the congregation in Mrs Captain Tolland's whitewashed meeting-room clutched their tract-pamphlets or, in the case of the officers, their hymn-books, but not Verity. Since childhood he had known every verse of the hymns that the Wesleys had brought to Cornwall, the great stirring tunes of the Whitsuntide revival. He liked this one. It was what he had been brought up to think of as "a strong man's tune". Pink-faced with exertion, chest thrown out and mouth wide, he launched into the final verse, his voice clear above the rest:

"Changed from glory into glory, till in Heaven we take our place . . ."

As he sang, the intensity of his determination suggested indignation rather than devotion. The harmonium squeaked, off-key, and he gathered himself for the final effort:

"Till we cast our crowns before Thee, full of wonder, love, and praise."

Then Captain Tolland prayed in a rather rambling extempore manner, the assorted soldiers and civilians sitting on the wooden benches, crouching forward a little and scrupulously avoiding the kneeling posture of the Established Church. With eyes closed tight in concentration, Captain Tolland prayed for the spiritual amendment of those present, for courage to resist manifold but unspecified temptations, and for the conversion of the heathen, which alone could bring enduring peace to the troubled lands of India. Verity mentally wished him luck with the last part of the prayer, while telling himself that if Captain Tolland had ever come face to face with the Nana Sahib or Azimullah Khan, he might have pitched his request at a less optimistic level.

Then it was over, and the members of the congregation were filing out, the officers to Mrs Captain Tolland's tea, the other ranks to a less elaborate refreshment in another hired room. As Verity passed the hostess, he paused.

"Mrs Captain Tolland, ma'am?"

"Mr Verity?"

"Might there be a place for me, ma'am, in the party of soldiers that's a-going to visit St Paul's Cathedral in Calcutta? I know o' course that I ain't a soldier, but the rate I'm going on I shall be leaving India without seeing any of it!"

"Of course you may come, Mr Verity." Mrs Tolland's broad face radiated her public smile. "Captain Tolland would welcome any member of the class-meeting."

"Much obliged, Mrs Captain Tolland," said Verity, as though he felt some explanation must be offered. "Only it's on account of my cousin."

"Your cousin, Mr Verity?"

"Yes, ma'am. I ain't no connection with India myself, of course, but I 'ad a cousin born here in Calcutta in eighteen-forty-one. Never seen 'im, and never shall now. Poor little fellow died at a few months, but he was baptised in the Cathedral, I heard. And being as we're to have a chance to look at the register and so on, I thought I'd like to come."

"Indeed," said Mrs Captain Tolland, "indeed," and then she looked almost knowingly at him. "But you shall see your poor cousin again."

"Oh, ma'am?" said Verity, as if alarmed at the prospect.

"You shall," she said, "for here we see as through a glass darkly, but then face to face."

"Oh," said Verity, relieved, "of course, ma'am. Not see 'im in Calcutta was all I meant."

And with that he pulled himself clumsily to attention, gave an awkward little bow, and turned towards the door. As he paused in the porch of the building, lowering his head a little to set his hat straight, he noticed with despair how the thighs of his Sunday-meeting suit were already beginning to take on the shine of wear, from the action of the black cloth on Mrs Tolland's wooden benches.

Verity and the party of soldiers, led by Captain Tolland, passed into the west doorway of the great neo-Gothic cathedral its square tower like one of the English "wool churches" of the Middle Ages. The interior, with its long airy nave, echoing vaults of the roof, and stained glass in profusion, was a medley of England's own cathedral vistas. Only in the memorial tablets, decorating the walls of nave and transepts, was there an incongruity, the names English and the places Indian. Verity read the fates of provincial chief justices who had died after many years up country in the service of John Company, of civil engineers assassinated in some local rebellion, of officers and men who had died in lone battles on the Afghan frontiers, or in the pitched fighting of Chillianwallah. Under the tower arch, sculpted by Chantrey, Bishop Heber in white marble knelt fully-robed in timeless devotion.

Captain Tolland's party were led with an air of courteous boredom past the treasures of the cathedral library, and then viewed with staunch disapproval the extravagance of the communion plate presented by the Queen on the occasion of the cathedral's consecration ten years before. The contents of the vestry excited greater interest, as members of the party, one by one, chose a volume of the registers shelved there to trace the birth or baptism of some remote ancestor in the diocese of Calcutta. When Verity's turn came, he took the volume for 1841 and fingered through it for a moment.

"Why!" he said presently, "Here he is! John Clatworthy, baptised 18th of March 1841. That's my cousin, that is!"

He peered at the entry closely, beaming at the discovery, turning it this way and that. Then he stood back, apparently satisfied. The tour of the building continued, the red tunic'd soldiers being left to their own devices for the last ten minutes.

"'ere!" said Verity suddenly to the corporal at his side, "where's my 'at? I gone and put it down, and I ain't picked it up."

With an expression of great purpose he strode off towards the vestry. Presently he reappeared, carrying the tall black chimney-pot hat which he had judged appropriate for such a visit as this.

"Forget me own name next!" he said softly to the corporal.

"Something dashed rum has happened," said Martock as Verity eased his large rump on to the tall counting-house stool at the opposite side of the double-sloped desk.

"Rum?" said Verity hopefully.

"Your Amy Stockwood and Miss Judith Perry were both to be shipped back to England, Amy to some of her family, and Judith to be trained up as a charity governess."

"That ain't rum," said Verity firmly, scowling at a sheet of paper that awaited his attention. "It was orders."

"Wait a bit," said Martock, "Amy Stockwood is safely in her berth on the *Princess Victoria*, two days out for Madras. But as for Judith Perry . . ."

"What about her?"

"The morning before the *Victoria* sailed, old fellow, it seems that Miss Judith ran away from the garrison missioners and hasn't been seen or heard from since."

"Ran away?" said Verity, as though it were a personal affront. "When she was to be took to England and made a lady of, in a manner of speaking?"

"Well," said Martock reasonably, "of course she'd never been in England before and that may have troubled her. But any garrison orphan would have jumped at the chance, let alone one who'd had the things done to her that she had."

"It don't make sense," said Verity firmly, "not yet, at least."

"However," Martock resumed, "your Mr Lopez is in a jolly old wax about it. And so is Colonel Farr, only as Colonel Farr is still on the way from Cawnpore, we only know he's waxy from what we're told."

Verity stood up.

"I say, old boy," said Martock gently, "it ain't tiffin yet!"

"I don't care about tiffin, Mr Martock. I'm owed a debt and I'm going to collect it, in the line of duty. I did a good turn to a native, and now he's going to do me one. That poor young lady may have been took by force for all we know."

"Just one thing you'd better know, Verity," said Martock, getting to his feet. "Force isn't likely."

"Meaning?"

"Meaning that girls aren't taken from garrison orphanages by native dealers. And there's something Massoumeh said."

"Yes?"

"Look," said Martock, "just because a girl has long hair and a beautiful innocent face makes no odds. When she lives as this one did in the zenanah, she may hate it fit to kill herself. But lots don't. Not even all the English ones."

"Meaning, Mr Martock?" said Verity with impatience.

"Meaning what Massoumeh said. There were two tales at Gwalior. One said that Miss Judith fought and carried on each time the Nana took her. The other tale said that, after the first time, she was mad for it, shaking her bubbies and backside at him like a nautch-girl on the rampage."

"Mr Martock," said Verity simply, "it ain't worthy of you to repeat such things."

"No," said Martock cynically, "but it might be worthy of you to remember them."

Verity left in a dignified silence, walking through the streets of Fort William and across the Maidan towards the emporium of Abdul Karim. It seemed years ago, rather than weeks, since he had passed this way on the night of Captain Groghan's downfall. Karim's bazaar shop with its false coins nailed to the wooden counter appeared unaltered, even to having the identical goods displayed for sale. Karim emerged from behind the curtain of the interior, saw Verity, and acknowledged him with a deeply respectful salaam. Verity heard the babbling of gratitude, and recognised Karim's vow that all his possessions, even his very life, should be at the disposal of the sergeant sahib.

"Now there ain't no need for that, really there ain't, Mr

Karim," said Verity generously. "A police officer don't expect rewards for doing what was his duty anyway. However, I wouldn't say no to a little information, if you could oblige me."

"Whatever the Sahib desires!" said Karim earnestly.

"It ain't much," Verity brushed his moustache thoughtfully, "only a young lady that's been missed, a Miss Perry, Miss Judith Perry. She was supposed to have been on shipboard, for England, but seems to a-ran away instead. We think she must have run to the bazaar. P'raps she's made an arrangement with a man, or she may have found a house to work in, if you take my thought. Now, you ain't heard of such a girl in the bazaar in the last few days?"

"No, Sahib," said Karim uneasily, "I hear of no girl at all."

"But if there was such a one running loose in the bazaar, or even in one of the pukka whorehouses near the Chowringhee, a man of your knowledge would come to hear of it?"

"Assuredly, Sahib."

"But she might have gone to live with a man by private arrangement and none of us be any the wiser?"

Karim inclined his head in a little gesture of regretful assent.

"The Sahib speaks truly," he said softly.

"Then if you can't help me there," said Verity, undeterred, "you might still show your thanks for me having held Captain Groghan off you."

"Yes, Sahib?"

"Yes," said Verity firmly. "Now you can tell a faker a mile off, where coins and valuables are concerned. Ain't that so?"

"Assuredly!" Karim's eyes glinted with professional pleasure.

"You'd know a jool from a glass imitation, I'll be bound."

"As surely as the Sahib can tell an honest man from a liar."

"However," said Verity, "lots of imitations is honestly sold. There ain't no crime where there ain't no deception."

Karim laughed.

"I do not deceive, Sahib!"

"Course you don't," said Verity, "but might you have

heard of some very big imitations being made in Calcutta?
Might you happen to know if any honest craftsman lately
turned his hand to an imitation of the Kaisar-i-Hind
diamond?"

"Oh, Sahib," said Karim happily, "I can answer you truly.
The craftsmen of Calcutta make baubles for ladies. They
could not imitate such a mighty stone. Why, a man must first
have something in front of him to imitate. It could not be."

"You ain't heard of such a thing lately?"

"No, Verity Sahib. Not lately, nor ever."

Verity polished his hat-brim on his sleeve.

"Then, Mr Karim," he said, "I'll ask you just this. Might
you have heard of anything at all unusual in Calcutta, since
our last acquaintance?"

"Of what nature, Sahib?"

"Of any nature, Mr Karim."

"No, Sahib," said the trader with deliberation. "But now
I will tell you what I know myself. Business is bad since the
troubles began last year. Many of the sahibs have gone with
the army to Cawnpore and Lucknow. Others have gone to
England. The city is more empty than it ever was, many of
the great houses at Garden Reach and on the Chowringhee
stand idle. Only the servants remain, and servants are not
good customers, Sahib. That is what I know, Sahib, and all
I can say. Your task may be hard indeed."

"So it is," said Verity sympathetically. "Why, Mr Karim, I'll
make you a promise. If everything should go as I hope it will,
and if I'm listed for England, I'll buy a little thing from you
before I go, to please Mrs Verity."

"I would make the Sergeant Sahib a special price," said
Karim, momentarily forgetting his indebtedness and lapsing
into his professional patter.

"I'm sure you would, Mr Karim," said Verity thoughtfully, "I never doubted it."

"Found her?" inquired Martock sceptically, as Verity reappeared.

"I might have, Mr Martock. Time will tell."

"No, it won't." Martock turned on his stool. "There's a

cipher from Colonel Farr at Raniganj. The minute he gets
to Calcutta tomorrow, Miss Judith is to be looked for and
found as a material witness."

"Witness to what?"

"God knows," said Martock, turning to his work again.
"But I can tell you, my son, that you're in for a roasting."

"Oh no, I ain't, Mr Martock!" Verity's moustache fluttered
a little with the sharp exhalation of amusement. "I just got
some information from Mr Karim what may be the finding
of Miss Judith and the saving of us all. I ain't going to be
roasted. Mr Martock!"

"The Bishop's chaplain says you will be," Martock murmured.

"What are you talking about, Mr Martock?"

"The Bishop's chaplain," said Martock simply, "was here
an hour ago to speak with Mr Lopez. Funny thing. Mr Lopez
being a shade tawny don't go white or red when he's upset,
but a colour as though he'd turned liverish. Never did see
him so yellow."

Verity set his tall hat on his desk.

"What's that to me?"

"Only," said Martock, "that they swear there's been
criminal damage to St Paul's Cathedral, sacrilege the rever-
end gentleman called it, and it's all down to you. They want
your hide for it, old fellow."

Verity thought about this for a moment. He was about to
question Martock when the door opened and the corporal of
the guard said briskly, "Sergeant Verity to Mr Lopez's office
at once!"

It was an interesting exercise in authority. Lopez enjoyed
the acting rank of Inspector, which was nominally though
not effectively superior to Verity's long-established rank of
Sergeant. Moreover, Lopez, for all his brutality with
prisoners, had a manner of addressing his sergeants as one
man of the world advising another. He lounged back a little
in his chair, his finger-tips placed together, his dark eyes
directly on Verity's, and the faint drawl of southern
European intonation colouring his English words.

"You bloody fool!" he said softly. "What in hell's name made you deface the cathedral registers?"

"Ain't *defaced* nothing, sir," said Verity firmly.

"There's a strip torn from the bottom of the very page you were supposed to have looked at, the entry for 1841 that was shown you during Captain Tolland's visit. What could you have wanted with it?"

"Just it, sir. What could I have wanted? Why should I tear out what I could easily have got from the copies made for the registrar's office here?"

"The strip torn away, Sergeant," said Lopez softly, "contains the entry of Miss Judith Perry's name. Let us put aside accusations of who may have torn it out. Why was it torn out, Sergeant Verity?"

"Couldn't say, sir. With respect, sir."

Lopez gave a little gasp of irritation.

"Listen to me," he said, "the fate of this girl, the disappearance of the diamond involves us all. If there is something in the entry of her birth which may bear on this, I swear to you that no one shall stand in the way of a proper investigation. But your behaviour is making an investigation impossible."

" 'ope not, sir."

Lopez stood up and faced Verity, his dark face smooth and expressionless.

"Sergeant, we may speak freely here. You feel, perhaps, that Colonel Farr has not always given you the assistance you require. You disapprove of my summary methods of questioning our prisoners. But I know of your past reputation, as an honest and resourceful officer. Tell me what you need to pursue your inquiries, and you shall have it. If I cannot give you the assistance myself, I will use all my influence to obtain it from those who can."

"Greatly obliged, sir," said Verity uncertainly.

"We must trust one another, Sergeant," said Lopez finally.

"Funny thing," Verity remarked conversationally, "I had a friend who wrote to me and said he'd trust Mr Lopez with his life. Corporal Fred French, that we spoke of before, that was in your intelligence department in Calcutta. You recall, sir?"

Lopez nodded.

"Well, sir," said Verity, "Corporal French was never wrong about a man, and what 'e says goes for me too. Now there is two things you might do that'd help me famously. One is to let the matter of the cathedral register lie a day or two before it's brought to Colonel Farr's attention."

"And the other?" Lopez asked cautiously.

"I'd like an hour," said Verity confidentially, "to write a line to Mrs Verity. I ain't had the chance for weeks, and I don't want her worrying as to what might have become of me."

15

Alone in the strong-room of the Granary Barracks, Verity prepared the contents of the safe for Colonel Farr's weekly inventory. There were several items still kept there, including the casket and "performing box" which had yet to be returned to Maun Singh after the disappearance of the Kaisar-i-Hind. He hummed a little tune to himself as he arranged the items on the table, opening and closing the cedarwood box once or twice to see its trick floor in operation. He shook his head in reluctant admiration. Then he picked up the lid of the casket with its large, crowning emerald. It looked better from a distance, he thought. Close to, the lid resembled mere cast-iron set with cheap stones.

"All show," he said aloud. "All sham."

Then he looked at the emerald and thought that a man might have hidden the Kaisar-i-Hind itself in a stone of such a size. But the brilliant green fire of its surface was genuine beyond any doubt of his. And, in any case, a man could hardly hide a diamond in a solid jewel.

With the care of a craftsman, Verity turned the lid over and examined the underside of the emerald which was set through an opening in the peak of the tall pagoda-roof shape of the casket. But he shook his head again, as though there were something in all this which was far too sophisticated for him. Then he put the lid down, felt in his pocket, and produced his knife. He unfolded the blade, sat down at the table, and began to work with great concentration, his tongue pressed hard between his teeth. Gingerly, for fear of causing too much visible damage, he drew the knife-blade firmly across the top of the emerald. There was no mark that he could see, only a deposit of dust from his pocket which had been on the blade to begin with. He turned the casket lid and repeated the process on the under side. Tiny fragments of mineral broke from the stone under the pressure of the blade, the little flakes turning a paler green as they were detached from the deep richness of the emerald.

"Ah!" said Verity with great satisfaction, "now there's a phenomenon!"

He tipped the fragments of mineral on to a sheet of paper, folded this carefully, and put it into his pocket. For several minutes he held the casket-lid up towards the window, turning the emerald this way and that against the light. Sadly he put it down again.

"And now I know how it was done, as well as by who," he said in a whisper. "But finding where it is mayn't be so easy."

Far away down the corridor, the rhythmic crash of boots on flagstones announced the approach of Colonel Farr's escort for the ceremony of the weekly inventory.

"I have cause to think, sir," said Verity, smartly at attention, "as this is a matter you'd wish treated very discreet."

"Do you?" said Farr wearily. "Then please explain yourself!"

They were alone in Farr's office, the monsoon rain beating like drumsticks on walls and windows.

" 'ave the honour to request, sir, that I may speak in total confidence, and that I may treat your observations similarly."

"Well?" said Farr cautiously.

"Reason we ain't found this Miss Judith, sir, is we been looking in the wrong places."

"Good God, man!" said Farr, his face reddening, "Do you have the damned impertinence to waste my time over this? Of course they were the wrong places. We should have found her if they were the right ones."

"With your permission, sir," said Verity firmly, "the wrong *sort* of place. We been searching the bazaar and the native 'ouses."

"Whereas you," said Farr heavily, "'would have gone with a justice's warrant to search Government House?"

"Something of that, sir," said Verity calmly. "I been thinking about this and about words I got from the man Karim. Now, if this young person run off from the orphanage, she'd hardly go to offer herself to the first native in the bazaar. It might happen, but it ain't likely. She might have taken to a life of sin in a bawdy 'ouse, but from what I saw of her I don't think it's likely either."

"Go on," said Farr quietly, as Verity paused.

"Well, sir, the man Karim was talking about houses that were empty on the Chowringhee and such places, owing to the persons having left. Just servants, native servants there for the most part. Who knows what may happen in such places? If this young person run off to a life of sin, I'd say she knew the man she was going to, and I'd say he was a man of substance who lived in such houses as those. Only I don't see it's likely to be a man that's been there long. Not a *respectable* man."

"You mean," said Farr softly, "that she's gone to a native servant in one of the big houses where the master and mistress have left?"

"No, sir," said Verity. "It might be, but I think there's more to it. Would you know of such 'ouses, where the master might have left and let it to another gentleman? That must happen."

"Not often," said Farr, "not in the middle of a sepoy mutiny."

"All I was saying," said Verity persuasively, "is that I'd feel happier, as a detective officer, if we was to direct our attention in that fashion tonight. I don't see much good coming of the bazaar again."

Farr nodded, tireder and older than Verity had ever seen.

"Just one thing, Sergeant," he said: "What other reason have you for this? I shall keep your confidence but spare me the trouble of lying to me."

"Well, sir," said Verity unhappily, "it's the person Karim."

"Yes?"

"Yessir. When he was talking about the empty houses, anyone might have listened and heard him. But unless it mattered to someone they wouldn't have cared."

"And they did care?"

"They cared, sir," said Verity. "They cared so much that a message was brought yesterday of Mr Karim, or what was left of him, being found in some reeds by the river bank. The men who found him only knew him by his clothes."

Colonel Farr passed a hand across his face.

"How does this concern Miss Perry?"

"Just it, sir," said Verity triumphantly. "He spoke of those houses just after I'd questioned him for news of her. Of course he swore he knew nothing of the girl. Then I asked him if there was anything odd happening in the city just now, and he mentioned how the Europeans were leaving some of the big houses to their servants, and either going to the war or else going to safety in England. I had a feeling he was hinting at something he couldn't say. But there must have been someone in the shadows, or perhaps standing behind the curtain of the shop. And what that person heard him say did for the poor mark."

"Why should this Karim favour you with such information?" asked Farr doubtfully.

Verity puffed his cheeks out a little.

"If you recall, sir, there was a matter of Captain Groghan and a native, a little while ago. Well, sir, the native I prevented Captain Groghan from assaulting was this Karim. Proper grateful 'e was. Wanted to sell me everything cheap."

"'And he mentioned the Chowringhee?"

"Chowringhee, sir, was the word. And houses where the servants was left in charge. Can't be that many, sir."

Colonel Farr stood up and buckled on his belt and holster.

"Report at six," he said. "You and Sergeant Martock."

"Much obliged, sir," said Verity sincerely, "but you won't say a word of our direction to any man, sir?"

"Sergeant," said Farr dryly, "I take care in making bargains. But the bargains that I make are kept."

In the lamplight, the open carriages, broughams and landaus bore their passengers along the broad drive of the Chowringhee. By night the broad lawns of the Maidan and the foliage surrounding the cool water tanks seemed black as the surface of the swift-running Hooghly. On the other side of the carriage-drive the tall houses in Georgian stucco were flushed pale gold by the light upon their façades except where the moon picked out some remoter surface with a white marble brilliance. Set back in their darkened gardens, the elegant houses were half-screened from the road by trees curtained with creepers of fragile growth, banyan and the red star-shaped blossoms of "flame of the forest", flowering tendrils, almond and bougainvillaea.

Above the rattle of the carriage wheels Verity heard the incessant tom-tom beat of drums from an Indian temple somewhere beyond the European quarter, the rhythm echoing, obsessive and sinister, in his mind. They had passed Theatre Road and Middleton Street, checking every house in these adjoining thoroughfares which had been temporarily vacated by its owners, according to Colonel Farr's list. Farr and Lopez, in grey civilian clothing but with belts and leather holsters prominently worn, rode in the first carriage with two uniformed Provost-Marshal's guards. Verity and Martock, the latter in his red tunic and blue overalls, rode immediately behind.

Only Farr had the complete list of houses to be visited. He pursued the routine investigation with a face like Judgment Day, as Martock observed. As each visit passed without revealing a sign of the girl, Farr's mouth grew tighter and his expression grimmer. Verity noticed that even Lopez, who seemed as much puzzled as any of the others by the proceedings, had begun to look sidelong and questioningly at his superior officer.

Just beyond Middleton Road, where the houses, though

still spacious, assumed a more suburban appearance, they
turned again from the Chowringhee. There had been rain
early in the day, which the sun had turned to an overcast,
miasmic heat, but now the dark storm clouds were rolling
inland from the Bay of Bengal, and Verity noticed that the
lightning which flickered on the horizon was almost pink in
colour. As he saw the carriage in front of them reining in,
he adjusted the belt round his greatcoat, and carefully
positioned the holster containing the Colt revolver. It was
one of the single-action type, issued by the Ordnance in
1855, and bearing the familiar WD stamp with a broad arrow.
It was not quite the weapon he would have chosen, since it
was not self-cocking but required thumbing back of the hammer between shots. However, he could shoot as well with it
as with anything, and it was hardly likely that he would have
to get off a number of shots in rapid succession. One would
probably do.

Once more the search-party repeated the routine which they
had followed at half-a-dozen other houses. Led by Farr, with
Lopez a few paces behind him, Verity, Martock, and the two
Provost-Marshal's guards walked smartly up the short drive-
way between the moist, sweet-smelling shrubs and trees with
all the precision of an escort detail. There were lights in the
house as Farr ordered one of the guards forward to pull the
bell at the double door, while he himself stood squarely to
meet whoever should open it. The lights in the other part of
the house grew dimmer and then faded, while another glow
appeared just behind the door, as though someone had put
up the light in the vestibule. Then the door opened to reveal
a native butler in white tunic and trousers.

"Mr Allon," said Farr abruptly, "I wish to speak to Mr
Allon."

The butler looked at the men outside. He had no need to
ask who they were or what they might have come for. Their
general appearance spoke for that.

"Mr Allon is not here, Sahib. He has gone away to England
and the house is let."

"To Mr Kavanagh, an East India merchant," said Farr, finishing the excuse for him. "Very well, then I shall speak to Mr Kavanagh."

Lopez stepped forward, looked hard at the Indian servant, and said cynically, "Unless, of course, Mr Kavanagh has gone away too. Perhaps Mr Kavanagh has gone up country. Is that not it?"

"It is so, Sahib."

And then Verity, without quite knowing why, said, "Only thing is, Mr Kavanagh's been seen about Calcutta. He ain't a stone's throw away."

Then several things seemed to happen at once.

Lopez swung round, his eyes flashing angrily at Verity's interruption.

Colonel Farr, addressing the butler, said, "I have a warrant to search these premises for a missing person, a Miss Judith Perry . . ."

And then the butler slammed the stout doors to in the instant before Farr could hurl his weight against them.

"Martock!" said Farr abruptly, "Cover the front of the house with one of our guards. Mr Lopez, take the other round that side, to the back. Sergeant Verity, round this side with me! Quick as you can!"

They ran through the damp shrubs and bushes, stumbling against uncovered roots and uneven turf. By the time that Lopez and Farr sighted one another from opposite ends of the rear façade, it was clear that the native servants had bolted. Their soft footfalls were hardly audible any longer as they sped nimbly through the trees and creeper which formed a garden-jungle at the rear of the house. There was a pause, hardly more than a moment. Then Farr said, "By God!"

She had been crouching by one of the bushes, trapped there by their sudden arrival, hiding until their attention should be distracted.

"Miss Perry!" said Verity softly.

There was no hope of catching her from where he stood. She ran barefoot and silent towards the cover. A moment more and she must be lost. But Lopez, who was nearer to her, heard Farr's oath and Verity's exclamation. With an astonishing burst of speed he sprinted after her, the helmet falling from his head and rolling across the lawn. But even more astonishingly, Verity lumbered forward after them. He could hardly catch Lopez, let alone Judith. Yet that hardly seemed to be his intention. He ripped open the holster at his side, and drew out the heavy Colt. Though the strongest instinct was to run onward, he forced himself to stop as soon as he had thumbed back the hammer. Resting the barrel over his arm, he sighted the black shape ahead of him and gave the trigger a strong, even squeeze. There was a roar, a thunderbolt flash, and the heat of the barrel penetrated his clothing until he felt it on his forearm. Lopez ran on. Verity cocked the revolver and fired again. Lopez stopped, motionless, almost as though he had been transfixed by some remote but delicate sound. With a face set like stone, Verity took his third aim, fired, and saw the back of the man's head dissolve in a dark liquefaction as he fell.

Then he dropped the Colt on to the wet turf and heard the first spots of rain, the prelude to a tropical storm. He knew that Colonel Farr, behind him, had been shouting desperate commands throughout the incident. Now the Provost-Marshal's guards came up, panting with exertion, and he stood quite still as they put handcuffs on his wrists.

Farr arrived, completely unnerved, his voice shrill and his face trembling.

"You bloody fool!" he shouted. "Don't you know better than to use a hand-gun in pursuit? You couldn't even trust a musket not to wound a man at that range. Your marksmanship has killed a brother officer instead of a native enemy!"

"With respect, sir," said Verity, in a low but firm voice, "there ain't nothing amiss with my marksmanship. The first round missed, I own it. But the second two went just where I aimed them."

There was an awful pause as the witnesses realised the implications of the words. Then Farr, with a voice that was broken with bitterness, said, "I would have given you credit for jumping at shadows and shooting wild. But you have signed your own death-warrant now, and I can do nothing for you."

Farr rode back alone in the first carriage. In the second vehicle, Verity sat with a Provost-Marshal's guard on either side of him and Martock facing him. They rode in silence, which was broken at length by Martock's anxious philosophising.

"You always have acted rum, old fellow," he said gently. "At times you're too brave for me. Sometimes you've been a fool. But this is no folly. For what you've done tonight they'll hang you twice over. That's the truth, and you'd better see your way to believing it, double-quick!"

16

"I ain't saying," Verity remarked reasonably, "that Mr Lopez wasn't foully murdered. All I am saying is that *I* never done it."

Captain Tolland shook his head.

"My poor fellow," he said sadly, "my poor Verity! How can I bring comfort of any sort in your agony so long as you drive me from you by wicked falsehoods?"

They sat side by side on the wooden trestle bed which had been set up in one of the pleasanter cells of Fort William.

"Captain Tolland, sir," Verity's hand movements expressed the conviction of a man speaking the truth for the twentieth time in succession, "if I said I *had* murdered, or even injured Mr Lopez, then I'd be guilty of falsehood all right. And many poor souls would be in peril as well as my own. There it is."

Captain Tolland switched deftly from spiritual adviser to practical man.

"Look," he said, "first there must be a court of inquiry into the incident. If the finding warrants it, you must then be charged with Mr Lopez's murder. If that charge comes to trial, every other person who was with you at Mr Kavanagh's house on the night in question is bound to be a witness to your guilt. If you can think of nothing but merely to stand before your judges and contradict the testimony of honest men, there can be only one verdict and only one sentence."

"This trial," said Verity in a tone of great confidentiality, "it'd take place here, I suppose, not England?"

Tolland nodded mournfully.

"And whatever came after?" asked Verity again.

"It would. I, of course, should be witness to your brave and upright character. If there were to be a commutation by the Governor-General, you would serve your life-term in an Australian penal colony. That is the best you can hope for."

"I can hope," said Verity righteously, "that no free-born Englishman shall be made to suffer for what he never was guilty of."

Tolland brightened a little.

"Then you can vouch that some other person discharged a revolver in the grounds of Mr Kavanagh's house?"

"Not that I know of," said Verity philosophically.

Captain Tolland stood up.

"Then I am wasting my time," he said forlornly, "and yours."

"No you ain't, sir," said Verity, standing man-to-man. "You been bringing spiritual comfort to a member of your class-meeting. In a cell like this, it means a lot to a man. To me it does, anyhow.'

"I have prayed with you," said Tolland thoughtfully, gazing meditatively at the barred window, "but in your present obstinate spirit, what more can I do? I ask God to bring you to a proper confession of your sins. But, remember, whatever may happen, I shall be with you until the end of your tribulations."

Verity seemed clearly touched by this.

"That ain't something I shall easily forget, sir," he said throatily.

Captain Tolland turned to the cell door, beyond which the guard waited.

"I beg you to think carefully over what I have said, my poor friend. I shall come to you again tomorrow."

He was about to knock for the guard when Verity said suddenly, "Captain Tolland, sir!"

Tolland turned to him.

"I ain't the least wish to commit any irregularity," said Verity humbly, "but I was wondering if I might ask you to obtain one or two small articles for me. You and Mrs Captain Tolland have always been good to me since I first came to Bengal, and I know you'll understand I ain't asking charity. I shall pay whatever the reckoning may be. But if I might have a ink-and-dip, I could somehow recollect my thoughts better. And the other thing is a smelling-bottle."

"A smelling-bottle?" asked Tolland with a frown of disapproval.

"I know it ain't usual," said Verity simply, "but I come over that faint sometimes, being confined here I suppose, that I don't think anything short of it is going to bring me to myself. I don't mean a lady's smelling-bottle of course. Just one of those little black sort – Featherstone's."

"Fainting-fits!" said Tolland firmly, "Unsteadiness! Delusions! If you had been ill, my poor fellow, if your mind and body had been injured by your sufferings at Gwalior, that might be your complete defence!"

"Defence, sir?"

"If you were not in possession of your faculties when the tragedy occurred, that might go a long way towards saving you, if it could be proved. Why, you might be examined by medical men to support the testimony!"

"Captain Tolland, sir," said Verity, looking hurt. "I ain't lunatic and never have been. The most important thing for me to prove is that I've been in possession of my faculties all the time."

"Then I can do no more," said Tolland helplessly.

Verity became cheerful once more.

"Don't say that, sir! Why, there's one other little thing you might do for Colonel Farr as well as me. There's Mr Saunders, the government apothecary. Now, he's got a message for me. Of course, I know I mustn't receive messages where I am. But I wonder if you'd be so good as to send to him, ask him what it was, and give the answer to Colonel Farr? I can't play the game above the board better than that, can I?"

"I don't like it no more than you, Mr Verity," said Corporal Wadman self-consciously, "but after your dodge at Gwalior, the Colonel ain't taking a chance of your escaping from here. Locked in with you, I'm to be, as if I was a prisoner myself. I'm to watch you when you wake and when you sleep. You're not to be out of my sight for any reason at all, not for a minute. I'm more sorry than I can say, Mr Verity. 'Tisn't what I should have chosen for a duty at all."

"You got no cause to fret, Mr Wadman," said Verity generously. "A man that does his duty needn't reproach himself with it."

"Still, don't sit easy," said Wadman ruefully, "keeping a death watch on a man that 'aven't even been tried."

Verity sat at his little table, opposite Wadman, the quill, ink, and smelling-bottle ranged before him.

"You *try* and sit easy, however," he said hopefully. "And if you ain't no objection I shall just compose a few lines by way of a letter."

"You aren't to be stopped from that," said Wadman, shifting anxiously on his chair, "unless you should appear to act suspiciously."

Verity chuckled.

"Now, Mr Wadman! 'ow can a man be suspicious when all he's doing is writing?"

"I couldn't tell that, Mr Verity. I never learned writing, and all the garrison schoolmasters never made me a scholar at reading."

Verity looked up from his slip of paper.

"Ah, Mr Wadman, a man should learn writing! If you was to learn writing, there's no knowing where you mightn't end, a man of your character. Why, you might be a great man in India!"

"My dear soul!" said Wadman, addressing himself, "'ow long might it take to learn writing, Mr Verity?"

Verity inspected the tip of the quill, sharpened to the finest possible nib.

"Well, o' course, Mr Wadman, it ain't easy. There's a craft and mystery to the pen, and we who can write some sort of hand know how hard it comes."

Then, with Wadman's eyes admiringly upon his movements, he opened the Featherstone smelling-bottle, which Captain Tolland had brought, prepared the quill with a moistened finger, and dipped it in.

"What a smell!" said Wadman indignantly, as the pungent fumes of ammonium chloride caught sharply in his throat and nostrils, "that's never part of writing a good hand!"

"Always start with a clean pen, Mr Wadman! Nothing like it for bleaching away any old ink or impurity. Why, you only watch this."

He took a slip of paper, covered with writing of one sort or another.

"Now, Mr Wadman," he said cheerily, "you learnt some reading, I daresay, so have a good look at that word there."

"Perry," said Wadman with difficulty.

"Very good, Mr Wadman. Now, we take the quill from the smelling-bottle and we draw it over the last letter of the word."

"Well, I never!" said Wadman delightedly, "it's disappearing."

"Bleached," said Verity knowledgeably. "It's an old trick with a Featherstone smelling-bottle. So instead of Perry, we have Perr. Now I'll show you something funnier still."

With great care, he held the quill steadily in his large fist and touched the last of the four remaining letters. Wadman leant forward, watching intently.

" 'Tis going," he said excitedly.

"But not gone," said Verity happily. "Now, Mr Wadman, whereas the letter 'y' disappears entirely, the letter 'r' disappears only to reveal another letter 'r' underneath."

"Why," said Wadman indignantly, "there's another word underneath, what has had this word Perry wrote on top of it."

"Mr Wadman!" said Verity admiringly, "Who says you

never learned writing! You might understand the craft of it better than any man, if you had a mind to. Now let's see what this word might be that's been overwrit. The two letters 'r' ain't different. But now that 'p' is an 'f' inked over, and that 'e' is nothing but an 'a'!"

"Farr?" said Wadman doubtfully. "Not Colonel Farr, however?"

"No, and not anyone else either, Mr Wadman," said Verity with an expression of plump joviality. "Just a game, that's all, to 'elp pass the time that you're obliged to spend here. And now, if you please, I really must turn to the matter of writing a letter."

On the day before the court of inquiry was to open, in a temporarily requisitioned hospital ward of the Granary Barracks, Captain Tolland paid an afternoon visit to his fellow Wesleyan. Verity asked after Mrs Captain Tolland and the class members. Then he said, "I got a request, sir. Before the court of inquiry, I should like to have the honour of an interview with Colonel Farr."

Tolland shook his head.

"That cannot be," he said abruptly, "Colonel Farr has constantly refused all communication with you. Such an interview would be improper before the court of inquiry sits."

"I wanted to confess my crime," said Verity, looking as humble as he knew how.

"To discuss that, before the sitting of the court, would be the greatest impropriety of all," said Tolland hotly.

"No, sir," said Verity with gentle insistence, "you don't understand. I ain't talking about the shooting. This is another crime that Colonel Farr knows nothing of."

"And you could not confide in me?" said Tolland sadly.

"Colonel Farr is my commanding officer, sir, and I must report it to him as my military duty. If I'm held to have acted wrong, then I shall make amends in prayer with your guidance, sir."

"How can you not have acted wrongly, if you have committed a crime?" asked Tolland with irritation.

"As to that, sir. I must abide by Colonel Farr's judgment."

"My poor Verity," said Tolland bitterly, "I see little hope of heaven for you, in your obstinate and unregenerate state!"

But when he left the prisoner, Captain Tolland went straight to Colonel Farr.

Verity was handcuffed, half an hour later, for the few minutes' walk to Farr's office, two guards marching ahead of him and two behind. Farr sat in his leather chair, arms spread out across the desk. Verity stood to attention before him, except that his handcuffs obliged him to hold his arms rigidly down to his loins rather than at his sides. Two guards remained in the room at Farr's command, one standing either side of the prisoner.

"Very well," said Farr, the iron-grey of his trim beard and hair framing a hard, bleak face, "say what you have to say."

"With permission, sir," said Verity smartly, "I wish to confess to a criminal offence, sir!"

"Not connected with the business before the court of inquiry?" Farr asked suspiciously.

"No, sir. Connected with my 'aving committed criminal damage to St Paul's Cathedral in Calcutta, sir!"

Farr looked at him with a blend of distaste and incredulity.

"So be it," he said at length. "Explain yourself."

"Sir," said Verity, "I have to confess, sir, to 'aving defaced the baptismal registers in the cathedral vestry. In particular, I am the person who tore out from the register the entry for Miss Judith Perry, the young person as is now absent from the garrison mission."

"Very well," said Farr, "you shall be charged with removing the legal entry of baptism from the register."

"Forged entry, sir, not legal," said Verity softly, his chin tucked upwards in plump self-confidence.

Farr turned to the two guards.

"Wait outside," he said calmly. "If some impertinent allegations are now to be made against this young woman's character, I shall hear them in private."

Verity waited patiently while the guards withdrew and the door was closed.

"Now," said Farr, "get to the point."

"Why, sir," said Verity coolly, "you know the point better'n any man. Of course, the copy of the entry in the *government* registry is sound as a bell, it having been done after the cathedral register was altered. That's why I had to go back to the original. Now, Colonel Farr, sir, any man of constabulary training knows the easiest forgery is the one built on letters that's there already. And a detective officer soon gets to see when that's been done, even though he mayn't read at once what was written underneath. O' course, I saw her name was altered and she could never have been Judith Perry, though she may have been called so from a month old in the orphanage. Perry might come from Parry, of course. Then I thought she must have been Judith Terry – or Berry even. But the only way, sir, is what we call 'bleaching-down', taking off the over-writing and seeing for ourselves what was written underneath. It takes a bit of practice, sir, and oh dear me, I never did think I should be obliged to do it in a prison cell, using a smelling-bottle and quill!"

Verity paused and chuckled richly at the thought.

"And then," he said innocently, "she was Judith Farr. And her father was James John Farr. Your very name, sir. And the mother, sir, was never your good lady, but a poor spinster who swore to give your name to the girl, before she made away with herself and left the foundling to the care of the missioners. Embarrassing it must be for a ambitious young staff officer to find his name so freely taken and used in the baptismal register. A few strokes of the pen altered it, but couldn't alter what the native servants knew, and what they found such good use for sixteen years later!"

"Sergeant," said Farr disdainfully, "'I do not commit forgeries. A man may father a bastard in India and be thought none the worse of. Lay an information if you wish, and be damned to you."

"Oh no, sir," said Verity quickly, "you ain't a forger. The over-writing had that slope to it which we in the detective police gets to recognise as a woman's writing. No, sir. If this was done by anyone, it was your lady wife who would have committed murder to save your name and hers. But I never came here to accuse or lay informations, sir. Only to confess what I did."

"My wife lies in St John's churchyard," said Farr slowly, "and no malice of yours can touch her."

"I ain't no wish to malign her, sir," said Verity nervously.

"You have murdered Mr Lopez, you have failed entirely to protect a most valuable jewel. Think of your own short-comings while there is still time left to you."

The narrow blue eyes sparkled with fury.

"Why," said Verity, "I almost clean forgot. Might you have had a message, sir, from the government apothecary, brought by Captain Tolland?"

"Yes," said Farr sourly: "Chromium oxide, whatever that may be."

"Ah," said Verity, and stood in deep thought.

"Is that all?" Farr's voice broke sharply across his meditation.

"Yes, sir," said Verity, "except for one little fact. Might you still have the letters which the Nana Sahib sent to you? The ones they made Miss Judith write from Gwalior?"

"Letters?" shouted Farr. "What letters, damn you?"

"After they tormented the poor young lady, sir, they made her write down all that had been done to her, in a letter to her father. And they made her say that she'd get worse next time unless he was to prove 'elpful in the matter of the jool, sir. Now, when we had no idea of who her father might be, it was nothing but stupidity. But Mr Martock and the woman Mass-oo-mer and a dozen others might swear to those letters, which must have been written to you. And, in that case, you must have been number one for having thieved the jool, sir. With respect, sir."

"Damn your impudence!" roared Farr, "I have never seen such a letter!"

"Course not, sir," said Verity truculently, "you wasn't to be wrote to. You was to be murdered and the letters found in your effects afterwards. I'd swear they're lying in this building now."

"And do you have the damnable effrontery to charge me with theft, sir?" Farr's voice rose to a shout in the last words.

"No, sir," said Verity firmly, "I did think for a bit that you might have the jool, but it wasn't in character. Now I know who took the diamond and how. It wasn't you."

"Who was it?" Farr inquired as if suspecting a trap.

"Thomas Kavanagh," said Verity.

"Who?"

"Thomas Kavanagh, sir."

"The man in whose garden you shot your colleague of the search detail?"

Verity nodded.

"Shot him in the back, twice!" said Farr disdainfully.

"Sir," said Verity, "after he fell dead, and was picked up, where was his revolver?"

"On the ground," said Farr impatiently, "a few feet off."

"So it can't have been in his holster. He'd drawn it ready to use. The natives had run off, and the only person in his line of fire was Miss Judith."

"My God!" said Farr, as though he had suddenly thought of something else.

"Now why should he want to shoot her?" asked Verity with great innocence, "unless it was to see that she never told her tale to you or the rest of us?"

"No," said Farr at length, "no. It won't do."

Verity became confidential.

"Sir, it's my duty to tell you that I ain't going to stand any trial alone. There must be witnesses."

"Who?"

"Corporal Fred French."

"Who?"

"Why, sir, you remember your Mr Lopez saying how he remembered Corporal French, who was under his command in Delhi? How he hoped the brave fellow had escaped with his life?"

"Yes, yes," said Farr irritably.

"Corporal French and his Colonel too will be giving evidence that Alfred French was never in Delhi, never in the

Intelligence Department, and never set eyes on your Mr Lopez. And then there's the wig."

"Wig?"

"Yessir. Did the man I shot have a wig?"

"No, of course not."

"The real Mr Lopez did. Just a small one where he was losing his hair. I got that from someone who *was* in Delhi but never really knew him, and who gave me my good opinion of him."

"And you ask us to believe, Sergeant, that the man we knew as Mr Lopez was Thomas Kavanagh – whoever he may be?"

"Couldn't have been the real Mr Lopez, sir."

"And where is he?"

"Dead and buried, most likely, sir," said Verity, "which gave the conspirators their chance. A man looking like Mr Lopez arrives in Calcutta, escaped from Delhi like so many others. He's a man of means, formerly Intelligence Department, and is recruited to help the work. No one else here knows him by sight, but his face fits the general description, and we all know how brave and resourceful an officer he's been. Kavanagh, whoever he might be, has an English father, a native mother, and a real name we shall never know. He might do as Portuguese Indian."

"The diamond?" said Farr reluctantly.

"As to that, sir, Lopez *alias* Kavanagh must have had help from one of Maun Singh's lot, in the pay of the Nana Sahib. Of course, the diamond never was in the performing box, but in the lid of the casket. You told me that just now."

"Did I?"

"When you said 'chromium oxide.' It's what they make imitation emeralds from, so good that you can't tell them from real. Now, I tried that emerald with a knife blade, the stone being harder than metal. And so it was at the top, where the blade never marked it. But underneath it came away. Jewellers' paste. Under the top part of the emerald there's a space just big enough to hide the diamond, though now it's all filled in with chromium paste. I daresay it's not a hollowed emerald, only a stone cut to leave a space underneath, but it looks like a jewel the size of your fist. Now even if the Kaisar-i-Hind went missing, you and the other officers would search every man in the tent before you'd smash up a prize emerald on the chance there might be a diamond in it. Your so-called Mr Lopez had all the time in the world to get it out of there. And as we all thought the diamond had gone before he came near the casket, when you called him, he was the one man it seemed that couldn't have thieved it."

"But the lid was inspected," said Farr.

"By the alleged Lopez," said Verity firmly.

"And by me! Do you think I couldn't tell the difference between an emerald and a diamond peeping through the top?"

"But you wouldn't a-seen a diamond, sir," said Verity patiently. "All the time Massoumeh was doing her dance, that diamond sat on its bottom, and was never shown upside down. I'll swear that underneath it was coated with that green chromium, what will come off again. If you looked at the underside of the lid, you'd have seen no diamond. These ain't street conjurers, sir, these are professionals."

"All right," said Farr, conceding the point for the sake of argument: "Suppose Lopez had the diamond, and could put it in the hollow of your truncheon, and devise a trail of clues to lead you to Gwalior. What then? Why send a fake diamond which must discredit the Nana Sahib's cause?"

"With respect, sir, it was only me that said it was faked. No one else but the Nana Sahib ever got near enough to see whether it was real or not. He must have known it was faked too, though he never let on."

"What in God's name does the Nana Sahib want with a fake diamond?"

"Oh, he doesn't want the fake, sir. He had the real one. Only the real one was kept in a safer place."

"In Gwalior?"

"No, sir. In Calcutta, most likely."

"Sergeant Verity," said Farr heavily, "tell me what all this is about. Sit down if you want to."

"Much obliged, sir. Quite 'appy to stand. It ain't difficult, sir. We just made a mistake over the Nana Sahib. We believed him when he said he was going to be an emperor and all the rest of it. So did his own poor dupes. Well, I seen him, sir, and all I can say is I've known Ratcliffe Highway magsmen that looked more imperial than 'im. He ain't even a proper heir to the Moguls, only a poor boy that was adopted by an old man that took a shine to him. He's a prime thief, however, and 'e can treat a doxy rough as a bawdy-house bully. And he won't stick at murder."

"The diamond?" said Farr softly.

"Just it, sir. Any villain who's up to the move knows that there can't be better than even chances of winning such a mutiny, however loud they shout. So just in case there should be trouble, he has a bolt-hole to run to and a pot of gold to live on. The real jool."

"The Nana Sahib has taken to the jungle," said Farr, "somewhere in the direction of Assam."

"Who saw 'im?"

"Reports from native spies," said Farr vaguely.

"Sir," said Verity, "where would you hide a leaf?"

"Eh?"

"Policeman's litany, sir. Where would you hide a leaf? In a tree. Where would you hide a corpse? In a graveyard. Likewise, where would you hide a native felon? Among the biggest gathering of other natives. And there ain't natives gathered in bigger numbers anywhere than in Calcutta."

"Absurd!" said Farr, "Never in Calcutta!"

"Is it, sir? If he'd got a bolt-hole and a diamond, there's no other place he could do better in. You can trade easy here and never be noticed. It's those reports about 'im being up a tree in a jungle that sound absurd to me. Who do you suppose may have been in the so-called Mr Kavanagh's house that night? Why did they run like hares when they saw Mr Kavanagh dressed up as Lopez? We might have been a few yards from the Nana Sahib then."

"Absurd!" said Farr again.

Matters had reached a deadlock.

"Sir," said Verity presently, "how might I stand now, with regard to my freedom?"

"You have no freedom," said Farr sternly, "unless the Governor-General orders your release. You should know that."

There was another pause.

"One thing, sir," said Verity, as if trying to be helpful: "We know now, don't we, that Dhingra couldn't have murdered Miss Amy Stockwood, 'er being still alive?"

"Yes," said Farr shortly.

"And there was no reason why he should confess to what he hadn't done, when he was standing with the noose round his neck. But anyone who didn't want the trail of the Nana Sahib followed too close – and who knew he had took Miss Amy – might have *said* Dhingra confessed to murder, so as to stop the hunt."

Farr grunted.

"And Sergeant Martock says," Verity continued, "that the report of the said confession came from you direct."

"Mr Lopez was in attendance at the execution," said Farr. "He was my informant."

"Just so, sir."

Another silence followed. Farr looked up, met Verity's wide-eyed reproach, and looked down again. At last he stood up.

"Very well, Sergeant. You will remain here under guard. I shall go to Government House at once and seek your release from arrest, with my own recommendation. However, I shall give orders to the guard commander here that if you attempt to evade custody in the meantime, you are to be shot!"

Verity beamed.

"You got no idea, sir, what your recommendation means to me."

Farr grunted again.

"Only," said Verity, "I 'ope the search for Miss Judith may go on soon. I know she ain't your daughter in anything but name, but if she's to be found, there ain't time to lose."

17

"And then," said Verity, dropping his voice almost to a whisper, "they was persuaded to take the private correspondence from his desk — what would otherwise have gone unopened to his dependents — and they read it. Sure enough, four letters from Miss Judith when she was a prisoner, written to her father but sent by the natives to Lopez *alias* Kavanagh. Sure as fate, Mr Martock, they would have murdered Colonel Farr somehow, and this Lopez *alias* Kavanagh would then have planted those letters among the Colonel's effects. And they knew I should have found out by then that Miss Judith was his daughter. No wonder Lopez *alias* Kavanagh was so keen to assist me. Don't you see, Mr Martock? Colonel Farr would have been fingered for the diamond theft, and him being dead there'd be no argument over it."

Martock shook his head.

"It's still dashed rum, old fellow. I ain't saying I'm not glad to see you well out of it, but if Lopez wasn't Lopez, he must have been caught sooner or later."

"You never really met a swell mobsman, or anyone of that style, have you, Mr Martock?" said Verity, as though sympathising. "So soon as Colonel Farr was dead, the false Lopez would give it a week or two, then he'd quietly resign his duties and go on ship for England or Timbuctu. The story would be of a brave man that escaped from Delhi, served in Calcutta, and then went about his business. And all the time the body of the real Lopez is lying in a ditch, where the natives that murdered him left him, and by now is all eat up by the crows. That's the size of it, Mr Martock."

"But there's no reason he should help mutineers and rebels," said Martock feebly, "real Lopez or not."

"Course he don't love natives nor mootineers," said Verity. "He's done it for money, like any other heavy swell in the game. As for impersonation, why, Mr Martock, it's an art.

Some of the speelers from the flash-houses off Regent Circus have got it so pat that they could tell you they was your own mother and you'd never doubt it!"

Martock drained off the remainder of his porter and set the tankard down on the table of the sergeants' mess where they were sitting.

"So you saved Miss Judith from the gun of a man who wasn't Lopez after all," he said, as though pondering the unfairness of it all. Verity had said nothing of the girl's parentage, judging that to be Colonel Farr's own affair. But as the two men stood up he remarked, "But I ain't saved her altogether. She's yet to be found."

Martock laughed cynically.

"You'll find her easy enough, in one of the smart whore-houses, all spread out and getting the kind of treatment that keeps a doxy cheerful!"

"No," said Verity softly, "it ain't that at all. Mr Martock, while I been under lock and key, has there been any search to see if this Kavanagh *alias* Lopez had another house any-where."

Martock chuckled.

"We ain't all green, old boy! First thing that was done. Not a sign of such a place anywhere."

As the two men walked out into the twilight, Verity thought about this. Then he took a slip of paper from his pocket, on which was an inscription in pencil.

"Mr Martock," he said presently, "might you ever have been to Garden Reach?"

"No," said Martock sharply, "nothing but big houses in their own grounds, by the river on the outskirts of Calcutta. NCOs aren't invited to Garden Reach, not you nor I."

"Not even by Mr Allon?" asked Verity innocently.

"Who?"

"Mr Allon, the owner of the house off the Chowringhee that we went to, the night Lopez *alias* Kavanagh met his end. That butler fellow said Mr Allon had gone to England and let the house to Mr Kavanagh."

"And that's all about that!" said Martock firmly as they

passed through the Maidan gate of Fort William into the cooler openness of the city.

"Mr Martock," said Verity, "I ain't been out of arrest for more than a few hours, but the first thing I did was to inquire for the latest annual of the *Calcutta Register*. I always been a reading man, and it's no hardship to me. I found Mr Allon, off the Chowringhee, and I found his name for a country sort of house at Garden Reach."

"Also let to Kavanagh?"

"No," said Verity, "not let to anyone. Left empty."

Martock gave an audible exhalation of relief.

"Nothing to it, old fellow," he said happily. "Man goes to England. Man lets his house off the Chowringhee. Other house stands empty, ready for him whenever he returns."

"Stop a bit," said Verity, "I made inquiries at the shipping office, in the person of a detective officer."

"You'd no bloody right!" said Martock severely.

"Right or wrong, I did. No party by the name of Allon has took ship from here since the sepoy trouble began."

"Damn it," said Martock, "he went overland to Bombay by dak and then took the Suez steamer!"

"In the middle of a mutiny, Mr Martock? Funny way to run, if you was frightened of the mutiny. And I had time to do just one other thing. I went to the place off the Chowringhee, where the late tragedy occurred, not to the house itself but to the one next door. I inquired after Mr Allon, who they must have seen sometimes, what his appearance and behaviour might have been before he went away. They described him Mr Martock, and that description was the dead spit of the person who called himself Lopez and Kavanagh. This dodge of letting houses ain't nothing but a blind. As for names, the man had so many, he'd probably long forgot the true one."

"A matter for Colonel Farr," said Martock flatly.

"No," said Verity, his voice resolute, "there's reasons I can't go into why it's better Colonel Farr shouldn't be first at Garden Reach. Now, Mr Martock, I'm going to bespeak that hackney cab with the driver that's asleep. I know I saved your life at Gwalior, but I ain't the man to remind you of

that by way of forcing favours from you. However, if you did
happen to wish to show appreciation, of your own free will
of course, you couldn't do it any better way than keeping
company with me to Garden Reach."

At the approach to Garden Reach, Verity's heart sank. The
pretty villas with their green verandahs, their English gardens running down to the edge of the Hooghly, the white
children in the care of their native ayahs, presented a prospect of domestic tranquillity which stretched for mile after
mile. But the house of Mr Allon, at the farther end of the
riverside suburb, appeared at last. It was dark and silent,
with no sign of any light burning.

"Stands to reason," Martock observed, as they took a lantern and left the hackney cab in the road, "if Mr Allon called
himself Lopez, and is now dead, there wouldn't be anyone
here. If he had accomplices, they'd be the last to use this
place once he was found out."

"They mayn't know he's been found out," said Verity
thoughtfully, as they trod the broad gravel drive side by
side. He thought to himself that it was for all the world like
stretches of the Thames he had once seen from the Great
Western line, the neat, secluded villas in their river-gardens.

Martock gave a sceptical grunt.

"Whether or not they know, they ain't sitting here in the
dark, old fellow."

They reached the sham-classical portico and regarded the
front door.

"Don't ring," said Verity softly, "just listen a bit."

They listened. Presently there was a rustling and a scratch-
ing, which seemed to come from somewhere behind the
door.

"Rats," said Martock. "Whole place smells of rats."

Then there was stillness, broken only by a bird calling as it
swooped low across the darkened surface of the river beyond
them. Verity had closed the shield over the window of the
lantern, but now he opened it just enough to allow the
merest glimmer. With hand cupped to Martock's ear, he
breathed moistly.

"Very careful, Mr Martock. Walk where I walk. I'm going to see what can be found out by shining through the windows before I rouse anyone who may be in there by banging at the door."

Martock watched the dim shape of the bulky sergeant creeping forward in a ludicrously conspiratorial manner. Reluctantly he followed. Several of the windows on the ground floor of the house were shuttered, but there was no sign of light behind them. By shining the lantern under the corners or through cracks in the frame, it was possible to glimpse angles of interiors, parallelograms of light which showed anonymous articles of heavy furniture draped in white sheeting. A few windows were unshuttered, most of them at the rear of the house where only the evening sunlight would fall, and where perhaps a caretaker might still be in residence.

One after another the windows underwent Verity's scrutiny, and each time there was nothing to contradict the supposition that the house had been long closed up by its owners. If the self-styled Lopez and his confederates had ever been there, they had certainly left no evidence of their visit. Undeterred by this, Verity began to examine at his leisure the unshuttered windows at the back of the house. There had clearly been some occupation here, perhaps by a servant, since the furniture in some of the rooms was uncovered. On the other hand, there was little that warranted covering. The second sparsely furnished room revealed a few wooden chairs, a bare table, and a black marble grate. Whatever carpeting there might have been seemed reduced to a moth-eaten underlay.

Verity cast the yellow glimmer of the lantern on cornice and ceiling, cobwebbed and grimy. He drew patterns of light on the black marble of the fireplace and on the green walls. High in the vault of the ceiling, the broad fan-blades hung motionless. Like the rest of the house, this apartment seemed sealed and airless as a tomb. He had almost completed his survey, when he felt his heart jump to his throat with shock at a cry from Martock that was half a scream.

"Oh God! Look!"

Verity turned, certain that Martock must have seen something behind them in the darkness. But Martock was pointing at the window, just where the reflection from the glass blotted out a small area of Verity's own field of vision. Verity shifted the lantern a little and, to his horror, saw the yellow light fall on a nose and mouth. He drew back a step, both in dismay and also to give the light a broader field. The features that stared out at him were smooth and ageless, a study in the placid evil and cruelty which only the most barbarous degeneracy might breed.

"I knew him from the mouth alone!" said Martock shrilly. "You can have my word on this, Verity. It *is* the Nana Sahib."

With the lantern darkened they stood back.

"What's he doing just staring out like that?" Verity asked nervously.

"Shine it again," said Martock without enthusiasm.

Verity slid back the shutter of the lantern. The Nana Sahib sat at the wooden table staring out at them. His eyes and features were motionless.

"He's dead!" said Martock.

"Can't be," said Verity uncertainly. "A dead body would have putrefied straight away in this heat. And he wouldn't be sat up like that if he was dead. More like he's been put in some trance, or perhaps given some drug."

"One thing," said Martock, "he can't be alone here. Even if the sepoy mutiny's collapsing, you'd never find the Nana Sahib without one or two hangers-on."

Verity recovered his composure.

"Look, Mr Martock, I don't want us to be caught in a trap. I may not have the storming of zurr-narr-narrs off to a tee, but there ain't much I don't know about taking a flash-house. You must stay here. See 'e don't get out through the window. See 'e don't move, in fact. I'll find a way in. If I'm in trouble I'll call, and you must come. But if you see there's not much you could do, go for assistance. Whatever you do for the moment, don't take your eye off that cove in there!"

And Verity disappeared, leaving the lantern with Martock, but taking from his pocket a packet of lucifers and a thin metal probe.

"Why," he said, fingering the probe affectionately, "I'd wager they never even heard of the real Bramah here! These backdoor locks 'ud open easier than a china-pig!"

But the door to the servants' quarters was secured by a padlocked chain, and that was easier still. Martock heard the wood scrape open and waited anxiously in the silence that followed. Presently he heard some banging and then Verity shouted.

"Mr Martock, quick as you can!"

Martock ran towards the open door, only to find Verity heading him off.

"Mr Martock! Drop that lantern! Whatever you do, don't bring it in!"

"Not bring it?" said Martock, perplexed.

"Do for the pair of us," said Verity enigmatically. He thought for an instant. "Take it back to the outside of that window and lodge it there, so it shines in. Then follow me."

Mystified and faintly resentful, Martock hung the lantern on one of the shutter-fastenings, where it lolled awkwardly, casting a yellow aqueous light on the interior of the room. Then he followed Verity into the darkness.

"Strike a glim and put up a light, old fellow," he said hopefully.

Verity stumbled over a small piece of furniture.

"Not on any account," he said grimly.

They felt their way along the wall of a darkened passage and came to what must have been the door of the room. There was light behind the door from the lantern which Martock had hung outside the window. In the faint luminosity of this Martock could just see that Verity held a small metal implement in his hand, about the size and shape of a nutcracker. Verity turned.

"Right!" he said. "Ready? Door's locked, keyhole jammed. Must be forced."

He inserted the edge of the tool between door and frame, there was a sharp crack, and the door itself flew open.

"Get back!" said Verity at once. "Stand clear!"

But Martock was choking already from the acrid vapour which filled the room like thin smoke and which was responsible for the watery quality that the lantern light had assumed. Then, as Martock drew back, his eyes smarting and flooding with tears, Verity dashed forward, seized a small wooden chair, whirled it over his head and brought it down in a shattering of glass against the large window, on the opposite side to the lantern. Then he withdrew and joined Martock.

"Charcoal!" he gasped at length. "Charcoal fumes from that grate. That's why he never decomposed. He could a-been there like that for weeks! A naked flame might a-sent the room up!"

Presently the fumes had cleared a little by the draught from the broken window and the two men crept back to look more closely at the grotesque figure which sat upright at the table. They now saw that there was an open book upon the table, and a candle quite burnt down, so that the grease had run into a broad circle round the dish. Preserved from decomposition by the deadly fumes in the sealed room, the Nana Sahib had dried into bones with a fine paper of flesh over them. When Verity touched the corpse, moving it slightly, the yellowed skin sounded like a drum, and its joints creaked like a puppet.

"Look at this!" said Martock suddenly, pointing at the book, whose pages were discoloured by exposure to the fumes.

"Don't touch it whatever it is!" said Verity sharply, peering closely, "Mr Martock! It's a finger!"

"With a ring on it!" said Martock absurdly.

"And it ain't one of 'is fingers," Verity completed a grisly inventory. "But I recognise that finger. At least, I recognise that ring. When a man thinks he's about to die, he sees things very plain. Now I can't swear I ever saw that finger, but I'll take my oath on the Bow Street testament that I seen the ring. I was buried to my neck, waiting to have my head tore off, and Mr Azimullur Khan was crouched there, crowing over me. And I can remember, clear as I see it now, seeing that ring on his finger. Square sort of a stone with that watery blue about it."

"It mayn't be his finger, however," Martock replied doubtfully.

"No," said Verity, "but I noticed another thing, likewise. When I said their jool was a fake, that Nana Sahib took it quite calm, as if he knew already. But Mr Azimullur looked at 'im like thunder, more as if he'd had something put over on him. I fancy the thieves may have fell out after they left Gwalior. I'd even wager that the rest of Mr Azimullur is dead as that finger, and that this Nana Sahib could have told a tale about that!"

And Verity began inspecting the hands and arms of the corpse.

"One man might have killed both," Martock suggested hopefully.

Without replying, Verity took the dead right hand, seeing a tiny fragment of red material held between finger and thumb. But the bones were locked hard by death and he failed to loosen their grip. As though it had been the most normal thing in the world, he took the little metal probe, with which he had forced the door, angled it between the stiff finger and thumb, and twisted hard. There was a crack, so unmistakably of human bone rending that Martock's stomach turned at the sound. The finger and thumb dangled loosely, releasing the scrap of cloth.

Then Verity stepped away. His bulk had been pressed against the dead shoulders during the use of the probe, but as he turned away, he heard the corpse behind him move. Swinging round, he just saw the rigid, brittle figure hunch forward at the shoulders. The trunk slid to an awkward angle in the chair, but the head bowed with sudden force, falling until the face hit the hard surface of the table with a dry, hollow impact. Even before he looked closer, he knew that the dead features, covered by skin as fragile as dried paper, had been damaged beyond recognition.

"How can a man that's stiff and dead bend his neck?" he whispered, as though asking the question of himself. Then he squatted down and, by the glow of the lamp, made out a dark stain on the floor, just behind the chair.

"Shine the lantern on him!" he gasped, straightening up again.

Martock obeyed, his mouth twisted with distaste.

"Look!" Verity gestured indignantly, "Look at that! Someone must a-cut his head half off! Gone through the bone almost! See, here? Only held by the skin in the front! That's how it fell so easy. It was just lodged on his neck, and I must have moved him when I was opening his fingers!"

He took out his pocket-book and folded away the scrap of cloth, rather more than the size of a half-crown, which the Nana had held. Then he said to Martock, "P'raps, you'd just help me put 'im to rights."

"Let him be," said Martock, drawing back a little.

"Why, Mr Martock! I'm surprised at you! He can't hurt anyone now. I can manage alone, however. Unfortunate he should have hit that table such a smash, the skin being so dry and brittle. There's hardly more than skull to him. Don't look much like the Great Mogul now, do he?"

"Doesn't look like anyone," said Martock edgily. "And I don't think he ever did. It was only seeing a face through the glass, and you keeping on about the Nana Sahib, that made me think so."

"Mr Martock! You ain't saying we haven't got the Nana?"

"I'm saying," Martock insisted, "that you and your prying about has shook me up so much that I don't know what I've seen and I don't know what to think. There's hardly a decent light from this lantern, and all you've got is a man's finger and a head with no face!"

"There's been murder done here, Mr Martock, and police officers have their duty to identify the victim and apprehend the criminal."

"Much chance there may be of that!" said Martock resentfully.

Verity became smugly confidential.

"Ah, but then you ain't really a Scripture-read man, Mr Martock!"

"I daresay not," said Martock, looking bewildered.

"Whereas, if you'd been brought up a Wesleyan, or in a garrison orphanage, you'd know Scripture stories so well as your own hand. Even the apocryphal stories that only the Pope believes."

"Don't go prosing on, for God's sake!"

"Mr Martock! 'ave you never heard of Holofernes?"

"No."

Verity studied the trunk of the corpse, still in its macabre posture, with an air of proprietorial admiration.

"Why," he said, "Holofernes was a great 'eathen general, just like the Nana Sahib. Among his enemies was a young person of great beauty, by whom he became infatuated, took her and made much of her. But all the time she was 'arbouring thoughts of revenge. One night, after a great carousal, Holofernes lay sleeping, sodden with drink. Then along comes the young person and, quick as a knife, cuts off his head! You no idea how much the temperance preachers used to make out of that story!" And Verity chuckled at the memory of it.

"The Nana Sahib wouldn't drink," said Martock. "Against his religion."

"But bhang or opium would do as well."

"And the young person?"

"The young person in the story," said Verity confidentially, "went by the name of Miss Judith."

"What rubbish! You mean to weave a tale like that in court?"

"No, Mr Martock," said Verity softly, "what I weave in court is a noose, and the party that finds it sitting round his windpipe don't generally get it off again. No, the story was for your improvement. Now, if you please, we'll give immediate notice to Colonel Farr of what's happened here, so that the house may be searched proper for the Kaisar-i-Hind jool. Then he may either comb the bawdy-houses for Miss Judith or have it done by the missioners. There ain't anywhere else much that she could have run to."

But when Martock, who left Verity to guard the premises, returned at last with Farr and two corporals, the Colonel's manner was unpromising.

"Well?" said Farr, "What's this bloody tomfoolery? Nana

Sahib? Haven't you been told, Sergeant Verity, that the Nana Sahib has been *seen* by our most trusted native spies in the jungles of Assam? That thing over there! You claim to identify that as the Nana Sahib? And this finger as Azimullah Khan? My God, man! And you call yourself a detective officer!"

Then Farr ordered the two corporals to proceed with their unproductive search of the house.

"Sir," said Verity, his plump face awe-stricken but determined, " 'ave the honour to request that certain places may be searched without delay in an endeavour to find Miss Judith."

"Places? What places?"

" 'ouses of a bad reputation, sir," said Verity unwillingly.

"Damn you for a foul-minded prig!" said Farr. "Miss Judith returned to the missioners at four this afternoon, of her own accord. I shall see to it that she is on the next ship for England. And, Sergeant Verity, if I have any say in the matter, you will occupy a berth on the same vessel. I do not take kindly, sir, to officers who drag me from my quarters in the middle of the night because they think every dead native must be the Nana Sahib! Be damned to you, sir!"

And Colonel Farr strode off to soothe his feelings with the aid of a silver flask.

18

Inspector H. Croaker, of the Private-Clothes Detail, "A" Division, Metropolitan Police, presents his compliments to Colonel Farr, of the Provost-Marshal's Office, Calcutta, and begs to acknowledge receipt of Colonel Farr's memorandum of the 25th of May last.

It has given Mr Croaker great pain to hear of the wilful and insubordinate behaviour of William Clarence Verity, Sergeant of this Division, since his secondment to Bengal. Mr Croaker has read with dismay the shocking details of this officer's cowardly assault upon Captain Groghan. If either Colonel Farr or the Captain should contemplate proceedings against the offender, Mr Croaker will be pleased to furnish an affadavit of Sergeant Verity having been paraded before him and reprimanded in November 1856 for an assault upon a member of the public.

Mr Croaker need hardly say how sincerely he regrets that the folly and incompetence of this police officer should have aided the loss of the Kaisar-i-Hind jewel. Mr Croaker has learnt of the gravity and displeasure with which that loss is regarded in high places. But Mr Croaker must be allowed to say that, in agreeing to the secondment of this officer to Calcutta, he had not the most distant contemplation of Sergeant Verity being entrusted with any but the most mundane duties, to which alone his capacity fits him.

Mr Croaker has read with some surprise Colonel Farr's request for the immediate return of Sergeant Verity to the Metropolitan Police "A" Division. Mr Croaker cannot, of course, refuse to accede to such a request, but must be permitted to say that he had envisaged the period of secondment in Bengal as lasting for several years, rather than for a few months only. However, Mr Croaker concedes that it may be best to allot the officer in question some routine constabulary duty on a homeward-bound vessel. Since Mr Croaker is not at present short-handed in his Detail, it would be agreeable to him if the vessel chosen were one proceeding by way of the Cape, rather than by the short Red Sea route.

Inspector Croaker has the honour to remain Colonel Farr's obedient servant.

H. Croaker, Inspector of Constabulary
Whitehall Place, London
12th July 1858

Colonel James John Farr, CB
Provost-Marshal's Department
Granary Barrack
Fort William
Calcutta

19

"Cheer up, old fellow," said Martock brightly, "there's no sense in looking as though you might be bound for Botany Bay, instead of home to England, which is where you've wished yourself ever since I first saw you here!"

Up and down the wharf on which they stood, trunks and portmanteaus were strewn in abandoned little settlements of luggage. Here and there the loin-clothed porters scurried, bent double with the weight of European possessions on their shoulders.

"For all that," said Verity, acting as manly as he knew how, "it ain't the way I should've liked to end it, Mr Martock. I *did* save Amy Stockwood, and I *did* square the game with the Nana Sahib and Mr Azimullur, and I don't care what may be said about them being 'id in a jungle. I *know* they're dead. I seen the evidence. The thing that bothers me is the jool. I lost it, in a manner of speaking, and I ain't found it. It could be anywhere. I heard that once, centuries ago, it was an eye in a 'eathen idol. You only think, Mr Martock, how many idols there may be in India, and twice as many eyes as figures."

"Never you fret yourself over the diamond, old friend," said Martock. "We have our ideas whereabouts in India it may be."

"Whatcher mean?"

"You shall hear all the news when we have it." And with that, Martock took his portly acquaintance by the arm and steered him reluctantly along the wharf. The wharf itself was lined with the half-rotten hulks of ancient East Indiamen, their sails reefed and the sky a mass of spars. A small bum-boat was in attendance to ferry out passengers and their luggage to the *Hastings*, a trim, freshly painted paddle-steamer which lay anchored in the middle of the Hooghly, dark smoke rising in a steady plume from its pale-brown stack.

At the place where the bum-boat was moored, the two

sergeants faced one another, and then Verity took Martock's right hand in a firm grasp, as he had done in the cell at Gwalior when his captors led him out to face death.

"I never really thanked you enough, Mr Martock," he said, "for the handsome way that you and the other gentlemen of the sergeants' mess saw me off last night. I shan't forget that easy, all the singing and the generous sentiments that were expressed."

"Pleasure was ours," said Martock gruffly.

"If I'd only 'elped to find the jool, I could go home a happy man now."

"I expect you may have helped more than you know," Martock observed innocently. "And you've still got duties, even on ship. Looking after Miss Judith all the way to England. My word, what wouldn't I give to have sole charge of that little madam, all alone on a ship and nothing else to do!"

"Now, Mr Martock!" said Verity in gentle reproof. "Now really!"

He stepped across from the lower level of the wharf into the boat, where his portmaneau as well as the other passengers and their luggage was waiting.

"Don't forget," he called, "Mrs Captain Tolland would be very happy to see you at the class-meeting and tea after. She said as much. Do try and go!"

"Yes," said Martock unconvincingly, "rather!"

The boatman untwisted the mooring-rope and cast off.

"And don't worry about the jewel," called Martock through the hubbub of farewells. "It's been found!"

Verity's round, moustached face was expressionless with dismay. "Found?" he cried desperately.

"In Gwalior. Weighed almost five ounces. Colonel Farr's orders that you weren't to be told while you were in India! You're a yard out to sea already!"

"No!" bawled Verity, "The real jool is more than that! You've got the fake again!"

"Mistake," called Martock calmly. "Lost some weight in cutting!"

"Fools!" In his agony, Verity struggled to his feet and

seemed about to run to the stern and attempt a flying leap
across the several feet of muddy river-water which now
separated him from the wharf steps. The passengers nearest
him pulled him down into his seat again as the boat began
to rock.

"Nice and gentle!" said the boatman of the *Hastings*.
"The stout gentleman ain't been himself for a bit. Wounded
'ero, as the thin gent on the wharf was saying."

By now the little boat was half-way across the stretch of
water to the waiting steamer. Verity's expostulations were
lost among the wharfside noises. But Martock could still
glimpse the red, open-mouthed face beneath the flattened
black hair, the mouth under its waxed moustaches thrown
wide in a helpless cry of "Fake!" Martock watched the unwilling passenger helped across the sponson of the paddle-
wheel and, a few moments later, heard the blast of the
steamer's whistle. With a slow but mighty effort, the finned
wheels began to turn, the *Hastings* moving forward to the
accompaniment of cheers uniting those on board with their
friends ashore. At the river bend, where the space between
the banks grew wider, the ship turned stern-on to the spectators, and the distant beat of paddles faded towards Garden
Reach, Diamond Harbour, and the open sea. As the vessel
disappeared, Martock caught a last, fleeting sight of a figure
pacing the after-deck in a mood of fuming determination.

Colonel Farr had followed Inspector Croaker's suggestion to
the letter rather than in the spirit. The *Hastings* was des-
tined for the Cape route, but she was a more speedy vessel
than some of those which plied between Bombay and Suez
on the shorter return to England. Whatever the speed, Verity
had reached the depth of misery within a few days. The food,
which he shared with other passengers of non-commissioned
status, took away all appetite at first appearance. The pea-
soup resembled nothing so much as a poultice, while the
bluish-red mutton tasted as though it had been cooked in
the engine-room boilers. Only the high tea of devilled biscuit
and pale ale was safe from the culinary ineptitude of the
ship's cook. The officers returning from India, who had their

cuisine improved by the doubtful addition of hot pickles,
sour claret, and bilious sherry, spent their days smoking
furiously, throwing away every second cheroot hardly
touched, and talking interminably of clubs, balls, steeple-
chases, hunts, and women.

Day after day, Verity sought the shade of a deck-awning
and watched the brilliant azure of sea and the cloudless sky,
the broad wake of the paddler stretching behind and the unattainable horizon always featureless ahead of them. Soon
some of the officers produced muskets or rifles and took up
places by the rail, waiting to shoot at any "flying fishes", as
dolphins were termed, which might loop out of the water.
One or two paid their attentions to Miss Judith instead, as
Verity watched their hopeless intrigues. Two of them walked
the deck with her, arm in arm on either side, while a third
walked behind to hold the parasol above her, and a fourth
marched in front, carrying her novel. Then, when the first
rumours of her recent history began to spread, the attentions
of the subalterns dwindled to a more distant politeness. She
was, it was said, no 'spec' for marriage, and even the most
lecherous young gentleman could hardly bring himself to
bed a girl after she had given the natives first pick.

From a deferential distance, Verity kept watch on her,
fulfilling his duty to Colonel Farr. She walked the deck,
generally alone, in her green or pink dress with its narrow
waist and matching parasol. The sweep of her light brown
hair helped to shade her face from the sun, so that she retained the same pale oval beauty, her regular features illuminated by the wide hazel eyes. She kept her gaze straight
ahead of her, and cast her eyes down demurely when a man
passed. At dinner, she sat modestly, avoiding both conversation and the eyes of others. Verity thought to himself that
she had the makings of a governess in her external behaviour
at least.

The infantry subalterns, disappointed of a lucrative con-
quest, turned violently against her in their conversation. On
a warm evening, a little after dinner, Verity was watching
the luminous foam churning back from the paddle-wheels
on the twilit sea, when he heard the voices of two men, well-

fed and wined, as they paced the deck. In the stillness, they must have been audible to most of those on the deck itself and even to some in the cabins and saloons.

"Miss Judith!" said the young man to his companion, "I tell you, my old chum, that Miss Judith can sit on her dignity at dinner looking as though butter wouldn't melt in her . . ."

"Mouth?" said his companion, and they laughed uproariously.

"From what I *heard*," said the first, "she's melted a native or two between her legs, and she ain't always sat on her dignity!"

Verity emerged from the shadows.

"P'raps, gentlemen," he said, "you wouldn't mind keeping your noise to yourself. I ain't particular to 'ear it, and nor are the rest of the passengers."

"And who might you be?" asked the first subaltern.

"I'm a police officer," said Verity gently, "charged with keeping the peace on this ship. I hope you won't take it amiss, gentlemen, but anyone who behaves like this for the future is to be put ashore at the next anchorage. I speak with the Captain's authority, o' course."

"Put us off at the Cape and be damned to you!" said the second officer.

"Oh no, gentlemen," said Verity anxiously, as though to correct a misimpression, "the Captain ain't anxious to wait until our next *port*. Just an anchorage. That'd be Minicoy by the Eight Degree Channel, more of a rock than an island. You might get shipped from there in a twelvemonth, but it ain't likely, and you'd be the only Englishmen among the natives. So if you ain't particular to pass a while there, p'raps you'd just remember the deck is a public place and to be respected as such."

In the weeks that followed, Verity felt rather than heard the cold hostility which built up against him among the junior officers. It seemed, however, that some of their seniors regarded him with a more kindly eye. Later still, they were many degrees south of the Cape, on a gusty day. The tropic seas had gone and in their place Verity found the wind dead

in his teeth, drenching rain in showers, interspersed by a
drizzling atmosphere that was somewhere between a Scotch
mist and a shower bath. The waves were thick and dark,
while water dripped from every rope and rail. Below decks
even the tumblers and the cutlery in the saloon looked as if
they had broken out in a cold perspiration. It was as Verity
was turning towards a companionway from the deck that he
drew back a little and said, "Why, Miss Judith, you surely
ain't going out for a stroll on the deck in this squall?"

"No," she said, as though advised by him. "No. Perhaps
not."

"You'd best let me escort you back," he said gallantly. "It
ain't at all the sort of day to be out there. The way the ship
pitches when them wheels miss the water, why it could throw
you clean over the side. What a way of dying that would be!"

He saw her shiver, and put his hand on her shoulder to
steer her towards her cabin. When they reached it, she
opened the door, entered, and turned to him in a businesslike manner.

"Come in," she said, wide-eyed with a faint mockery.

He stepped self-consciously after her. Judith removed her
coat and gloves, then sat down on a small wooden chair.
During this moment Verity glanced round the little state-
room, taking in the pale oak panels, the bed, the commode,
the blue plush of the upholstery, the carpeting, and the pink-
shaded lights. Martock, he thought enviously, would have
travelled in this style and had his way with the girl throughout the voyage.

"You've been good to me," said the girl forlornly, after
a pause. "You saved me at Gwalior, and I heard how you
spoke up for me on the ship. I don't deserve speaking for.
Gwalior made me bad, and I've been bad ever since."

"'ave you now?" said Verity, stretching out his hand and
stroking back the long curtain of hair from her features, as
if to observe her more clearly.

"I'm bad every night, if I can be," she said.

"What a little lady like you needs is a man to be bad with,"
Verity chortled, appalled at the sound of his own vulgarity
but seeing no other way of attaining his object. Then, to

his surprise, Judith stood up, her young back straight, lips parted, and eyes defiant.

"Teach me!" she said.

Verity chuckled again.

"Why, miss, I ain't got time for that now. I got duties to be attended to, however much I got to mind you!"

"Tonight," she said, "after dinner."

"Well!" said Verity, "Well, you ain't a girl for being backward!"

"I was cured of being backward," she said quietly, "at Gwalior."

"I daresay," he said, looking at her slyly, "I daresay you were. A girl that's been cured of backwardness can always show a man something!"

"Tonight, then," she said determinedly. "The door of the cabin shall be on the latch."

"O' course," said Verity, "if it's your invitation, and if you don't change your mind . . ."

"I know my mind," she said bitterly, "and I know what good comes of being an obedient charity girl! The minute I'm engaged for a post in England, I shall have to please the man who pays me. But so long as I can, I'll please myself."

Verity turned away.

"Then if I should find the door on the latch," he said softly, "I shan't wait for asking."

The rest of the day he thought of Martock and Martock's philosophy. To be sure there were girls who experienced what Judith had experienced and then remained shocked and withdrawn, fearing the approach of any man for the rest of their lives. But if Martock was right, and Verity began to think he must be, there was another type of girl, and Judith was one of that kind. For her the experiences at Gwalior had been a self-discovery, a sudden realisation of hidden lusts. However much she might have screamed and struggled at the time, she was haunted and aroused afterwards by the thoughts of what had been done to her. So, at least, Martock argued. It was strange, but not as strange as Massoumeh with her Persian beauty choosing the zenanah and its slavery to the sexual vices of a despotic master, its unnatural passions between the girls themselves, and its ever-present threat of savage retribution, even of death in its most unspeakable forms. Judith had not returned willingly to such horrors, in the manner of Massoumeh, but she seemed as much the slave of her zenanah experience now as she had been, unwillingly, the concubine of the Nana Sahib at Gwalior.

Verity was no expert on female psychology, but he knew that girls were sometimes of a very different sort. Long ago, before he left England, there had been a frightened little doxy with an almost Eastern beauty about her and dark cat's-eyes that gave away nothing. Her clever keeper had her in such fear of the gallows that she even scuttled about the streets like a frightened little mouse. Lieutenant Dacre must have believed, Verity thought, that he had her on a string, especially when he made her an accomplice to murder. But the villain drove her to a feeble defiance by his cruelty and then, in a mood of savage vengeance, had ordered his two bullies to use a whip on Miss Jolly's bottom, the three men laughing at her during the ordeal. And in that moment, thought Verity, he had turned the trembling little street-girl into an executioner. There was something undeniably rum about the way such young women acted with men.

At dinner, he could hardly eat for excitement at what was about to happen. When the meal was over, he went to his own berth and made himself sit there, watching the clock-hand creep a score of times round the second-dial. Afterwards, he got up and walked gently towards the more spacious accommodation on the *Hastings*, the carpeted and oil-lit passageway with the cabins which included Judith Perry's. He reached the door, lifted a hand to knock, thought better of it, and turned the handle instead. The door was unlocked. It had crossed his mind several times that this might be a trap to compromise him in some way, but it was hard to see what she could gain from it and, in any case, in his present state of anticipation he hardly cared.

He pushed the door open, stepped inside, closed it again, and took the tentative precaution of sliding the little bolt across. There was no sign of Judith at first, though a brush and comb on the miniature dressing-table suggested that she had recently completed the evening ritual of brushing and braiding her long brown hair in preparation for bed. Entering the cabin further, he stepped round the pink screen which the shipping company provided so that when a cabin was shared by two female passengers there should be some degree of privacy. Judith was lying on the bed, exactly as though she had not heard him come in. She had removed some, but not all, of her clothes. Her long slim legs were still encased in lilac stockings, a plum-coloured corset left her shoulders bare and ended in a waist so tight that her pale hips seemed to swell rounder and fuller by contrast. From the waist to the knees she was still covered by loose-fitting open drawers. Verity's heart jumped at what he saw. Her hair lay in a pair of braids across her slender shoulder-blades, and she appeared ready for bed, in every sense of the phrase.

He sat on the bed beside her and she turned on one hip to face him.

"Miss Judith!" he said admiringly, "I quite thought you was having me on this morning. I never thought, I never dreamt even, that I should be with you like this!"

He made no attempt to remove his black frock-coat, but with his fingers he touched the tight young breasts just where the frill of the plum-maroon corset crowned them.

"I hardly thought you'd come to me," she said softly. "There aren't many on this ship who would. They all want me to be bad with them. But once they find out that I was bad, against my will, in India, they won't come near."

He could feel the breasts hardening through the silky material.

"They're boys!" he said knowledgeably. "It takes a proper man to understand a young woman's wants."

And he began to stroke downwards from the breasts across the firm, slightly rounded shape of her belly. Judith arched back on her elbows, so that he might handle her more easily.

"Mind you," said Verity, "I'm putting a great power in your hands, aren't I, being your beau for the rest of this voyage? Only think of the 'arm you might do me if you chose!"

"But why should I harm you?" she asked, wide-eyed.

"As you say, Miss Judith, why should you? What good might it do you? None at all!"

His hand was level with her navel, where the hem of the corset was covered by the waist of the loose pants, his fingers pointing downwards. He noticed that she opened her knees a fraction in anticipation. This, at least, was no pretence.

"Miss Judith," he said, his forehead a little moist from perspiration and his voice trembling perceptibly, "would you have any objection to take those drawers off?"

Without answering, she lay on her back, raised her hips, and slid them to her feet, sitting up to remove them and lodge them on the bedside chair. Verity's fingers reached the hem of the corset as she lay back, and he looked at the little triangle of light brown hair which shaded away between her thighs.

"I do like to see a girl in a corset," he said confidentially, "in a nice corset."

"How funny," she said, looking at him quizzically. "I thought men preferred a girl with no clothes on at all."

"Lots do," said Verity, peering carefully, "but I like a girl in a corset. P'raps you'd like to turn on your front and I'll show you a trick worth knowing."

"You might take your coat off," she said mockingly, "and the rest."

But she turned over and Verity examined the view, the braids of hair tied with two little ribbons and lying across the pale shoulders. Then the frill of lace edging the top of the corset, just under the shoulder-blades, the tight waist, and the corset ending with another frill that trailed across the top of Judith's backside.

"You no idea how much I like a corset on a girl!" he said again.

She turned her head in faint disapproval.

"Perhaps you like the corset better than the girl," she said.

"And there, Miss Judith, you mightn't be so very far

wrong. Only I do like you a bit, in a general way, as it happens."

She tried to struggle round to face him, but Verity pinned her down firmly with one hand, while his other hand went to his coat pocket. He took something out and Judith renewed her struggles, as though convinced that he was about to use some device on her. Now she had crossed her legs hard, one knee pressing into the back of the other, and her soft pale buttocks were clenched, as she strove to close her body to him.

"And I don't think," said Verity gently, "that I ever took to any corset quite as much as this one of yours. Though, of course, I have seen it before, in a manner of speaking."

Judith stopped struggling, though without relaxing the tension of her body.

"That's foolishness," she said quietly. "Now go and leave me alone."

"P'raps it's foolish," Verity conceded. "What I meant was I'd seen a bit of it, a bit of lace from this border at the back. Now, it being at the back, o' course you wouldn't notice so easy as if it had been tore off elsewhere. But the shape of the missing bit is quite distinct, and the pattern easily remembered."

He was holding up a scrap of paper, with a design traced on it.

"Paper!" she said bravely. "Foolishness!"

"Fits the pattern and the tear to a tee, however," said Verity optimistically. "Now I ain't got the cloth, that's with the Intelligence Department. But I have seen it. It was me and Mr Martock that took it from the dead hand of the Nana Sahib. Seems he wasn't quite as sound asleep as you thought, and when he felt himself being murdered, he must have begun to struggle and his hand tore off a bit of lace from the woman who was his bed companion."

"Foolishness!" she said again, her face buried in the pillow.

"Is it, miss? I tell you what I think it is. A young person that was hardly ever out of the garrison orphanage is took to Gwalior by natives and made to live as an easy woman.

And she ain't altogether averse to it, but the better part of her swears revenge on her seducer who brought her to such ruin. But 'aving been brought up in the garrison orphanage, she understands the native lingo pretty well, and she hears the plans made at Gwalior by the men that have took her. P'raps she even tries to become the favourite of the one that calls himself Mogul Emperor, and wheedles it out of him. P'raps she has a way of getting it from young women that *are* his favourites. She may hate the man like fury, but what she learns from him might make her a very rich young woman. I'm right ain't I, miss?"

"Much good shall it do you," she said, for all the world as though she were a little governess and he her pupil.

"As to that, Miss Judith, we shall see. Well, then, the so-called Mogul Emperor has to run for his life to Calcutta. But the girl soon finds him, whimpering after him and begging him to pleasure her as no other man can. And then she takes a 'orrible vengeance, only leaving a scrap of evidence behind her. That's the tale you might tell, miss, when all this comes to court for murder."

Judith turned to face him fully, her eyes flashing with tearful anger.

"And if I did?" she cried. "Is there a man or woman in Bengal would blame me?"

"They mightn't *blame* you, miss, if they *believed* you. I may know it was the Nana Sahib in whose dead hand you left that scrap of cloth, and so may you. But the Governor-General swears that the miscreant has escaped to the jungle and is still alive. If you come to court, Miss Judith, it'll be for murdering a poor innocent native what never harmed you. And I'm the one man that could defend you — only I shouldn't be believed if I said it was the Nana Sahib."

"It wouldn't matter if you were believed or not," she said with sudden primness. "A girl isn't hanged for killing a native, however innocent he may be, if she's suffered what I have."

With a determined gesture she turned on her side, so that her back was towards him and her face almost concealed.

"Why, Miss Judith," said Verity, "who talks about hanging? Who talks of prison even, for one in your state? Ain't you a victim of delusions and erotomania? Wouldn't Colonel Farr himself be glad to have you looked after where you should be? You'd have to go back to India first, to appear for trial, but courts and families always have a way of disposing of their awkward customers."

"I should go to England," she said with a desperate effort to appear self-possessed.

Verity shook his head.

"Now there, Miss Judith, you make a mistake. Really you do. I seen a hundred cases like this. And I heard Colonel Farr's opinion on your behaviour. Now, when the court hears from me and Mr Martock how mad you acted after Gwalior, dumbstruck and silly, and how mad you acted on this ship, there's only one place for you, and it ain't England."

"Where, then?"

"The madhouse, Miss Judith. You got blood on your hands, a fire of hell between your legs, and you ain't safe anywhere else."

She stared at him.

"You think I'm mad?"

Verity stroked his moustache.

"No, miss, I don't. But private madhouses, what is run by medical gentlemen to line their own pockets, happen to be full of a lot of people as sane as you and me. They get put there by their families, so that their estates may be enjoyed by others, or because the courts are persuaded to it. Places of that sort is more secure than Newgate itself. And I promise you, Miss Judith, once you was in a madhouse, you'd go on your knees and beg to change places with the worst-treated girl in the zurr-narr-narr of Gwalior. Now, there's commissioners in lunacy that come round after a year or two to see that everything's done proper. But when you tried to speak with them, to tell them how cruelly you was ravished by mad and sane alike, how the guards beat you, how you were made to work at oakum till your fingers bled, you'd just be told not to plague the gentlemen with your delusions."

She sat with her knees drawn up, her forehead resting on them, sobbing helplessly. Verity had hardly dared to hope she would believe him so easily.

"Now," he said, "I shall have to get a guard on this cabin and report all this to the Captain. There ain't no call for you to dress further, because they'll want you in your under-things if a strait-waistcoat is to be put on you."

"But you know I'm not mad," she cried, pulling at his sleeve. "You can see it!"

"In this matter, miss, people generally sees what they want to see."

"Whatever it is you want," she said softly, "you shall have it. If you order me to sell myself in London for you, I'll do it."

"Why, Miss Judith!" said Verity, mocking her, "All I want is for you to be a happy, sensible girl. Now, if I must, I shall go and give orders for that strait-waistcoat. And if that happens, you'd thank Jack Ketch for putting the rope round your pretty neck to save you from years of living torment. However, it's just possible I might say nothing. In that case you shall land in England a free woman. Why, with your manners and appearance you might make a very genteel governess in a good family. You might fall in the way of a fine gentleman. He might take a fancy to you, even marry you, and you become a fine lady."

He let her think about this, and then he added, "Likewise, you got a body for a girl of sixteen that a proper young woman might envy. And you ain't shy with a man. You might work in a flash bawdy-house and enjoy the pleasuring and be well rewarded. You might even hook a rich young fellow, or a rich old fellow. Lots of rich old men would pay a fortune to set up a girl as young as you for their mistress. Now, I ain't saying it's *right*, I'm just saying what might happen if you wasn't to be put in a madhouse for the rest of your life. You might have carriages, and servants, and jools even."

She sniffed back her tears.

"Tell me what you want," she said softly.

"The jool," said Verity with satisfaction, "that Kaisar-i-Hind that caused all the trouble."

"You fool," she whispered, "how could I have it?"

"Oh, you got it," said Verity confidently. "It's only you that could have. When all the rest had gone, there was you and the Nana Sahib, and the real jool, at the house in Garden Reach. Now you took a lot o' care to make it seem that you killed him on acount of him ravishing you at Gwalior. But, then, you ain't averse to being ravished, are you? So why should you go to such trouble over him? However, what you did know from Gwalior was that he had the real diamond in Calcutta and was going back to it, if his army was beaten. Why, miss, all that business of cutting off his head to make it look like the act of a poor demented creature, that was nothing but show! It wasn't to hide the murder, only to show that you was deranged with grief when you did it, so that you'd go free and no one ever think it might have to do with the diamond!"

"I have no diamond!" she cried desperately.

"Well, miss," said Verity wearily, 'I'll put this to you. I hope, for your sake, that you got it. If you have, and if you put it in my hands in the next two minutes, I shall walk out of here, never speak to you or of you again, and I shall return the jool where it belongs. Otherwise, I shall go directly from here and make arrangements for that strait-waistcoat. If you really ain't got the jool, then it's your misfortune, but it don't alter my purpose. Unless I 'ave it, it's the mad'ouse for you. I can't say that you deserve much better in any case."

She lay on her side, knees drawn up a little, and wept.

"Look at it this way," said Verity encouragingly: "What use is a jool hidden away if you're in a madhouse and can't get it? And ain't it better to be in London without it, but to have the world at your feet? And how is a silly foolish girl, that was overcome with greed, going to sell a fine stone in London — even if she has the chance? The first sharp you showed it to would have it off you in two minutes and give you no more than a split lip in exchange!"

She wept a moment longer, not answering him. Then she became a little calmer, sniffed, and stood up. She opened a hat-box, reached under the rim of its lid, and stripped off a length of gummed tape with a tiny package in tissue paper, the size and shape of a small egg.

"There's a sensible girl," said Verity soothingly as he took it from her. "And, oh my, how it do sparkle in this light! The sooner this is in a little snuff-box and locked in the purser's safe, the happier I shall be. Only to think what trouble this handful of devil's glass has caused!"

"You can't have known I had it!" she said furiously.

"No miss," he said reasonably, "I never promised myself so much as that. I only thought you was the one person still alive who had every chance to lay hands on it, and every reason. Why, you was poor and might make yourself a rich lady with it. You'd been brought up poor, and there's nothing like that for giving a girl a taste for gold. And once you'd been ravished at Gwalior, it didn't make sense that you'd go on the rampage in Calcutta just to kill the man that did it. You ain't the kind, too meek and mild by far, as you've shown yourself on this ship. And if you'd needed men to pleasure you, then you *would* have gone to a bawdy 'ouse, instead of back to the orphanage. No, miss, when I heard you'd gone back to the missioners, I reckoned you'd got whatever it was you wanted. Only being methodical in my way, I didn't see straight away what it was. No, miss, even tonight I didn't know for sure that you'd got it. Though I did think that genteel young ladies of sixteen don't generally take a fancy to be pleasured by my sort, unless they want to do some sweetening for another purpose. But I *did* promise myself that if you *had* got it, I was going to leave this cabin with it in my hand."

She had turned away from him, and Verity looked wistfully at the tall pale beauty of her body, the braided hair touching just below the top of her plum-red corset.

"Now," he said, patting her whimsically, "you ain't a bad girl. You ain't the sort. I shan't interfere beyond my duty, which is to see you safe in the care of Miss Lammle in Cheyne Walk. A real martinet is Miss Lammle but when you leave her hands you'll be more genteel than ever. Why, Miss Judith, even when you're undressed alone in your room at night, you'll still be a proper little governess through and through!"

And then with a final pat that was half a caress, Verity drew himself away from her and left her in a thoughtful mood.

20

Sergeant William Clarence Verity, of the Private-Clothes Detail, Whitehall Office, presents his compliments to Inspector Croaker, and has the honour to report his arrival from Calcutta, per steamship Hastings.

Sergeant Verity also has the honour to request Mr Croaker's urgent attention to the enclosed package, containing a stone of the first water, having 300 facets, weighing some 5½ ounces, and answering in every way to the description given in Calcutta of the Kaisar-i-Hind jewel at the time of its disappearance. Sergeant Verity was unable to locate the stone previous to leaving Bengal, but had the good fortune to discover it secreted upon the steam vessel Hastings.

Sergeant Verity has been concerned to hear of an imitation of the said jewel being found at Gwalior and being described as the original. From his own knowledge of the two specimens, Sergeant Verity is able to swear that cannot be the true stone, being a good ounce short in its weight. He trusts that his own discovery of the enclosed specimen may suffice to correct any erroneous report now being spread.

Sergeant Verity now holds himself at Inspector Croaker's disposal and has the honour to remain Mr Croaker's obedient humble servant.

W. Verity, Sgt.
2nd of January, 1859

"I imagine, Sergeant, you think yourself very clever in

this matter," said Inspector Croaker bitterly, his thin, yellowed face drawn into a mask of vindictiveness.

"No, sir," said Verity firmly, standing at attention, his gaze directed above the head of the Inspector sitting at his desk before him. "No wish to be thought clever, sir."

"Then perhaps, Sergeant," said Croaker softly, "you wish us to think you a wag? Eh?"

"No, sir," said Verity, looking down at him uncomprehendingly.

Through the window behind the Inspector's back he saw the reassuring familiarity of the Thames below Westminster Bridge, the busy little paddle-boats puffing smoke from their tall stacks, the barges with rust-brown sails, and the coal wagons with their heavily-built horses lining the Westminster wharf.

"Sergeant Verity," said Croaker impatiently, "you are surely aware that during the period of your voyage news reached London of Colonel Farr and his subordinates having found the Kaisar-i-Hind diamond at Gwalior? You perhaps do not know that Her Majesty's personal commendation was despatched to Calcutta, and conveyed to the Colonel by Lord Canning as the newly designated Viceroy of India."

"Can't help that, sir," said Verity determinedly.

"Oh yes, Sergeant, you can help it. You can help it by not sending me a cheap imitation stone and asking me to congratulate you on having saved the Kaisar-i-Hind. You can help it by not seeking to advance your own glory at the expense of an honourable man."

"It ain't glory or honour, sir," said Verity, his face creased with anxiety, "it's what's true that matters! I seen that Gwalior jewel, and it's a fake. It weighs light, and it don't answer the description we were given by Colonel Farr of the Kaisar-i-Hind, after it vanished. But the one I found *does* answer it."

Croaker became a little more conciliatory.

"Sergeant," he said, "you are perhaps not to blame for that observation. It is now agreed that in the confusion of the disappearance there was a mistake. The description given was of an imitation of the jewel. Since the specifications of the real diamond have lately been found to vary from the description, that must clearly be what happened."

"Sir," said Verity helplessly, "if you think that, let the jool I found be examined by any diamond merchant!"

"Certainly not," said Croaker sharply. "Do you suppose I have no more thought for the reputation of Scotland Yard than to go along with a cheap imitation and ask if it might not be the Kaisar-i-Hind? Do you suppose that I would even contemplate casting such an aspersion upon the gallantry of Colonel Farr? Am I to announce publicly that the Colonel, Lord Canning, and even Her Majesty have been duped in the most shameful manner? Do you imagine, Sergeant Verity, that our officers in India do not know a real diamond when they see it? Your suggestion is quite preposterous!"

There was a pause while Croaker gathered his energies for a final blast against the plump perspiring sergeant. Verity interposed quickly.

"Sir, in the light of your remarks, I 'ave the honour to make a request, sir."

"Well?"

"Sir, this stone I found, being as it's nothing but a piece o' worthless glass, I was wondering, sir, if I might be allowed to have it as a sort of keepsake of my time in 'indoostan, sir."

"No!" squealed Croaker, "You may certainly not! That item is going under lock and key until such time as it forms part of a collection of police exhibits, illustrating criminal activities of one sort or another. A museum of crime."

And Croaker sat back proudly at the thought of this pet scheme.

"And when might that be, sir?"

"It will be," said Croaker, "when officers of your kind devote themselves sufficiently to their duties to control the criminal element of this great city and allow us some leisure for reflection."

"I see, sir."

"I doubt," said Croaker, "that you do. In the space of your secondment, you have criminally assaulted Captain

Groghan, you have lost a priceless diamond, which was only retrieved by the pertinacity of Colonel Farr. You have shot dead an enemy spy who might otherwise have been interrogated and made to give information of the greatest value. You have spread the most mischievous story of an unidentified headless corpse being the body of the Nana Sahib. You have committed criminal damage in the vestry of St Paul's Cathedral in Calcutta. And, as for your voyage home, there is every reason to think that you were instrumental in the ruin of a young person of sixteen years of age – sixteen years of age, Sergeant Verity! – and were only saved by the natural modesty of the girl in refusing to lay an information. You are not here because I requested your return, but because the authorities in Calcutta have ended your secondment. Perhaps you think that is a record to feel proud of?"

"No, sir," said Verity meekly, "I never felt proud all the time I was away. Not proud of myself, that is."

"No," said Croaker, "you were too busy making such a damned nuisance of yourself that you could work a passage home! Well, Sergeant Verity, you shall find I have some duties for you. There is a general reluctance among our officers when it comes to a night-beat in the rookeries. A man grows shy of suicides, and woundings, padding-kens and graveyards. You've rather missed your share while you were in India. I think the general opinion is that six months of the night-beat would begin to square the account."

And Croaker raised his face, his dark eyes small and glittering. He was almost recognisably in a state of happiness at the prospect.

"Face!" said Verity indignantly, "I never in my life saw so many people all trying to save their faces!"

As they lay in bed, Bella trailed her toes down his leg affectionately and said, "But fancy them swearing your diamond was glass when it must have been real. Why would that be, Mr Verity?"

"Ain't I just told yer?" said Verity impatiently. "It's face!"

He stared indignantly ahead of him and saw, by the remains of the fire in the grate, the outline of the cradle at

the side of the bed. Much as he had longed for Bella and
Paddington Green, he had hardly been prepared for her to
present him with a son, now eight months old. The infant
had the round, red face of its father, and the beginning of a
head of flat black hair. Indeed, with the addition of an
artificial moustache it might almost have passed for a miniature of Verity himself.

"Mr Verity," said Bella softly, stroking the side of his face
with her finger, "what was you on about in your letter,
hoping I was an example to the neighbourhood? Example
o' what?"

"All that you should be," said Verity sternly.

"And wouldn't I be?" she cried.

"Course you would. It was a manner of speaking, that's
all."

She continued to rub his leg with her foot and then said
reproachfully, "What I heard of the sojers and the native
women, where you was, they could do with some examples
there! I 'ope you were one, Mr Verity!"

"Why, Bella! Mrs Verity!" he said in dismay, "I never so
much as had a thought all that time except 'ow I could keep
myself 'olesome for *you!*"

"Didn't you?" she said happily. "Oh, Mr Verity, if only
'er Majesty knew how much you've done for 'er, while you
was in India, she'd invite you to Buckingham Palace and
thank you for it herself!"

"Much chance o' that," said Verity sceptically. Then he
thought for a moment.

"Funny," he said, "it don't seem possible that I been to
India, and been took a prisoner by 'eathen, and been led out
to death, and escaped, and seen the end of the Nana Sahib,
and lost the great jool, and found it, and saved poor souls
from the zurr-narr-narr, and now 'ere I am, back in bed in
Paddington Green, as though it had none of it ever happened!"

"What's a zurr-narr-narr?" asked Bella innocently.

"Why," said Verity, "why, it's a sort of convent place. Only
'eathen, of course."

"You mean it's religious?"

"Oh yes," said Verity eagerly, "very strict. 'eathen, of course. But very strait-laced."

Bella seemed satisfied by this. They lay in silence for a little while longer, Verity with his arm twined round her. Clear on the winter night, a church clock towards Marylebone chimed the half-hour. Bella nudged him with her plump little arm.

"Go on, Mr Verity," she said, as though reading his thoughts, "Go on!"